THAT FINE
LINE

CINDY STEEL

Front Cover Design: Melody Jeffries

Editing: Editing Fox

Proofread: Amy Romney

Dad,

Remember those early mornings when you would kick the footboard of my bed with your rubber milking boots to wake me up and tell me that you needed me to go milk the cows? Even though I hated it at the time, I appreciate it now. I would thank you for singing me your good morning song so horribly off-key, but I wouldn't mean it. Mostly, thank you for being the kind of dad who taught your kids to love the land and never took himself too seriously.

PROLOGUE

FOURTEEN YEARS EARLIER
The Incident(s)

I woke up that morning with my stomach feeling... iffy.

I had begged my mom to let me stay home, to no avail. She thought I was trying to get out of going to school because that day was our second-grade classroom talent show.

Though I had an intense fear of speaking in public, Mrs. Perkins had insisted that everyone was required to participate. So I did the only thing I could think of that might impress my class without me having to say much. Raised with an older brother obsessed with roping anything in sight (including me), I brought his lasso to demonstrate my roping skills—the perks of being raised on a farm.

Mrs. Perkins, a large dynamite of a woman with a booming voice and rotund bosoms smooshed into a white button-down blouse, called my name. With shaking fingers, I tucked my stringy, brown hair behind my ear and stood up on knobby, scraped knees. The freckles on my nose and cheeks seemed to burn with self-consciousness. At eight years old, I was a spiny wisp of a thing. My stand-out features were my oversized feet, emphasized by my stick legs and gangly arms.

The snickers from the class—and more specifically, Cade Williams and his friend Luke—offended my young ears as my best friend, Tessa, and I made our way to the front of the classroom. I pulled the rope from the waist of my skirt. Tessa stood opposite of me, near Mrs. Perkins's desk, standing straight and still—my target for the talent show. Moving back about ten feet, I held the rope, ready for the signal from my teacher to start.

"She's not a real cowboy," Cade said, the unruly patch of dark hair on the back of his head standing to attention as he bobbed in his seat. "She's just a girl."

"Yeah, and she's wearing a dress!" Luke laughed, his twisted top incisor catching just a bit on his lip as he closed his mouth.

"Boys!" Mrs. Perkins gave them a sharp look and then nodded to me. "Go ahead, Kelsey."

My fingers holding the rope tightened as my nerves gave way to determination. Shy or not, I was also blessed with a spirited personality that wasn't inclined to being made fun of, especially not by Alfalfa and Snaggletooth. Turning away from Mrs. Perkins, I stuck my tongue out at the boys, pulled the rope over my head, and began moving it in a circular motion. All the eyes in the classroom were on me.

Trembling, I let the rope go, watching in defeat as it missed Tessa's blonde head completely, landing on the floor before Cade's desk in the front row. Tessa's face fell with disappointment for a moment, before she nodded her head, prodding me to pick up the rope and try again. The class burst out laughing, but none louder than Cade.

Pointing at me, he mocked, "Kelsey can't rope. Kelsey can't rope."

"Cade!" Mrs. Perkins snapped her fleshy fingers. "Stop that right now."

He stopped the chanting, but as soon as the teacher's back was turned, he mouthed the words to me again.

Anger fueled my insides. How dare he. He had never seen me

rope at home against my brother Logan. I was good, and I was going to prove it to him. Pulling the rope back toward me, I wrapped it carefully into a coil. Taking a deep breath and drowning out the snickers and murmuring, I once again circled the rope high above my head.

I exhaled my breath at the same time the rope left my fingers. The class sat, waiting in anticipated silence, moving their heads along with the rope as it soared through the classroom. It flew through the air; past the chalkboard, past Tessa, past Mrs. Perkins, and made connection exactly where I was aiming.

The neck and shoulders of Cade Williams.

After a collective gasp, the class sat in stunned silence. As the shock on Cade's face gave way to anger, I matched his glare and slowly pulled the rope toward me, tightening the cinch around his neck.

Once she had registered that I had potentially come unglued, Mrs. Perkins bounded over to Cade. "Kelsey! Drop that rope right now!"

While she loosened the knot around his throat, I dropped the rope and stuck my tongue out at him once again as I ran to sit down. Cade's face grew red as the class snickered and pointed at him. I guess you could say this was the start of a very bad day, for *him* as well.

After lunch and recess, the queasy feeling in my stomach had become decidedly worse. I thought about going to see the school nurse, but then I would have had to talk to Mrs. Perkins again, and after what happened earlier, I decided to take my chances. That afternoon, the entire first and second grade filed into the gymnasium to see a woman sing fun songs in crazy voices. She had come the year before, and I had loved singing along so much that I hadn't wanted to miss out on seeing her again.

So, there were many reasons for not going to the nurse when the sick feeling got progressively worse during the assembly.

It was also not my fault that Cade was sitting directly in front of me on the gym floor. Even when he and Luke walked in and made faces at me, they still chose to sit right in front of Tessa and me, probably trying to block our view.

The singer was on a rousing chorus of Apples and Bananas when I took a turn for the worse. My stomach tossed and churned, and I became increasingly afraid to make any sudden movements. I scanned the crowd for Mrs. Perkins and found her talking to another teacher on the other side of the gym.

I shot my hand up in the air, waving frantically, trying to catch her eye. Still nothing.

I was losing time. Desperate time. And then suddenly...

Time ran out.

I was in the midst of standing up to run out of the gym, teacher be hanged, when I lost it.

All of it.

Chunky, projectile vomit spewed from my mouth as the wide-eyed kids in my row suddenly re-lived the prison-grade spaghetti, meatballs, and green beans we had all ingested for lunch. And chocolate milk.

But perhaps no kid re-lived the horrifying second helping more than Cade Williams. Unfortunately for him, I was in the middle of standing up, which put me at the perfect angle for a direct hit. The brown and pink spaghetti slime gushed down the back of his head, both sides, and the front of his face. The unbending patch of hair finally yielded at the weight of the sour-smelling sludge, now piled high atop his head. Upon contact, he jumped up and whirled around, spraying chunks of vomit onto the unsuspecting bystanders. Staring at me, with brown eyes flashing the depths of his misery, the look on his face could only be described as complete and utter horror.

My stomach heaved a few more times, but for the most part, I felt surprisingly better. The room held a collective gasp as hundreds of captivated eyes stared at Cade and me. The two of us gaped at each other in the most excruciating face-off.

I wanted to die.

By the looks of it, Cade wanted me to die as well.

The quiet could only last so long, especially from the innocent among the crowd, who soon realized it was puke juice that had been flung onto them. The room soon erupted with crying, wailing, laughing, pointing, whispering, and my extreme humiliation. Mrs. Perkins finally rushed over, ushering Cade and me out of the gym.

The three of us trudged toward the nurses' office; the only sound between us was the click of my purple, plastic sandals with a daisy flower on top. The throw-up had gotten on my shoes and feet, making my heel slip with each step forward. I had thrown up in front of the entire second grade. The despair I felt fled out of my eyes in the form of heaping tears and hiccuping sobs. Cade was most likely crying because he had someone else's regurgitated spaghetti goo dripping from his body throughout the hallway. Walking between us, Mrs. Perkins attempted to comfort us both, while trying to discreetly encase her nose in her shirtsleeve.

After being scrubbed down as best as the nurse could manage without removing our clothes, we were left alone in the office to wait for our parents. I sat on the long medical bed staring at the floor, my shoulders slumped. Cade still hadn't said a word to me. He sat dejectedly in a chair, his legs bent at the knees, his arms around his shins as if protecting himself. From me? Most likely. My stomach still felt a bit unsettled. His brown hair had been rinsed out in the sink and was now plastered to his head, water dripping down the sides. The silence weighed heavily in the air.

As did the smell.

Swallowing hard, and with my head hung low, I muttered, "Sorry, Cade."

He said nothing. I looked up and found him glaring at me.

"This is war."

Confused, I asked, "What?"

"This is war."

"I didn't mean to throw up on you."

"Well, you did."

"Cade, I said I was sorry. Just forget it."

"That's easy for you to say, you don't have my barf dripping all over you!" Even I had to admit that he made a fair point.

"I still didn't mean to!"

"This. Is. War," he growled, with all the dramatic ferocity an eight-year-old boy could muster.

The nurse walked into the room at that moment. "Kelsey, your mom is here."

Standing up, and with one brave glance back at Cade, I plugged my nose for good effect and said, "I'm glad I threw up on you now. You stink!"

Then I stomped out of the room.

So began the next ten years of my life with Cade Williams. Ten years of tricks, pranks, and intense paranoia. My only therapy, beyond revenge, was by way of a hard-bound, rose-colored journal. The well-worn pages were filled with girlish lists and musings, as well as all the intimate and colorful details of Cade's lavish misconduct. Not mine of course; I was only a poor victim of his horribleness. I mean, beyond the simple retaliation necessary for my survival.

There were just *so* many pranks.

Summer Checklist

1. Meet with florist & decorator
2. Pick wedding colors
3. Ride Ace every day
4. Cattle Drive
5. Run ~~four~~ three miles twice a week with Tessa
6. Parker-proof house for the 4th
7. Seriously, pick flowers and wedding colors ASAP
8. Summer softball league with Tessa!!!!
   (Added by Tessa who def should not be reading my journal)

My left leg tapped against the floorboard to the beat of Imagine Dragons' latest song on the radio. I had one hand out the window of Tessa's truck and one cleated foot on the dash as we belted out the lyrics. We wore matching red team shirts and were driving along the back roads toward the town softball field. Though I hadn't planned on being home for the summer, something about this scene felt right. Sentimental even. The warm summer wind whipped my honey-brown locks into something Medusa would be proud of—minus the snakes. As I tucked my hair back behind my ear, the sunlight hit the rock on my princess cut engagement ring just right, and I couldn't help but admire it.

"Stop looking at it."

I yanked my eyes upward and gazed at the green hayfields rolling by, trying to keep the smile off of my face.

Tessa laughed, her silky blonde hair pulled up in a high ponytail. "You can't even stop smiling."

My eyes once again found their way down to the two and a half karats sitting atop my left ring finger. Yes, TWO AND A HALF. I'd never been a jewelry person, but this ring... this ring looked *good* on my finger.

My phone buzzed on my lap. Tessa leaned across the seat and spied the caller ID. She groaned, good-naturedly, turning the radio down. "Keep the embarrassing love talk to a minimum in my presence, please. I got my fill of you two at college." Her emerald eyes flashed me a teasing look to let me know she wasn't one hundred percent serious; only about ninety-five percent.

I smiled sweetly before swiping the phone on. "Hey, baby cakes. I miss you so, so, so, so, sooooooo much."

Tessa reached across the console of her dad's diesel truck and smacked my arm while I laughed.

A deep chuckle sounded in my ear. "Tessa with you?"

"Yup. And now I have a bruised arm."

"You should put me on speaker so we can get her *really* embarrassed."

I looked over at Tessa. "Do you mind if I put him on speaker?"

She shuddered. "Don't even think about it."

"She said next time for sure. What's up? How are you?"

"Good, just saying hi. I'm headed out with some friends in a bit, so I'll call you later tonight."

I lucked out in the fiancé department. Parker called me like clockwork at 8 pm on the dot. At least that had been his pattern since Tessa and I moved back to our hometown of Eugene, Idaho for the summer, exactly two days ago. But still... lucky.

"What are you and Tessa up to?"

I glanced sideways at my friend before answering. "Tessa made me join the town softball league for this summer. I only agreed because she promised to drop our runs from four miles to three if I said yes. So, I really had no choice."

Tessa caught my eye and mouthed, "You're such a baby."

I just grinned.

"You could just run by yourself whenever you wanted," Parker said in my ear.

"Whenever I wanted? I doubt running thirty seconds a day would do much."

Parker laughed and I imagined the deep dimples in his cheeks piercing through his skin, and suddenly I wished I were miles away in California with my fiancé. We chatted a bit longer until I ended our conversation by making kissing noises into the phone until Tessa began to gag, and then I hung up.

I tossed the phone on the seat and leaned back, sighing happily. "It feels like old times."

"Sitting next to you while you phone-make-out with your boyfriend doesn't feel nostalgic to me."

I laughed. "I'm talking about it just being you and me riding around Eugene. I can't believe it's been so long since I've been home for longer than a holiday or a weekend."

Tessa glanced over at me, a slightly accusatory expression on her face. "And just think, we only had to get rid of the fiancé for the summer to make it happen. Don't look at me like that, I'm just kidding," she added. "I loved being the third wheel everywhere we went."

"I know. You've always had the worst time getting dates. Guys really hate that hot blonde, funny, girl-next-door type. And the bodies on runners these days. Bleh."

She laughed. "Shut up."

It was true though. My beautiful friend with high cheekbones, tan skin, and a perfectly sculpted body (full of muscles and shapes that mine had never known) would never be a third wheel to anyone. Although it had been shocking to me that *I* had found my happily ever after before she did. I was definitely the Monica to her Rachel— although to be fair, Monica *did* get married first. Unless we count that whole drunken Vegas thing. Hmmm... I digress.

At school, I had been so consumed with Parker that my relationship with Tessa, even though we were roommates, had taken a backseat. It felt fun to be just us again for one last summer before I officially traded in my old cowboy boots for stilettos. Except I had never owned a pair of cowboy boots. Or stilettos. So I guess I would be trading in my knee-high rubber milking boots for two-inch platform heels.

Tessa turned the truck into the softball field parking lot and pulled to a stop against the chain-link fence. I looked out at the field in front of me. Dozens of young adults our age were scattered across the grass, stretching, practicing pitches, and catching grounders. I swallowed, wiggling my feet in my stiff cleats, suddenly very aware it had been three years since I last picked up a softball. And at least three years since I had seen any of our old friends.

"What if we did something else together this summer? Something that didn't involve softball and seeing everybody we know, that *still* has me only running three miles?"

Tessa applied a coat of cherry gloss to her heart-shaped lips in the rearview mirror. "Can't. I already told everybody we were coming."

"Who's everybody?" I asked, slightly panicked.

She grabbed her door handle and yanked it open, pausing only a second to say, "Kelsey Marten, do you want me to make it *five* miles?"

"You wouldn't."

"Out!"

Giving her a mock salute, I leaped to the ground and slammed the door behind me. A warm breeze carrying the smell of summer ruffled at the hair resting on my shoulder. Using the elastic hair band that lived on my wrist, I pulled my tangled tresses into a low ponytail, then slid my gray trucker hat onto my head, threading my hair through the hole in the back. The bright red team shirt hung large around my torso, so I did a partial tuck into the front waist of my black joggers, which seemed to help accentuate my... lack of boobage. But the shirt no longer looked like I was drowning in cheap cotton and hopefully took the attention off the one place I had curves on my body—my hips.

We grabbed our bags of softballs and mitts and made our way toward the fields.

"Listen," Tessa began, "I know you're only here because of me and that you're going to be busy with wedding stuff this summer, but thanks for coming. We only have three months left until you get hitched and I'm all alone with my cats. I just wanted some time with you."

I bumped her with my shoulder. "We were going to be crazy cat ladies together."

"I know. Look who went and ruined our plans. Parker would make the worst cat lady."

We walked in silence for a bit before I added, "If I admit I'm a tiny, minuscule amount excited to be here tonight, will I regret it?"

Her eyes lit up and she began bouncing. Tessa was a bouncer when she was excited. "I knew it! You love softball. I don't know why—"

"I know, but I also don't want Parker..."

"What?"

I kicked at a stray softball with my feet as we walked. "I just... feel bad that I didn't go to California with Parker, and I don't want him to hear about me doing fun things and him thinking I would rather be here more than with him." There, I said it. After our college graduation, Parker moved back to his hometown of Santa Cruz, California to work an internship at his dad's law firm for the summer. Up until the week before we graduated, I had been planning to go with him.

Tessa stopped walking and looked at me. "So you can't have any fun this summer because you think it might make him feel bad? He knows you love it here, doesn't he?"

Sure he does. We talked about bucking hay and cattle drives all the time. Insert eye roll. Of course, Parker and I have talked about my childhood. It was a significant part of my life. Yes, he loves teasing me about being a cowgirl, but that's about it. Because we've both moved on. As it should be. Because the only thing worse than being *in* high school are the people who can't move *past* it. And I desperately wanted to move past it. I had spent four years at college *trying* to move past it.

I came home and worked the farm the summer after my first year of college. I played softball and hung out with friends and had a great summer. Then I met Parker that next year at the University of Idaho. He stayed in Moscow all year round, interning at law offices, so to be near him, I had gotten summer jobs and stayed there as well. Moscow, IDAHO, not Russia. Trust me, we're not that interesting. Moscow is where the University of Idaho is located and where Tessa, Parker, and I went to school.

Here's the thing: I came home this summer so that my mom could have a part in planning the wedding. Years earlier, my older sister, Amanda, eloped with her fiancé and it really did a number on my mom. I don't think she ever really got over the disappointment of not helping her oldest daughter plan a wedding. So it feels like my duty as the current favorite daughter to be here so she can help me pick out a dress and flowers and do all the other wedding things her heart desires. Combine that with the fact that my dad also needed some extra help on the ranch this summer, I ended up changing my plans at the last minute, much to Parker's dismay.

But deep down in the pad-locked secret chamber of my heart—I *wanted* to come home.

I wanted to be with my fiancé too, don't get me wrong. After just a few days apart, I was already missing him like crazy. With his sandy blonde hair, blue eyes, and dimples for days, he looks like a true California surfer boy. Although, I don't believe he has ever actually picked up a surf board. But what he lacks in sport and playfulness, he makes up for in sophisticated direction. And he loves me. I had been a definite work in progress in the looks department, so I understand the importance of having somebody of Parker's caliber say he loves me. ME.

But...

It had been three years since I had been home for longer than a holiday or weekend. THREE. And there was nothing like summer on the ranch. No matter how I tried to talk myself out of it, my heart ached for Eugene. For one last summer at home. One last summer milking cows with my dad. Or playing basketball after chores with Jake and Dusty, my dad's ranch hands. One last cattle drive. It would be the perfect send-off to my new life in California.

There was one thing I hadn't counted on, however. Walking back onto the softball field of my youth, toward friends I had grown up with, made my hands clammy and my breathing shallow. I wanted the farm with my dad. I wanted dress shopping with my mom. But with each step closer to the softball diamond, I also got a ball of nerves in my stomach and the uneasy feeling that my carefully planned life had just taken a sudden U-turn, back to the uncomfortable existence I occupied before. The memories of high school, the good, the bad, and the pranks came back in full force.

I didn't have a bad childhood, for the most part. Except for some sketchy events that happened thanks to... well... no need to bring that up. I had good friends and enjoyed the sports scene, but overall, I had been glad to get out of high school. To grow up and move on. I had dedicated the past few years of my life to being somebody different, and I was suddenly terrified that all my efforts toward change would be lost by association.

Tessa hooked her arm through mine and pulled me through the grass toward the large, outdoor complex which sported four diamond-shaped softball fields with a snack bar in the middle. It seemed the whole town had shown up to cheer on their friends and family members with shouts and whistles. The unmistakable crack of a bat hitting a ball pierced through the air.

"Ahhh. Don't you miss that sound?"

A shimmer of anticipation ran through my body before I could squash it. "Nope." I shot Tessa the tiniest of smiles before she rolled her eyes.

"Stoooooop," she groaned. "You're such a liar. It's just a bunch of friends from high school. Jake and Dusty will be there. Holli and Margo said they were coming. You can still have fun without Parker." She released her grip on my arm and turned to face me as she walked backward. "I, for one, am just thrilled Kelsey Marten is off the market, so maybe some of the guys around here will finally notice me."

"You want a guy from *Eugene*?" I couldn't help the wrinkle in my nose when I said it. I couldn't think of any boy I grew up with that I would want to date seriously—let alone *marry*. There were some good guys here, sure, but there was something about watching the boys your age pick their noses throughout elementary school, and occasionally junior high, that just never screamed *come-hither* to me. I knew too much.

"Last I heard your hot brother was still from here."

"Ew." I gave her a light shove while she pulled away laughing.

We ambled toward the fields. I took a deep breath, this time smelling popcorn and barbecued hamburgers, and gave myself just a small moment to appreciate the fact that Tessa had dragged me out here tonight, although she'd never hear it from me. I hadn't meant to stop playing my beloved sport but college and degrees and boyfriends had a way of changing a girl's priorities.

"Who are we playing?"

"The Tramps. Jake and Dusty's team. So it should be a fun game."

"The Tramps versus The Sons of Pitches, huh?"

Tessa laughed. "I didn't pick the names. Here's our team."

She nodded toward the field in the lower east corner, where players in matching red shirts were talking, stretching, and taking a few practice swings. I spotted several friends from high school.

"Is Pete Jones home for the summer?" I asked in surprise as I scanned the players from the other team.

"Yup, I heard he's heading to Virginia State with Margo and Holli this year." You know those friends who always seem to know all the things? That's Tessa.

We were closing in on the field but hadn't been seen just yet. My nerves hummed as we grew closer.

We were spotted.

"Finally!" Margo said as the dark-haired beauty squealed and jogged over to wrap me in a hug. "I've been waiting for you guys to get home all week."

She pulled away, eyeing me up and down. "Girl, you look good."

The attention made my face feel hot. That's what dropping twenty pounds during sophomore year and growing your hair out will do to a person.

I laughed awkwardly and added, "So do you." Other than the fact that she wore a bit too much makeup for such a pretty face, I meant every word.

She refused to let it go, taking a step back to scan my body once more. "I'm serious. Your fiancé must be eating out of your hands."

More teammates sauntered over to offer hellos. I was surprised when the hugs and small talk from old friends took the edge off my nerves. Instead of the apprehension that had gripped me on the drive to the field, I found myself easily conversing with them as if the years hadn't been between us.

"Thank goodness the runt isn't on our team," a voice drawled from behind me.

Turning, I elbowed Jake lightly in the ribs as he pulled me in for a side hug. My head barely came to his chest against his tall, lanky body. Tonight, instead of his boots and cowboy hat, he wore gray sweatpants and his team shirt.

I relaxed at the sight of his friendly face. I also found my fake bravado. "I just feel bad that your team is going to get killed tonight, and you'll still have to face me at work tomorrow."

Jake's eyes lit up, dancing with anticipation. "Care to place a wager on that?"

Immediately, I was on my guard. Anytime Jake offered to place a wager on *anything* my heartbeat sped up to a thousand beats a minute. Before I could answer, Dusty walked up to us and gave me a fist bump. The boys were best friends and two years behind me in school. They had worked after school and summers for my dad since they were fifteen. Where Jake was tall and lanky, a rascally cowboy through and through, Dusty had the build of a football player but the temperament of a teddy bear. They were big in the rodeo scene and were starting to make a name for themselves. They were the best fake little brothers I could ask for—annoying, sweet, funny, and competitive goofballs. We got along wildly well and I adored them both.

I eyed their blue shirts sporting the logo 'Tramps' across the front. "Should I start calling you a loser now, or do you want me to wait?"

Dusty grinned. "Oh, you better wait. We've got a secret weapon coming tonight."

"Did you finally get your grandma to join your team?"

"Ohhhh, Kelsey's bringing the *heat*," Jake quipped, tugging my hair before he and Dusty moved away to play catch. "We'll see if you're still smiling after the game."

A whistle was blown before I could think about his statement, and the two teams moved to their prospective sides, amid good-natured ribbing. Our team won the coin toss and chose to bat first. Dave Nunez, our team captain, brought us together and called out the batting order. My wide eyes met Dave's when he called out my name as the third batter. He grinned at me.

"Don't embarrass us, all-star." Taking in my probably very white face, he added, "And don't throw up on anybody. It's just softball."

Always with the throw-up jokes. Swallowing, I forced a smile. "Funny. I'll be fine. It's just been a while."

Pure adrenaline began racing through me as the members of the Tramp team filled the outfield and bases. I bounced on the balls of my feet while my hands curled against the chain-link fence that separated the dugout from the field. I had forgotten about this part. The pre-game jitters. The excitement and anticipation. The clamminess. The way the world quieted when I was up to bat. It seemed like an eternity since I had played, while at the same time, it felt as though I'd never stopped.

But I had. Happily. Which made my sentiments that much more confusing.

We had one out and Margo was up to bat. I was up next and had just stepped out on deck, taking practice swings in the corner by the dugout.

"Let's go, Margo!" I called. The nerves inside my body had slowed to a dull buzz—the energy of the game overtaking my senses.

Two strikes. Pete was winding up to pitch again when a diesel engine roared to a stop behind the field. A loud, explosive pop sounded just before it went quiet again. The entire team of Tramps suddenly broke out into whooping and cheering, waving beyond the field at something or someone in the parking lot.

The sound of the truck... seemed familiar. Before I placed the noise, a feeling of anxiousness began to churn inside me, like knowing a train wreck was about to happen and not being able to do anything about it. Not that I had ever seen a train wreck, but it almost felt as if my body could sense what was coming before my brain caught up.

And then, my brain caught up. Got the memo. Landed the plane.

I whipped around to prove myself wrong. Fate would have other plans, however, because walking with a wide grin toward the field, as if he had no care in the world, was Cade Williams.

2

Journal Entry (circa - jr. high.)

I opened my locker today. There was a frog inside. I screamed. It jumped out and hopped down the hall. I had to chase it and grab it, which required me to TOUCH IT before it went into the teachers' lounge. I will get his locker combination if it's the last thing I do. Freaking Cade.

Instinctively, I pulled my hat down a bit lower on my head as he passed by my team's dugout, amid excited whoops, hollering, and handshakes from *my* teammates. He wore a blue Tramps shirt and jogging pants, so if I had to guess, this was the big 'secret weapon' mentioned by Jake and Dusty. A town prodigy, if you will. His older brother, Justice, played in college and currently plays in the minors. Cade had been a star player in high school, a starter at Colorado State, and was now set to follow his brother's cleats to the minors. He strode into the dugout where he proceeded to high-five, hug, and chest bump the rest of his fan club not currently on the field. He changed into his cleats and jogged out to replace the catcher. A few practice pitches into his mitt and apparently the world seemed delighted to stop spinning for Cade Williams.

My eyes found Tessa's and I wasn't surprised to see she had been watching me. She shrugged and smiled at me sympathetically. Tessa understood, better than anyone, just what having Cade here meant. I prayed he was only here for the weekend.

"Strike," the umpire called, jolting me out of my nightmare, or perhaps, *into* my nightmare. Margo had just struck out.

My turn.

Though I suppose most everyone's eyes were on me as I sauntered toward home plate, I felt only Cade's. Perhaps it was because as I made my way closer, he tipped back his face mask, a slow grin carving onto his face as he studied me. It had been four years since I had last seen him at graduation. It had been four years and a month, give or take a few days, since I had last *spoken* to him (or yelled at him —however, you want to look at it), since the disastrous prom night. A four-letter word escaped from my mouth as I approached. I lifted my chin slightly and met his eyes with a challenging stare. He tugged at his bottom lip with his teeth and took me in, the small dimple on his left cheek making an appearance as he did so. I moved into my place in front of him in the batter's box—determined to ignore him.

"Looking good, Red."

The breath I had been holding seethed out of me at the old nickname. So it begins.

"Wish I could say the same."

His deep chuckle met my ears as I stepped back and took a couple of practice swings. I wiped my clammy hands on my pants. Sweat had begun to form in tiny droplets all over my body and I was seriously worried about the bat slipping when I swung.

"You're not nervous, are you?" the moron behind me asked. "A big-time all-star like you."

"Do me a favor," I said, not looking at him. "When I'm ready to swing, do you think you could move up a foot or two?"

He laughed as he turned around and said something to the umpire.

The umpire called a time out. I stepped back as Cade stood and jogged around me to the pitcher's mound where Pete Jones was standing. He bent his head close to Pete's. I studied them discreetly for a moment while taking a couple of practice swings. They could pass for brothers with how alike they seemed. Cade and Pete both topped six feet by a couple of inches and both had done some intense physical training after high school—both being college athletes. Their bodies were lean, but instead of geeky, stinky, and pimply teenage boy vibes, manliness oozed out of them. There was an easy confidence in their movements and a settled, effortless air in their manners.

I didn't like it.

Pete was nice, but Cade would still be Cade, no matter how many years had passed. No matter how rugged that five o'clock shadow made his face look. The truth was in his eyes, and at that moment, those eyes were looking at me like I was a piece of meat dangling in front of a hungry dog. The conspirators glanced at me from time to time while most likely discussing ways to outsmart me with a pitch. Pete smiled and smacked him on the back as Cade turned around and sauntered toward me, his baseball hat turned backward on his head. Dark curls and pieces of his unruly hair stuck out beneath his hat. He only grinned while I stared at him dangerously, my eyes narrowed.

"Oh, don't worry about that," he said, crouching back down behind me. "It's just guy talk. Nothing to worry about."

Taking the high road, I focused all of my energy in a prayer heavenward—praying to have the ability to knock the ball out of the park, or somehow backward to smash into the catcher's arrogant face. Okay, so maybe the 'high' road was stretching it a tad.

The first pitch came. It seemed a little high so I let it pass.

"Strike."

"What?" I looked back at the umpire, making sure it wasn't one of Cade's groupies doing his bidding. The balding, middle-aged man with a hefty gut in the middle didn't seem overly partial toward the high school immortal squatting before him. I stifled my groan and focused once again on the pitcher.

"I thought it was a bit high too," Cade whispered.

"Shut up."

On edge now, I swung the second time, but Pete threw a curveball and I hit only air. The firm thud of the ball hitting the glove behind me might as well have been nails on a chalkboard.

"Good try, Red. It took me until about fifth grade before I could hit a curveball."

"It seems like I remember a state championship game where some low-life catcher struck out on a curveball."

"Low blow, Red." I glanced down at Cade just before he mimicked out some play to Pete with his fingers. He was calling the shots behind me like he knew what my weaknesses were. Or maybe he was only messing with my head. Oh, how I hated Cade Williams.

Tuning out every last thing he said behind me, I focused my attention squarely on Pete. The way he gripped the ball didn't look like he was preparing for a curveball, but I primed myself for one anyway. The umpire was calling strikes on high balls, so I made a rash decision to swing at anything coming my way.

The pitch was right down the middle. I swung. The bat chipped at the base of the ball. It popped up—high. Probably a foul, but I took off running anyway, dread filling my stomach. Somewhere behind me, I heard the rustle of Cade's movements and the crowd's cheers picked up. He caught the ball before I reached first base.

"Out!" the umpire shouted as the crowd erupted into cheers.

My heart sunk. It wasn't like this game meant anything. Heck, I didn't even want to *be* here. Nobody on my team seemed upset by the play, but embarrassment flamed my cheeks. I walked back to the dugout, handing out half-hearted high-fives to my teammates. I stole a glance over at Cade and was surprised to find him still watching me. He grinned and then saluted me before rolling the ball to the pitcher's mound and jogging toward the dugout with the rest of his team.

The next time my team was up to bat, Tessa sidled over next to me behind the dugout fence.

"You want news?"

"Nope." I gave my best effort at watching my team up to bat. I waited three whole seconds before adding, "Did he get injured or something?"

"No. According to Dave, just before graduation from Colorado State, he was all set to try out for the minors but then backed out at the last minute. Apparently, it was some big upset. I just heard he moved home for the summer." She gave me a sympathetic glance.

I snorted. "I don't care. I won't see him after this. Doesn't bother me at all."

"I can tell. I should just call you 'easy-breezy Kelsey' with how much this doesn't bother you."

I elbowed her before she got the hint that I didn't want to talk about him. I wanted to kill him. If he ruined my summer with his horribleness...

Ugh. The *whole* summer? I closed my eyes and took in a deep breath. Okay, it wasn't a big deal. It's not like I would be in a class-room with Cade again. I didn't even have to leave the farm if I didn't want to. We weren't in high school anymore. He couldn't rig another foghorn under my chair in English or leave an open can of tuna fish in my locker over the weekend. He's just some idiot I used to know. We had grown up. At least one of us had. If I wasn't around to play his games, he would have to leave me alone.

It took a few innings, but I managed to calm down and put the annoying catcher out of my head. Or rather, I channeled my energy into his demise on the field. Tagging him out once on second base helped a little. Even though he was still his smiling, annoying self each time I was up to bat, I had some decent hits that grew my confidence a few notches and earned a high five from Dave.

It turned out that Cade really was a secret weapon. The Tramps won 5 to 2, but even I was impressed at my team's ability to hold the college all-star to only five points. The game ended, and both teams gave a cheer and came together in a line to slap hands.

"How'd you like our secret weapon, Kels?" Dusty asked, giving me a fist bump in passing.

"Yeah, yeah," I muttered.

Instead of slapping my hand and moving on, Cade *grabbed* my hand and pulled me toward him, out of line.

"I gotta admit, I was kind of hoping you'd be around this summer." His self-assured grin made me want to gag.

I pulled my hand out of his grasp. "I hate to disappoint you, but I most definitely won't be *around* this summer."

His thick brows furrowed. "You going back to school?"

"No. I've graduated. I'm just here for the summer while I plan my wedding." I wiggled my left finger at him. I couldn't help but throw that little tidbit in. If I had to, maybe I could make it seem like Parker could kick his trash if he got out of line with me, though that might be overkill. "I'll be busy working for my dad, so although it's been a *pleasure*, this will be the last time you'll be seeing me."

"What?" Cade stared at me, stunned. "You don't know?"

"Know what?"

At my confused face, he threw his head back in disbelief and laughed. "It's even better than I imagined."

"What?" I asked again, the nerves in my body starting to hum.

At that moment, we were surrounded by both teams gathered

together laughing and tossing smack between each other. A sense of deja vu overcame me. It felt like four years of my life had never happened and I was right back in high school with Cade. My fingers twisted the rock on my hand as a reminder.

Four years at the University of Idaho *did* happen. My degree in Broadcast Journalism was burning a hole in my proverbial back pocket. I was getting married and moving on with a promising career ahead of me. I may be here for three months while I plan my wedding, but my mind would be in California with Parker. I would not engage. The old Kelsey had grown up and moved on.

Gradually, more and more people separated Cade and me. I no longer cared about what information he was taunting me with. Who cares if he's here for the summer? Although, this was now the official *last* game of my career in the hometown softball league. There was no way I'd be playing again. Hopefully, Tessa would have pity and still not make me run four miles. I found her in the crowd talking to Holli. Feigning a smile, I tucked my arm through hers and gave her the *look* —that SOS look between best friends that essentially said, 'get me the H out of here.'

Tessa, bless her heart, caught on perfectly, and soon we were edging away from the crowd, saying our goodbyes.

"Everybody's meeting at Daisy's for ice cream in a bit," Tessa said as we walked toward the truck. "I'm guessing that's a no for you."

I shook my head. "If you want to go, please do, but could you drop me off at home first?"

"Sure." Tessa was quiet. "I'm sorry Cade showed up."

"It's fine."

She burst out laughing. "Oh yeah, you seem perfectly fine. But I must say, you held your own against him on the field beautifully."

"It didn't feel like it."

"From the perm-a-grin on Cade's face, I don't even think he minded when you tagged him out on second. Did you see the way he looked at you when you first went up to bat?"

I brought my hands up to cover my face. "Ugh. What's he doing here?"

"I heard he's doing an internship or something."

Tired of talking about it and feeling dumb that I had made seeing Cade such a big deal, I forced myself to talk about something else the rest of the walk back to the truck, even though my mind was racing. All I wanted was to get home, go for a ride on Ace, call Parker, and pretend seeing Cade had never happened. Talking to Parker would help. He had a way of taking my mind off of things that didn't matter. Seeing Cade again threw me for a loop, but I'd just have to be extra vigilant about leaving the privacy of my home from now on. I would do wedding things, ranch things, and Tessa things. That's it. It would be great.

I had just opened the passenger door of the truck when a voice called out from behind us.

"Hey, Red! Tessa! Hold up."

We looked over to see Cade jogging toward us.

With him still out of earshot, I whispered to Tessa, "Do we have to?"

She nodded. I wasn't kidding, but she had the keys.

All my senses were on high alert as he moved closer. There was a calculating look in the back of his eyes as he approached, carefully hidden, but one I recognized from years of being his target; not unlike an animal in the wild about to pounce on its prey. My stomach clenched as he approached, my body's natural warning reflex around Cade.

He stopped a few yards away from me, putting his hands in the pockets of his dark gray jogging pants as his eyes took me in. I refused to allow myself a glance at the muscles peeking out from his sleeves, other than to quickly acknowledge that in the past four years, he had apparently gotten to be friends with a couple of guys named 'bench' and 'press.'

"Hey, Tessa, how's it going?" Cade gave her a friendly grin which Tessa returned, eagerly. My mouth dropped open as I stared at them.

"Good, Cade, how are you? You had some good hits tonight." She walked closer to him for a quick side hug. When she finally had the guts to look at me, she could only smile sheepishly. My eyes narrowed—excuse me while I extract the knife from my back.

When she stepped away, Cade turned and motioned for me to follow suit. I folded my arms and leaned against the truck.

He smiled. "Look, Red, I'm sorry we got off on the wrong foot. It's kind of surprising how easy it was to step back into high school mode."

I stared dumbly at him for a few long seconds. Other than the fact that he still blatantly called me Red, did he just... apologize? I glanced at Tessa as she raised her eyebrows.

He continued. "I mean, it brought back a lot of fun memories," he said with a laugh. "But I am sorry."

I still had not uttered one word. At this point, he had stopped talking and looked at me for some sort of response.

"Okay." Geez, that was bad. I tried again. "Thanks." Still bad, but hey, I had never dreamed of a moment like this happening, so I had never prepared myself for an apology.

"Anything you want to say to me?"

My eyes shot up to his to find a barely suppressed glimmer of laughter lurking in their depths. Caught off guard, the tiniest hint of a smile itched to break away on my face, but I stopped it just in time. It was time to give this guy exactly what he was asking for, which was probably the only way to shut him up. I released the most sweetly patronizing look I could muster and said, "Sure. I'm sorry too, Cade."

He nodded and stuck out his hand. I hesitated a moment. It felt like a trap, but when somebody sticks out their hand to shake yours, you do it. It's a reflex.

His hand was warm as it engulfed mine. I immediately pulled it away and wiped it on my shirt, fully aware of the growing glint in his eyes as I did so.

"I'm really going to enjoy working with you."

And there it was. The statement I should have been prepared for. The apology had been a decoy. I repeat, the apology had been a decoy.

"What?" My fingers gripped the door as my blood pressure rose.

His eyes danced with pure delight. I watched him try to swallow it, to hide it, but it couldn't be done. Elation radiated from him.

Something close to a smile formed on his face as he dropped the bomb he'd been waiting for all night. "Yeah, I'll be living on your ranch for the next few months. Your dad hired me to cowboy for him this summer."

3

Journal Entry (circa - high school)

Tessa and I walked the entire length of Main Street today, and we knew who lived in every house. Then we walked one street over and did the same thing. Then we ran out of streets. 52 more days until college.

My hometown of Eugene sat tucked away in central Idaho, thirty miles south of Salmon, and nestled at the base of the Challis National Forest. Besides my four-year stint at college, I have lived in Eugene my entire life, down the same half-mile lane, in the same single-level ranch-style home. The sky had softened into a cotton candy sunset out my window as Tessa and I left the baseball field and began to weave our way through green farmland before entering Main Street. It was the most happening street in town and boasted a hardware store, tractor parts store, thrift store, and even a tiny, run-down, and completely overpriced grocery store. Eugene was pretty, in a rustic sort of way; the way you might pick up a discarded penny from the sidewalk only to turn it over and see bright, shiny copper hidden on the other side. It was easy to overlook, but once a person smelled the sagebrush, heard the sounds of the tractors plowing the deep, rich dirt, or closed in on the rugged mountains surrounding the town, they might stop and take a second look.

Tessa tried three times to bring up Cade in the truck, but I had been shell-shocked into a numb silence, providing little substance beyond grunting and the occasional moan. She switched gears and brought up Parker, which was probably hard for her, bless her heart. Even thoughts of my fiancé couldn't bring me out of this mental stoop I found myself in. Finally, she grew quiet, turning down the half-mile dirt lane that led to my parent's house.

Cade Williams was working for my dad this summer. *I* was working for my dad this summer. Those were two sentences that should have never collided.

"Why didn't my dad tell me?"

Tessa glanced over at me, not at all surprised by my sudden outburst. Once the shock had begun to wane, anger was quickly taking its place.

"To be fair, you didn't tell your parents you were coming home this summer until a week ago."

"That means he had seven whole days to tell me."

"Maybe he knew if he told you, you wouldn't come home."

I banged my head against Tessa's passenger window. She was not wrong. I would be holding hands with Parker and walking along the beach right now, if I had known Cade would be working anywhere in my vicinity over the summer.

She pulled up to the brown brick house of my youth and put the truck into park. Though it was only the beginning of June, the grass in the sprawling yard was green and freshly cut. Towering pine trees surrounded the house and yard, and my favorite maple tree with the lush leaves, stood guard over the porch sitting to the left of the entryway. The lone porch swing swung just a bit, a testament to the slight breeze that had picked up as we left the softball field.

"You know what I think?" Tessa asked.

I looked at her and raised my eyebrows in reply.

"That this summer just got a whole lot more interesting," she grinned at me.

Needing to nip this conversation in the bud before Tessa ran away with it, I shook my head. "No, it didn't."

"Maybe not in your mind, but in Cade's mind, this summer definitely got a lot more interesting."

I groaned.

"What am I going to do? I'm planning a wedding. I'm engaged. I do not want to get involved in some huge pranking scheme. I don't have the time or the freaking energy, and I just... can't. What do I do?"

"I don't know. Your track record isn't great at ignoring him." She laughed. "Remember when you found out he was taking Jenny Miller on a date to The Ranch House?"

Despite my best effort, I could not keep the grin from escaping at the memory. It had been one of my better pranks. It took place early in our senior year, and it just so happened that my older brother Logan's best friend, Tommy, worked as a waiter at the diner. I was able to convince him to put a special ice cube, that Tessa and I had concocted, into Jenny's drink. An ice cube with a fake diamond ring inside. It was the first and last date for Jenny and Cade.

"He had to be kept in check," I countered.

"I'm just saying, he got worse because you pranked him back," Tessa insisted.

"It was self-defense!"

She laughed, rubbing her face with her hands. "I'm sorry. I feel for you, I do. I'm trying to think of how to handle all this."

"Ignoring him is the key. If I don't respond, he'll have to stop."

"While he works for your dad? Doing the same jobs you're doing?" Disbelief shone on Tessa's face as she snorted.

"What, you don't think I can?"

"I think you *can*. But do you remember it like I do? You're acting like it was all doom and gloom, but it was fun for you too."

"It wasn't fun. It was self-preservation."

Tessa stared at me in amazement, shaking her head slightly. "Alright... well, when you finally give in to temptation, I'll be here, just like old times, to help you think of some good pranks."

I pulled on the door handle. "Nope. Not happening."

As I ran up the steps to my house, she shouted, "I give it one week!"

I entered the house breathless and ran down the hall to change my shoes. I flung my cleats in the back of my closet where I had found them and reached for another pair of shoes that hadn't been worn in a while. I tried to assess how long it had been since I had last ridden Ace. Had it really been a whole year? I tried to come home on major holidays and a few weekends every year, but I couldn't recall if Ace had been ridden during my last visit. The knee-high, brown boots were dust covered and felt stiff against my shins and knees as I tugged them on after such a long bout of neglect. So different from my usual heels. I threw on old sweatshirt on over my Pitches shirt and set off down the hallway.

Mom was sitting in the kitchen and was anxious to discuss wedding plans. Parker and I had opted for a short engagement, a mere three months, and had since thrown her into panic mode. She had already set appointments for us to meet with a florist, photographer, and a reception hall later in the week. I gave her a quick hug, thanked her, and promised I would feel up to discussing wedding plans the next morning. I grabbed a handful of carrots and slipped out the back door. I didn't even have the energy to discuss Cade with her yet. I wanted to save all my steam for my dad.

The traitor.

The setting sun had nearly met the horizon when I meandered behind the house, past my dad's shop, and made my way out to the corral. Dad must have felt my inner wrath in his choice of employee and stayed out of my way. Either that or he was still at the agriculture meeting in town and hadn't made it home yet. Ace jittered and snorted in excitement as he watched me approach the fence. I laughed as he nuzzled his nose directly into my hand with the carrots.

"Hey, boy," I cooed in his ear as I stroked his neck.

He shuffled and whinnied, and I couldn't help myself any longer. Leading him over to the fence, I climbed up onto a rung and threw my leg over Ace's back. Years ago, I had learned to ride bareback and had never looked back. It wasn't necessarily a preference, as I appreciated the comfort of a saddle, but I was much too lazy to saddle my horse as often as I wanted to ride him. If I took the time today, it would be too dark. I led him slowly around our corral until neither of us could stand the snail pace any longer. Leaning forward, I pulled the latch that opened the gate and spurred him onward. As if a fire had been lit behind him, Ace charged out of the corral, with me holding tight to his mane. The next few minutes were spent reacquainting ourselves as we flew through the hay fields surrounding my parents' home. Mountains of homework, packing, finals, and getting engaged had filled my days and nights the weeks before graduation, and it had been so long since I had felt the sense of freedom that only racing at top speed on the back of a horse could provide.

When we reached the base of the mountains just past our corrals, I pulled Ace to a stop, breathless but invigorated. A stubborn streak of orange was the only color still left in the sky and it was quickly losing brightness. It was too dark to trudge up the mountains behind my parents' house, though I looked at them longingly. The smell of hay and sagebrush filled my lungs and I let my head fall back as Ace sauntered back toward home. I refused to let my mind think about

Cade. I think I was in the denial stage of my grief. It was easier if I just pretended nothing had happened, that he wasn't going to be working for my dad.

The stars in the Idaho sky twinkled merrily, and the sounds of the crickets crooned in the distance. Otherwise, all around me was quiet. There were a few homes scattered in the distance, across the fields, but for the most part, we were completely isolated on the ranch for at least a mile in all directions. This was a far cry from Moscow. Though it was also a beautiful mountain town, I had lived in a noisy apartment just off campus with Tessa and five other girls. I couldn't remember the last time I'd been alone for longer than a car ride to the grocery store or class. And even that was a rare occurrence.

A popular love song cut through the still night air. My back pocket vibrated, causing Ace to stiffen and jerk.

"Easy, boy," I mumbled, leaning forward to reach into my pocket. "It's just Parker."

"Hey, babe," his strong, self-assured voice rang in my ear when I answered. I sighed and immediately felt calmer. Parker was one of those types who had his life mapped out since he was a child. His dad was a lawyer and Parker always knew that was what he wanted to be too. As far as I could tell, his dad would have been supportive of *any* of his son's dreams, so it wasn't even one of those cases where the parents force their will upon their kids. He just knew exactly what he wanted. He knew he would be good and that kind of confidence demanded respect. Parker would make everything better.

"How's my little cowgirl?"

"*Farm*girl," I corrected.

"What's the difference?"

"I have never once worn a pair of wranglers or a cowboy hat for anything other than a Halloween costume."

"Oh, that sounds interesting. What do you wear while working on the farm?" he teased. "No, wait, don't tell me. Let me see if I can imagine what you wear while you drive a tractor."

Delight at his suggestive words bubbled up inside of me even as I gave him a halfhearted scolding. Which just made him laugh.

"How was your night with your friends?" I asked.

"Boring without you. Are you still playing softball? It sounds like you're outside."

"No, we're done. I'm outside riding Ace. We're almost back to the house."

"We?"

"Me and Ace."

"In the dark?"

"It's just now dark, but the stars are bright and Ace knows where he's going. It's fine."

He made a noise like he wasn't sure he believed me. "Be careful. I don't want to be driving my wife down the aisle in a wheelchair on our wedding day."

"I promise we are almost back to the corral."

Something was on his mind. Parker was never one to chit-chat with no direct purpose. I don't think he was too worried about me riding a horse after dark. He treated his phone calls to his fiancé like he did everything else in life. They were direct and scheduled, with just enough sweetness to keep me anticipating his call every evening. I enjoyed a few more minutes of rare casual talk before he finally zeroed in on his purpose.

"So... have you found a dress yet?"

That didn't fall into the category of subjects I thought he'd bring up. "No," I answered him. "My mom and I plan to go in a couple weeks to look, I think."

I couldn't remember *exactly* when dress shopping fell on the intimidating wedding calendar that hung in my mom's kitchen, but it was soon. Ace and I had arrived back at his corral. I held the phone with one hand while I maneuvered my body awkwardly off my horse.

"What would you say if I told you I could help out with all that?"

"Help out with what?" I asked, wincing when my feet hit the ground. I forced myself to stretch the stiff muscles in my legs. Missing a few years of riding can really take a toll on the body.

"With your wedding dress. Would that take some stress off of you?"

What? He now had my full attention while I forced myself to walk gingerly around Ace's corral, working to loosen the tightness. "No offense, because you are a really good dresser, but I don't think wedding dresses are in your wheelhouse."

I could almost see him rolling his eyes through the phone, which made me smile. "I meant that we have access to a wedding dress for free if you want it."

"Free?" Free didn't sound like anything Parker's family would approve. In a family dynasty filled with wealth, free was definitely beneath them. And then dread filled my stomach. It was his mom's. What else could it be? And how could I possibly turn down the offer without offending my future mother-in-law?

"Is it your... mom's or something?"

"Nope. Better than that."

I almost sighed in relief having dodged that bullet, but I kept myself in check. "Whose, then? And why is it free?" And why would your family be concerned about a price tag?

"You've heard of Jennifer Harris, right?"

"The actress?" Of course I had. Tessa and I quoted her movies all the time.

"Yeah. She had a fancy wedding dress made by a designer friend of my mom's and she called off her wedding last week. In cases like that, the dresses usually go up for a bid between all the bridal shops in the area, but since my mom is a friend, the designer checked with her first."

"I still don't understand how this involves me. I can't afford a celebrity dress."

"Hendrix, the designer, will let you wear it for free as long as the wedding is professionally photographed and covered by a wedding magazine; Martha Stewart Wedding magazine, to be correct. After you wear it, my mom will get to sell it in her dress shop. She'll have the right to use the pictures for her shop as well. That way the designer and my mom each get some good publicity."

I stood in stunned silence for a few moments, trying to compute everything he had just said. Jennifer Harris. The actress. I would get to wear her dress. JENNIFER HARRIS. THE ACTRESS. Martha Stewart Wedding magazine? My mind exploded.

"Can I see it?" Was my voice breathless? It sounded breathless.

He chuckled. "I just texted you a picture."

I checked my phone. "It hasn't come through yet. I probably don't have good reception out here. So our wedding is going to be photographed for a magazine?"

"Yeah. It's good publicity for my dad's law firm as well." He paused. "Is that okay with you? I didn't think you'd care, so I already gave my approval about all the publicity."

"No. I just... I don't know. Jennifer Harris? Really?!"

Parker laughed. "Yup."

"I'm still confused on why they think I would be a good fit to wear her dress?"

"Because you're just as hot as she is," Parker said. "My mom showed the designer your picture and he thought you'd be perfect for it as well."

"She showed him my picture?" Flattery at his words ran through me, even if my skin crawled just a bit at being judged so superficially.

My phone buzzed. I put him on speaker and opened the picture. My mouth dropped open.

"Yes. A thousand times, yes."

He laughed. "I thought you might say that."

The dress was a soft white, with just the right amount of shimmer. Shown on the model, it was a form-fitted sleeveless dress with a slight mermaid hem splaying out at the waist, but the real eye-catcher was the plunging V neckline that dropped almost to the navel. It looked as though the neckline did the same in the back. Intricate lace and flower detail overlayed the dress in detailed precision. In a word, it was stunning.

"So, are you sure? Should I tell my mom you want to wear it?"

As the news processed, my initial excitement paused. I had come home to Eugene so my mom could be a part of the wedding plans. Though the actual wedding will take place in Santa Cruz, we would have a reception in Eugene after the honeymoon. She had been so excited to go dress shopping with me. She had a girl's trip to Boise planned to get pedicures, go out to lunch, and shop for a dress with her youngest daughter.

But this dress would be free. My family had lived comfortably on our ranch my whole life, but some years had been leaner than others, thanks to the varying prices of cattle, milk, and wheat. So "free" had to count for something. I didn't know the going rate of a celebrity-designed dress, but this seemed like a pretty big honor. But my mom...

Parker moved in for the kill. "Look babe, if you don't want to wear it, you don't have to. It's your wedding, not my mom's. We just thought that since it was free and a cool thing to tell the grandkids one day, that you might go with it. My mom will be pretty bummed, but like I said, it's your wedding, not hers, so if you want to pick out a dress with your mom in Boise, be my guest. She'll get over it."

I shook my head slightly. Yeah, I'm sure she'd get over it. And that would make family dinners together for the next fifty years delightful. No way. Besides, the dress really would be quite the thing to tell people at dinner parties. Not that dinner parties had ever been a part of *my* world, but they had most likely been a part of Parker's.

"Yes," I said. "I'd like to." As soon as the words left my lips, my mom's face flashed through my mind once more. Dress shopping with her would have been fun. Maybe we could still do it if I could convince her that shopping for bridesmaid dresses would be just as much fun. Burning guilt aside, the more I thought about it, the more excited I got about the dress. *Jennifer Harris's* dress. Me. I was finally catching Parker's vision.

Parker smiled. I couldn't see him smile, but I knew he did. "Great. Thanks, babe."

"Isn't it bad luck for you to see the dress before the wedding?"

"Too late. I've already got a pretty good visual of what you'll look like wearing it. And I'll just tell you, the wedding night can't come fast enough for me."

I laughed softly as I leaned against a fence, nudging my toe in the dirt.

"Oh, one more thing," Parker cleared his throat. "You're a size four, right?"

"Size four? No." My stomach clenched in a tight knot. "Is the dress a size four?" I mentally smacked my hand to my forehead. Of course, I wouldn't be the same size as a celebrity.

"Yeah. You can't be that far off, can you?"

"I'm a six on a good day. Can't the designer alter the dress a little?"

He sighed. "Not really. He won't alter it even if he could, because it would lessen the Jennifer Harris appeal. It has to be size four." He paused, waiting, using the power of his silence to intimidate and raise my anxiety levels. Well done. He would be a good lawyer one day.

Three months. I would have three months to lose a dress size. Okay, maybe a dress size and a half, just to be safe. I lost twenty pounds and two dress sizes in six months during my first year in college, so one more little size shouldn't matter. I'd probably be too stressed to eat much this summer anyway.

"Okay. I think I can do that."

"Thanks, babe." There were muffled voices on the other end of the line before Parker spoke again. "My mom said she'll bring the dress when we come out for the Fourth of July and you can try it on then."

Right. The fourth. Parker and his parents were flying out from California to meet my parents and discuss wedding details, which meant I had until then to lose a dress size, tell my mom I already found a dress, and avoid Cade.

Easy-peasy.

4

Qualities I want in a Husband (circa - junior high)
- ~ Handsome
- ~ Dark hair preferable but will settle
  for blonde, if there are dimples
- ~ Makes me laugh
- ~ Rich
- ~ Be a good dad (play with kids)
- ~ will help me wash dishes
- ~ Likes to cook
- ~ Treats me nice
- ~ Feeds me when hungry
- ~ Knows how to ride bareback
- ~ Does not like to prank

The next morning, after milking in the barn with my dad, we moved to the north corral to feed the cows. We had a good system; he would pick up and move the bales into position, cut the twine holding the hay together, and then I would use the pitchfork to pick the hay bale apart and fling it into the manger. Although the job was nothing to write home about, I found the monotony of feeding cows cathartic and I always enjoyed the one-on-one time with my dad, teasing and laughing, even though I was annoyed at him at that moment.

Dad had given Jake and Dusty the day off since they had a rodeo over in Missoula that evening. One of the many reasons they loved working for my dad was that he was generous with whatever time off they needed for their sport.

"What about Harold?" I asked my dad as I pitched a large chunk of hay into the manger. "I loved Harold. How about him?"

Dad looked like how you might expect a farmer to look. He wore dusty jeans, comfortable boots, and a button-down plaid work shirt. He carried a pen, notebook, and his phone in his shirt pocket, had skin tanned by hours spent working outside, and laugh lines around his eyes. He was handsome, I could see why my mom fell for him, but my dad's best feature was his sense of humor. Except now, of course. I didn't find him all that funny today.

He barked out a laugh as he moved another bale into place. "You hated Harold."

Hate was a strong word. It's not that I couldn't stand the old, retired farmer, it was more his breath and aversion to personal space that had offended me. He was the dictionary definition of a close talker. I wouldn't be over the moon excited for his presence, but I'd tolerate him just fine for the summer. "I didn't hate him, Dad. I was just thinking that I would love another chance to get to know him better. Why not call Cade up and tell him you had a better offer?"

He smirked at me as he brushed hay off his jeans. "Sorry Kels, Stitch asked me. It's his grandson. If you think *you* can say no to Stitch, be my guest. He's in the bunkhouse drinking his coffee at the moment."

I sighed. My dad and I had spent the morning in lighthearted banter as I tried my hardest to persuade him to look into other options besides Cade; not that I thought it would get me anywhere, but a girl had to try. I refused to go down without a fight, but I had my limits, and I couldn't say no to Stitch either. He was my dad's ranch foreman, a retired veterinarian, and was generally the quietest and grumpiest person on the ranch. But that grumpiness was counteracted by a twinkle in his eye that I just adored. His only downfall was his shared genetics with Cade.

Dad carried another hay bale and dropped it by the manger with a thud. He reached up and removed his cowboy hat and wiped the sweat off his forehead. I smiled watching him. His once full head of brown hair was a distant memory. He wore his hat more and more these days, and I was beginning to suspect he did so to cover up his bald spots. "Just remember, I hired Cade for the summer *before* you told me you were coming. So you can't be mad at me."

"And why didn't you tell me before I got here? You know how I feel about Cade."

He kicked the last bale of hay into the manger before walking over to me, throwing his arm over my shoulder and tucking me in for a side hug—my dad's specialty. "And take the chance of scaring you away? I'm already losing you to some rich, city kid. I just wanted one last summer with my most okay-est ranch hand."

"Your *best* ranch hand," I said, giving my dad a sharp elbow.

"If Logan or Amanda ask me about any of this, I'll deny it."

"When is Cade supposed to get here?" I asked, slapping the hay and dust from my clothes with my gloves.

"He should be here by 9 am to move his stuff into the bunkhouse."

I pulled a face. "Ugh. Why doesn't he just stay at his mom's house?"

My dad smiled. "He specifically asked if we had a room available *in* the bunkhouse. I'm not sure why he wanted to stay here."

My stomach sank. I knew *exactly* why he wanted to stay here.

I pulled my phone out of my back pocket and checked the time. 8:40 am. Crap. "Uhh... Dad? Do you have anything I could do today that won't put me interacting with Stitch's grandson?"

Dad shot me a warning look. "Kels, it's going to be a long summer if you don't change your attitude. Just be nice. Most people move on from high school."

"I know, Dad. I promise, I don't plan on this summer being a problem with Cade, but I just want to..."

"Hide out for a little longer?" He gave me a knowing look, but his eyes danced just enough to give me hope.

"Yeah."

"He's going to be with Stitch most of the day, learning the ropes. His number one priority is to get experience with a licensed Vet, but he'll also be doing chores and helping out around here just like you and the boys. So..." Dad drawled out the word as his eyes darted around the farm. "If you wanted to go work out near the orchard this morning and cut out the dead branches of those two birch trees we didn't get pruned last fall, be my guest."

"I'm on it!" My eyes lit up as relief flooded my body. "Thanks, Dad."

"Do you need something for this afternoon?"

"No, Mom and I are headed to Salmon to meet with a florist."

I laughed at my dad's disgusted face. Anytime I brought up something to do with the wedding, his reaction was the same. I ran to the shop where we kept the pruning shears and clippers and grabbed a pair of gloves off the shelf. Throwing them into a wheelbarrow, I ran like a fire was lit underneath me to the small orchard situated in front of our house. Though not heavily dense with trees, it provided opportunities to... keep to myself... if I chose. Even though I was planning to play nice, I would make sure to always be one step ahead of Cade.

Just in case.

The large white birch sat neglected in the south end of our orchard. I trimmed the tree as far as I could reach from the ground but found I needed to be up higher for the rest. I leaned the rickety ladder next to the tree and inched my way up toward the top, holding onto a strong branch above my head, not trusting the thirty-year-old ladder for longer than necessary, and pulled myself to sit on the thick tree branch. Clinging to the tree with my legs, I cut and pulled out the dead limbs and branches with satisfaction.

Though the monotony of the job had my mind wandering to my wedding plans and what my fiancé was doing right at that moment, I could sense the moment his truck turned onto the driveway. The blue jays above me immediately stopped singing, pulling their wings over their faces in terror. The squirrels and chipmunks, once happily munching on acorns at the base of the tree, scurried up the limbs to lose themselves in the leaves. The mice in the fields darted into their underground burrows. Even the snakes slithered back into their devil dens. A bitter wind picked up, causing the leaves in the trees to shudder. The...

I'm kidding.

But if my life were a Disney movie, that's exactly how it would have played out.

I would recognize that blue truck anywhere. Even from my position in the tree, I knew that as he moved closer, I would see a discolored dent in the rear bumper where Jenny Miller accidentally backed into it in ninth grade. It stood tall and heavy like a tank, and we had all been in shock when Jenny's truck was the one left unscathed. He hadn't demanded payment from Jenny and had refused to fix it up, claiming that the dent just gave his beloved clunker added character.

I watched helplessly as he sped toward my house, invading my personal space in a much more horrific way than Harold ever did. It wasn't like Harold ever put a whoopee cushion on my chair when I sat down in science class. He never put my car on cinderblocks in high school. He never left a peeled, boiled egg in my locker over the weekend. Harold's only crime was being a close talker and having breath that could curdle milk. Harmless, really—in the grand scheme of things. What had I been complaining about? He was a delight. So funny and kind. A great cowhand. Harold was exactly what my dad needed.

Then why wasn't it Harold's musty old Buick driving down the lane right now?

The truck came closer and without thinking, I climbed a branch or two higher. I felt vulnerable in the worst way, like a chicken waiting for the old man and the ax to arrive. The tree gave me everything I needed at the moment—a large and looming trunk with thick, leafy branches. Branches that provided protection from all kinds of unwanted varmints, especially the two-legged variety. As he rounded the bend near the house, I edged myself around the tree, stepping on branches, being careful to keep the tree between me and Cade's moving truck at all times.

I was like a ninja, with how well I kept pace with the truck. There was no way he could've seen me. Although, perhaps I could have chosen a more ninja-like outfit. I had on an old red t-shirt, jeans, and rubber boots that hit me almost to the knee. A high ponytail kept my hair off my neck and my face was free of makeup, which was a rare occurrence these days. I always had makeup on, I just hadn't felt the need to dress up for the cows at 5 am. It didn't matter though, because I was invisible.

Finally, the truck pulled up next to the bunkhouse, just underneath the large *Lost River Ranch* sign above the door.

I held my breath as the truck door opened and Cade stepped out. He wore a pair of faded jeans and a fitted t-shirt. His dark brown hair, as always, was shoved underneath his baseball hat. A bed frame and mattress, a few boxes, and garbage sacks full of Cade's belongings had been tossed haphazardly in the back of his truck, further proving that he was here to stay. All summer. Before he could slam the door shut, my dad stepped out of the bunkhouse and approached him with a smile.

A smile.

Betrayal didn't even begin to describe how I felt at that moment.

Cade grinned as they shook hands, both of them laughing at some remark. They were too far away for me to hear what they were saying, but I had no idea what my dad and Cade could have so much to laugh about. I could recall countless times my dad had commiserated with me regarding all the pranks he used to pull. It was one thing to understand that my dad hired him for the summer, but it was another *watching* them interact together. So friendly and casual. Like twelve years of my life hadn't even happened.

At that point, the tree started digging into places no woman wanted dug into, but I was stuck there as long as they continued to shoot the breeze. I shuddered to think what Cade's reaction would be if he were to see me in the tree. I knew very well what it might look like to an observer.

Finally, my dad motioned for Cade to follow him into the bunkhouse. Shifting slightly, more than ready to make my getaway, I forced myself to hold still a moment longer. My dad stepped through the doorway with Cade on his heels, but just before he closed the door, Cade turned back and looked toward the orchard.

Directly at *me*, to be precise.

My heart jolted as I drew in a sharp breath. He couldn't see me, right? I'd been so careful. Something else must have caught his attention. Then, ever so slowly, he raised his arm until he was pointing to exactly where I was hiding in the tree. From my limited viewpoint about seventy-five yards away, it seemed he even had the gall to slap a big, fat, irritating grin on his face. Then he strode into the bunkhouse like he owned the place.

Groaning, I let my head fall against the tree in defeat. There would be no scorekeeping this summer. NONE. I wasn't going there.

I wasn't.

But if I *were*, the score would be Cade one, Kelsey zero.

The dirty skunk.

Things to Eat on a Low Taste, Low Fat, High Sadness diet:

1. Chicken
2. Turkey
3. Fish (I'd rather die)
4. Fresh fruits and vegetables
5. That's it. That's all you get

The Blushing Lily flower shop was located on Main Street in the town of Salmon, about forty minutes north of Eugene. For all that was thriving in my little town, (eye-roll), they just couldn't seem to keep a flower shop in business. For the entire drive, I tried to naturally keep a wide berth around any and every subject that might eventually lead back to wedding dress shopping. It was a difficult task when I was my mother's last daughter to get married, and the only daughter who hadn't eloped. Thanks so much for *that*, Amanda. She had talked about wedding dress shopping with me since I was a little girl. Cue dagger in the heart.

My mom was a rational woman, I reasoned with myself as I asked her once again for her tricks on mastering her homemade rolls. She loved to talk about anything kitchen related, but her specialty was yeast. Other than stuffing my face with said rolls, I wanted nothing else to do with them, but I feigned polite interest to keep her talking.

I wasn't being a *chicken*. I was waiting for the right time. And the right time was definitely not on the way to a meeting. If anything, I would be telling her on the way home, as soon as we were five minutes from the house, so I could make a break for it the second the car stopped.

Bak, bak, bak.

Mom wouldn't freak out. She would be okay. I repeated Parker's words in my head, it was *my* wedding after all. It was Jennifer Harris's wedding dress. Jennifer Harris! And it was free. This was a no-brainer, except the part about losing a dress size to wear it. That was going to be a bit of a head-scratcher. The dress was gorgeous. THIS WAS NOT CRAZY. If anything, I'd be crazy not to do it.

I was going to break my mom's heart.

After learning everything I never wanted to know about making rolls, Mom swung into the empty parking stall in front of The Blushing Lily. Getting out of the car, we laughed about our similar outfits. We both wore jean capris and a floral top. Her short, light brown hair was curled loosely around her rounded face, making her seem sweet and earnest. She looked like the best mom from a nineties sitcom. She never saw the need to get her nails professionally done, shopped the thrift stores for new clothes, and would never be the queen of fashion (Eugene was always years behind anyway), but she was warm and inviting and gave the best hugs when you had a bad day and then stuffed you full of chocolate chip cookies.

The shop hit me with the earthy smell of fresh flowers the moment we stepped inside. The flower shop's building had a faint pink brick, dating back to the early 1800s. The air felt slightly damp inside, but earthy, like walking into a greenhouse. The exposed brick on the inside provided a nice, urban charm to the beautiful arrangements of flowers hanging, sitting, and leaning on just about every space, bucket, and shelf in the store. It felt cluttered and eclectic, and I found myself liking it immensely.

"Do you have any ideas of what you want for your bouquet?" Mom asked as we browsed through the baskets of flowers surrounding us. "Oh, those are pretty!" She paused at a basket of pink tulips. "And the boutonnieres?"

"I want long-stemmed Hawaiian Lilies for everything."

Mom shot me a curious look. "What?"

"Parker and his mom are special ordering them from Hawaii for the ceremony and the reception in California. I thought I'd just do the same for the one here."

My mom's mouth shut as she nodded and turned back toward the case. I relaxed the tiniest bit. Maybe this wouldn't be too bad.

"Are you sure that's what you want?"

Dang it.

"Yup. I looked them up on Google and they're really pretty. They'll be nice for the look we're going for in Cali."

More silence as we started moving again, both of us browsing the varieties of flowers. I could feel Mom was ready to say something else again when humming and rustling in the back room saved me from more questions. A moment later, a pleasantly plump, middle-aged woman stepped into our view, holding an armful of pink flowers. She released the garden onto her work-table sitting just behind the register. Her bright orange and blue floral dress was a striking contrast against the soft colored flowers surrounding her. The Taylor Swift song she was enthusiastically singing made me automatically like her. Mom cleared her throat, and she jumped a mile out of her skin.

"Oh!" Her hand pressed to her heaping bosom as her eyes shot over to us. "I'm so sorry! I didn't hear you come in. How long were you waiting?"

"We just walked in," Mom said, waving away any awkwardness with her hand. "We were busy admiring all the beautiful flowers."

"I'm glad you like them. We got a new shipment of Peonies today and I've been in the back basking in their glory all morning."

"Is that what those flowers are? Peonies?" I walked toward the woman, hoping my ignorance toward all flowers didn't embarrass me. I had no prejudice against any living plant, but beyond roses, tulips, and lilies, I pretty much knew nothing.

She glanced down and touched the flowers on the workbench gently. "Yup. They're my favorite." She laughed. "Actually, I say that about every flower I get into the shop. But they do rank pretty high in my book. Now, my name's Bev, how can I help you, ladies?"

I opened my mouth to speak, but mom beat me to it. "My daughter is getting married on September 5th in California, but we are having a reception in Eugene a week later." Mom glanced at me as she said, "their flowers are taken care of in California, but we'd like a fresh bouquet, some boutonnieres, and some table flowers, for the event in Eugene."

The woman's eyes shot toward me. "Oh, how lovely!"

I smiled, and before my mom could take over again and make me feel like a teenager, I said, "Thank you. We've decided on the Hawaiian Lily. My fiancé is special ordering them for our wedding in California. Is that something you could get in here? I just thought I'd keep the same theme going."

Her brow furrowed lightly. "The Hawaiian Lily?"

"Yes."

Bev frowned. "Hmmm... I have never heard of that before. It's a flower off the Hawaiian island, you say?"

"Yes. It's only grown in Hawaii."

Bev moved down the aisle to a computer tucked away in the corner. "Let me check and see what I can find. I don't believe my supplier would carry anything like that."

I leaned over and smelled a bucket of daisies hanging on the wall while she typed.

"Yes, nothing is listed. I could call and check to see if they could special order it, but it would carry a hefty price tag to get them off the island, I do know that. It's easier for coastal flower shops to get them in because it's one less stop they'd have to make. And most people around here have never heard of that flower."

That included me, but hey, if Parker's family wanted to spend their money on a beautiful exotic flower for my wedding, who was I to stop them? "Could you check to see if you could get them in?"

I looked back at Mom. "If it's really expensive, I know Parker's family would be happy to pay for it."

She gaped at me. "Kelsey, *we* are paying for the flowers at our reception. If they're too expensive, we'll just have to pick something else. You don't have to have the same flowers at both events."

I nodded, my cheeks reddening slightly.

Bev interjected. "I'll double-check with my suppliers and a few others I know to see if we can find anything. In case it's not available, do you want to take a look at what we have here in the shop and pick a second choice?"

My eyes flitted to the peonies for a moment. Visions of a wedding in a field surrounded by mountains came to mind when I looked at them. They were beautiful, but I heard Parker say something about his mom planning to supplement with white roses in California. Not sure what that meant exactly, but it sounded like that would be the more seamless choice. But I definitely wasn't scared or intimidated to order the wrong thing at my own wedding. Nope.

"Um." I glanced around the store. "How about just white roses? For everything."

Bev's eyes widened but held it together like a professional. "Oh. Great. Yes, that's always a beautiful choice. Very chic."

I smiled, relieved. "They should go with anything, right? No matter what colors I pick?"

Bev nodded. "Yes. You don't have colors yet?"

When I shook my head, she said, "Not a problem. When you

decide, just give me a call and I'll coordinate with the appropriate ribbons."

"Perfect. Thank you." I wrote down my contact information on a pad of paper on the counter and practically dragged my mom out the door. "Thanks so much, Bev. You have a beautiful shop."

"Thank you! Have a good day," Bev called out behind us.

I knew I was rushing and that I was going to hear about this from my mom, but suddenly Bev's shop felt suffocating.

We climbed into the car, but before Mom turned the key she turned to me. "Are you sure you don't want to look around a bit more first?"

"Is there something wrong with white roses?"

"No, they're beautiful." She put the car into reverse. I leaned my head against the seat and waited.

"They just... don't seem like you."

Bingo. There it was. I resisted the urge to pat myself on the back. To her credit, she waited until we were at least a block down the road before she said anything. That had to be a record.

Instead, I sighed. "Mom, I've grown up quite a bit since I lived at home. Tastes are allowed to change."

"Your tastes have changed to an exotic breed of flower that only grows in Hawaii?"

Sitting upright in the seat, I turned to look at her. "These are what Parker and I have picked for our wedding. It's mine *and* Parker's wedding, and he happens to like the Hawaiian Lily." Okay, pretty sure Parker had never heard of those flowers either, the more I thought about it. My future mother-in-law loved them, however. I didn't want to be too hard on my mom, so I smiled at her to ease the tension. "I think you'll like them too. Let's just wait and see if they're available."

Mom put her easy smile on her face and carefully erased the worry lines that had been there before. I've been my mother's daughter for almost twenty-one years, and I knew what she was doing, masking her worry, but I appreciated it all the same. "Okay then. How about we hit up Frankie's for celebration milkshakes before we head back to the grind?"

Frankie's Diner was a rite of passage for our family. Any trip to Salmon involved milkshakes at Frankie's. Occasionally, we'd splurge for the hamburgers and fries, but always, *always* milkshakes. It was tradition. They must lace it with some sort of addictive drug because I have never tasted ice cream as rich and smooth. I always ordered Rocky Road and it came out thick, stuffed with marshmallows, peanuts, and a toasted homemade marshmallow on top. A smile was half on my face before I remembered.

Size four dress.

Jennifer Harris.

Wedding magazine.

"Actually Mom, would you mind if we cut out early. I love Frankie's, but my stomach isn't feeling great right now."

She looked concerned. I didn't blame her. I had never once in the history of my life passed on a Frankie's milkshake. It pained me to start now. But beauty is pain. At least so I've heard.

"Are you alright?"

Once I assured Mom I would be okay, that I just needed to go lie down, we turned the car south and headed home. The conversation passed pleasantly. So pleasantly I didn't have the nerve to bring up the dress.

I blamed it on my dang stomach ache.

6

Reasons I love Parker Gillette (circa - current)

1. Looks good in a suit
2. Driven to succeed
3. Hard worker
4. Those dimples
5. Loves taking me out on dates
6. Calls me every night
7. Does not like to prank

"Hey, Kels. Wake up."

My shaking bed awoke me the next morning, but I kept my eyes closed. Maybe if I didn't make any sudden movements, he would go away.

"Kelsey…"

I popped one eye open. Dad stood grinning at me, dressed in his dirty milking clothes, complete with knee-high rubber boots kicking at the footboard of my bed. A darted glance out the window told me that dawn had not yet arrived—which was never a good sign.

He chuckled. "Sorry, Kels, I know I told you to be out at seven, but the weather's perfect right now. I've got to go bale the ends of the field before I put Cade in the tractor all morning."

"I thought Jake and Dusty were milking today?"

"They were, but I just got a call from Tom Bingham and our fence is down by his place. The cows scattered, so they're out rounding up cattle. Cade's in the barn right now."

I waited for his next statement with a growing sense of alarm.

"I need you to help Cade finish milking. He doesn't know our system yet. I should be back in an hour and then I'll come and save you." Never one to stick around once an order was given, he turned to leave but paused long enough to add, "And try to be nice, Kels. Don't kill him on his first official day."

"I could probably wait it out until day two or three."

He only snorted in response as he stepped into the hallway.

"Tell me again how Cade Williams ended up on this ranch for the summer?" I called after him.

"It's all Stitch's fault." His voice sounded muffled as he made his way down the hallway, his rubber boots squeaking on the linoleum once he reached the kitchen. He had more faith in me heeding his words than I did.

I lay in my bed, contemplating my fate. My ring snagged against a piece of loose thread on my blanket and I smiled, remembering Parker. Smart, handsome, successful Parker. I could handle anything this summer as long as I got hitched at the end of it.

"Kelsey!" Dad's voice came from the hallway, startling me out of my self-induced trance. He must have realized I hadn't moved to turn on any lights in my room yet. He knew me too well.

But I couldn't avoid this forever. So, at the pace of a dying turtle, I dragged myself out of bed and got dressed.

The walk to the barn was the shortest it had ever been.

I braced myself as I cracked open the door and peeked inside. The smell of bleach, warm milk, and manure flooded my senses. There was a lifetime of memories wrapped up in those smells. Much to my surprise, I found myself regarding the aroma quite fondly. Long hours spent milking cows with my dad and siblings, pull-up competitions on the pipes running throughout the barn, water fights, and long talks with my dad flowed into my thoughts like a warm hug from an old friend. Even before I stepped one foot into the barn, I was home.

With the barn set to milk ten cows at one time, five on each side with an aisle to stand in between, milking generally took about ninety minutes to complete. Each of the cows had milkers with four attachments suctioned to their udders. The milk, once drained from the cow, traveled through pipes to the large, refrigerated tank in the next room. Later that day, a milk truck would come and haul it off to the cheese plant in town.

My lifelong antagonist stood at ease in the middle of it all. I peered at him, unseen, as he absentmindedly bounced a small ball off the wall, caught it, and threw it back again. The barn was quiet with the hum of gentle pulsations while each cow was being milked. Cade's attention was engrossed by the boxy old TV my dad kept high on a makeshift shelf. It sounded like the morning news. He was dressed in a faded pair of jeans and a button-down gray shirt, complete with a ratty baseball hat on his head.

With a pit in my stomach, I opened the door wider and stepped inside. At the movement, Cade caught the ball and held my eyes as I ambled toward him. I had promised Dad I would be nice, so I gave myself an imaginary pat on the back as I kept my facial expression neutral, when my natural reaction to him was much darker. Cade watched me with interest while his mouth slowly curved into a provoking grin.

Before he could say anything, I stuck out my hand and burst into my 'nice' speech I had practiced on the way to the barn. "Hey." I choked out the rest as if I spewed venom. "How's it going?"

His gaze dropped down to my hand and back up again, his grin fading slightly. Just before I drew my rejected hand back to my body, he grabbed my hand in a squeeze.

"I'm good. Thank you for asking."

I moved to take my hand back, but he held on tighter.

"Did you finally decide it was safe to climb out of that tree, Red?"

Ugh. Again with the nickname.

"I was working."

"I'm sure you were," he drawled as he made a show of looking at the clock. "Speaking of work. You're a little late this morning. Women troubles?"

"Let's not assume *everyone* has the same problems as you." I smiled smartly, yanking my hand from his and moving past, bumping his shoulder in the process.

Chortling, he turned toward me. "If you were trying to hide, you shouldn't have worn the red shirt. You could have just waved and ushered me right to the bunkhouse." He paused a moment before adding, "But red is your signature color."

Ignoring his last statement, I countered, "You should be used to women going to such great lengths to avoid you."

"Whatever you say, Peeping Tom."

"What are you doing here?"

He squirted me lightly with one of the four water hoses we use to clean the cows, which hung down from the ceiling. "I missed you."

I gasped in shock from the cold water and grabbed my own hose for defense. "Do you really want to mess with the boss's daughter?" I wasn't sure it was wise to pull out my big gun this early, but I was rattled and rapidly running out of material.

"Oh, I've got lots of ideas for the boss's daughter. And he'll probably thank me for knocking you off your high horse by the end of the summer."

Okay. It was all there. Let me double-check... yup. All there. The wild and excited look in his eyes, the threat, and my stomach feeling like I was strapped to the top of a roller coaster about to plummet to the bottom. That was my cue to nip every atrocity banging around in his head, in the bud. Fast. I could not afford to have Cade messing with me all summer. I thought it might work if I just ignored him and dealt with it, but now I can see he wouldn't stop at that. Time to pull out the real secret weapon.

Begging.

I wouldn't even be opposed to mustering up some fake tears.

I got in his face (i.e., chest), *really* using my 5'6 frame for intimidation purposes. "Cade. I'm getting married, planning my wedding, and have a loving fiancé who I adore. I don't have time to waste dodging your immature pranks. And if you think I'm going to sink to your level and prank you back, you're wrong. So please, just stop. Let's work together when we have to and then stay out of each other's way."

There were a lot of emotions that flickered across Cade's face during my impressive speech. Amusement, though that one was nearly always there. Surprise. Was that disappointment? The last looked pensive, which didn't fool me for one second.

He flipped his hat around so it sat backward on his head, but not before giving me a brief glimpse of the unruly brown mop that lay below. "Red. I'm shocked you think I would sink to that level. Especially since we're both so grown up and mature now. I'm here to work for your dad. I would never dream of—"

"Being a redneck moron is the only thing I've known you to work hard at."

"I'm flattered you noticed."

I swallowed, my throat feeling like sandpaper, and ignored the growing smile on his face. "I've moved on from high school. Please tell me you have too."

"Really? Your time hiding up in the tree suggests otherwise."

"I was work..." I broke off. My stomach tightened and I felt like screaming, but I couldn't allow myself to give him the satisfaction. "Just stay away from me."

He looked at me for a long moment. "You're right. We've both grown up." My eyes narrowed as he continued. "We're both mature college grads now, so obviously we can't have any more fun."

I gaped at him, waiting. That couldn't be it. Of course, it wasn't, because when he opened his mouth to speak again, barely controlled excitement radiated from him.

"Listen Red, I get what you're saying, I really do. But I just can't find it in me to agree to no pranks."

"Cade!"

He continued, holding up his hand. "But I *can* promise that I won't start any pranks until *you* do it first."

I blew out a breath, my body relaxing for the first time since I arrived at the barn. "Rest assured, I won't."

"Good. Yeah," he nodded in enthusiastic agreement. "That's good. Very mature of you." He rubbed his chin as if deep in thought. "What was that one prank I pulled on you? My favorite one? Oh yeah, the entire varsity football team's sweaty jerseys and pads locked in your hot car all weekend. I forgot about that. Well, I always figured you'd want to get your revenge for that one, but I'm so glad to hear you've moved on. You're a saint."

I stared at him, still as a statue, not moving except for maybe the tiniest perceptible nostril flare as the smell of that horrible day came roaring back into memory. Then I smiled, a long, slow, Cheshire cat smile, while I balled my fingers into a tight fist.

"Of course, there are no hard feelings for that. It's all good." I stepped away from him and leaned forward to take a milker off a cow that had finished milking.

He stepped beside me, doing the same for the cow next to me. "That is *such* a relief. I can't believe how mature you are now. You know, since we're talking, I've always felt bad about that prank in junior high with the water-filled whoopee cushion in class. I honestly didn't know it would sound like that. So... explosive."

Yeah. He and I both.

"Stop. I know what you're doing, and it won't work. I'm not taking the bait. Not happening. No more pranks."

"No pranks unless you start it first," Cade corrected.

I raised my eyebrows. "Fine. Not happening either way."

He shook his head. "It *will* happen. Guaranteed. I give it one week, *maybe* two, and that's being generous."

When I said nothing, he smirked. "Pleasure doing business with you."

I pushed past him and spent the rest of my time in the barn desperately trying to ignore him. He chose a different childish reaction and found every excuse in the book to annoy me. He would bump into me, brush up against me to take off a milker, and slapped at my shoulder, claiming to swat at a fly. The more my jaw clenched, and I resisted the urge to retaliate, the more he seemed to find some sort of perverse enjoyment and smiled at me the entire time.

I would be the bigger person if it *killed* me.

But I had clearly underestimated my opponent.

7

Reasons Cade williams is the worst
    (circa junior high - current)
67. He's cocky
68. He thinks he's funny
69. He thinks I was hiding from him in a tree. ~~I was legit working~~
70. His stupid blue truck
71. He's related to Stitch (my most favorite grump on the ranch)
72. ~~He always smells good~~
73. He still calls me Red
74. wet whoopee cushion (mentioned previously but since it has
        been brought up again recently, I have lived through the
        humiliation once again in my head and decided it deserves
        another mention)
75. Second grade (same as above)
76. Prom night (same as above)

"Babe, did you get the picture of The Castle I sent you? I hope you liked it because I booked it. I had to pull a few strings, but we were lucky to get it with such short notice."

"Yeah. It looked really pretty. So, was there a cancellation? Is that how we got it?" I put the phone on speaker and tucked it into my shirt pocket. Yeah, that's right, I had a shirt pocket. It came in handy on the farm. I bent over to cut the strings off of a hay bale before tossing the chunks into the manger with a pitchfork. Parker never called during the day, so it had been a nice surprise while I was out feeding cows.

Parker took an interest in all the wedding plans. He had found a venue in Santa Cruz called The Castle. It boasted a beautiful tree-lined driveway, which led into a cobblestone courtyard where impressive spires of a beautiful castle filled the view. Behind the castle sat the Pacific Ocean. From the pictures on the website he sent me, it seemed gorgeous. Expensive. A place where a Jennifer Harris dress would shine. It had a grand ballroom, which provided a perfect place for a wedding, dinner, and reception afterward.

I had never been a person who planned every detail of my wedding from a young age. Instead, I had dreamed of the romance. The first date, holding hands, kissing, and the proposal. I hadn't given the other details much thought beyond, perhaps, a small country wedding somewhere. The image of my favorite meadow on my dad's pastureland came to mind. In the middle of the grassy field, next to a winding stream, sat a large willow tree. I had always thought it would make the perfect spot for a ceremony, but that was before I had experienced a bit of life *beyond* the ranch. Before I met Parker, who was born and raised in the city and had always planned to get married there. He would stand out like a sore thumb wearing his Italian leather boots in the middle of my dad's pasture. Funny, I hadn't thought about that field in years, but why get married in a muddy field, when I could get married in a castle?

"What are you doing right now? Did I just hear a cow?"

Parker's voice brought me back to the present as I kicked a loose chunk of hay back into the manger. "Yeah, sorry. My dad had a meeting tonight so I'm feeding cows."

"I've got to see this side of you. I really can't imagine it. Think you can wear a sexy plaid shirt, a short skirt, and pigtails on the tractor when I come for a visit on the fourth?"

"That would be fun considering your parents are coming with you."

He laughed. "What time is the party at Tessa's?"

I swallowed. I was excited to show Parker off to the town, but nervous for him to see it all. "It always starts around 6 pm. You sure you're up for it?"

"Will I need to buy me a pair of wranglers to fit in, or will I be okay?"

"It wouldn't hurt." I laughed, trying to imagine him wearing such a tight cut of pants. It wasn't easy.

"What happens at the party?"

"Dinner and dancing."

"Dancing? Can farmers dance?"

I snorted. "It's more like loud music and... swaying. Sometimes there's a country line dance. It's not pretty, I'll tell you that."

He laughed. "Why did you insist on going home for the summer when you could have been with your amazing fiancé in the best city in the world?"

"Believe me, every minute I'm here, I'm missing you," I told him.

Later that evening, after Tessa and I finished a four-mile run, we lay sprawled on our backs on the front lawn. Yeah, I was also under the impression that by agreeing to play softball, I would not have to run four miles, but Tessa claimed she said it was only a one-game for one-run kind of deal. Very shady business. Although, I couldn't deny the effect our runs, both at home and at college, were having on my calf muscles and cheekbones. Things I had never seen so chiseled on my body before. That being said, adding a whole extra mile was torturous. No matter how much we ran, I still hated every blasted step. Case in point: my Amazonian best friend was lying peacefully on the lawn, softly breathing the night air, while the wheezing walrus next to her wanted to die; after I killed Jennifer Harris and her size four booty.

"When do you move to Boise?" I asked Tessa, sitting up to stretch my legs. "By the way, I still hate you for not moving to California and living with me and Parker after we're married. I don't know how you think I'm supposed to do life without you."

She laughed. "I know. I bet Parker is devastated too. My program starts on September 3rd, so I'll probably move a few days before that." She sat up next to me, straightening her legs while she bent over to stretch her hamstrings. "I can't believe it will be our first year of life without each other."

"I'm sure they have a physical therapy school somewhere near Santa Cruz. Maybe you should think about it."

"Let's stop talking about it or else I'm going to cry. How's Cade? Any pranks yet?"

I filled her in on our new deal. I had been shocked at how quickly Cade had accepted my terms. It nearly made me laugh, how he thought I wouldn't be able to resist pranking him. I had this in the bag. My Cade problems were over.

Tessa snorted. "There is *no way* you won't be full-on pranking within two weeks. No way."

My mouth dropped open. "You know, the more you and him keep saying that, the more I am sure I will *never* prank him." I smiled, checking out my nails as if I had nothing else in my day to worry about. "So keep it up. You're just fortifying my resolve."

"It's too much in your blood. I don't care if you spent the past four years pretending like it never happened, you gave as good as you got from Cade. Admit it."

"I don't need to admit anything. We are not pranking."

"Remember the time you trashed the outside of his truck with cans and cookies and balloons like it was his wedding day, and then you wrote 'Still Single' on the back with whipped cream?"

I tried to fight the smile lifting my face, but it was a lost cause. It was hard to forget the priceless look on Cade's face, as well as half the school when he stepped out the double doors that day. After taking in the carnage, his eyes had immediately found mine, where Tessa and I sat casually by a tree on the school lawn in front of the parking lot, you know, just doing our homework and stuff. The way his devilish smile crept across his face as he shook his head at me had been emblazoned upon my brain.

"I only did that to get him back for rigging my computer to say BUTT every time I typed my name."

"Or that time you had Mike switch his shampoo bottle with hair dye in his gym bag?"

I laughed. "He kept his hair green for three days trying to stick it to me."

"I wonder if his dad appreciated that one?" Tessa asked. The sound of bellowing cows in the distance filled the air between us as we both grew quiet for a moment. Cade's dad had coached football at the high school. During school hours he taught American History and PE. Every kid in school had him, and everyone in the whole town loved him. Most of all Cade. Just when Cade would have been coached by his dad, he passed away from a tragic car accident when we were in tenth grade. The whole town had mourned the loss.

"I hope he did," I said quietly. At the mention of his dad, my mind was drawn back to that moment long ago when I was at the viewing with my parents and had worked up the courage to tell Cade how sorry I was for his loss. He had looked at me for a long moment, and I remember thinking it was the first time I had seen him look serious. He had no twinkle in his eye, no gleam, no spark, but then he pulled me close and hugged me, long and tight. No words were spoken and soon I whispered sorry again and moved out of his embrace. The next week, Cade rigged a foghorn to go off under my seat in our English class and it was as if that moment between us had never happened.

"Or the time he tied your ponytail to your chair in junior high, so when you tried to stand up, you were stuck to your seat." Tessa's voice pulled me back into the present, but the mood was over, at least for me. Tessa looked like she had a few more trips down memory lane up her sleeve. I cut her short.

"Do you remember prom night? Was that fun? He's the worst, and if I play his games now, then it's like the last four years never happened. I'll be stuck spending all my time being paranoid and constantly watching over my shoulder. Not to mention Parker's parents are coming to visit in a month. I can't have Cade running wild and unchecked."

Tessa nodded, the sweat glistening off her face catching the porch light and somehow making her look even more beautiful. "I see your point."

"Thank you."

"But I still have my doubts that you'll be able to hold off all summer."

"I will."

"You hens done clucking yet?"

Tessa and I turned at the sound of Jake's voice. He stood at the corner of the house holding a basketball. Even dressed down in basketball shorts and a t-shirt, the cocky cowboy in him shone through. It was the way he swaggered everywhere he went, not walked.

"You need me and Kels to show you how to play?" Tessa crooned as we helped each other up.

"Don't get too excited, you're just bodies on the court while the men do all the work."

I punched his arm while he laughed and dodged Tessa's attack.

"What kind of hit was that? You girls need to give up this running crap and hit the gym."

We fell into step beside him.

"What's with the hair on your chinny-chin-chin? Finally growing some peach fuzz?" I asked, rubbing at the scruff on his face for the simple pleasure of just being annoying.

"Is that talk in fifth grade about your changing body finally starting to kick in?" Tessa chimed.

He jerked away from both of us while his face broke out in a grin. "The ladies haven't once complained about any of my manly attributes."

While Tessa and Jake continued the banter, I only smiled. The nightly basketball games with the guys had begun being my favorite ritual. Even Cade's presence didn't dampen the lighthearted camaraderie on the court. The boys loved Cade, which was kind of annoying, but I was dealing with it. It began the summer I came home after my freshman year of college, and I had been pleased to see us pick up right where we left off three years earlier. Tessa wasn't always around to play, but when she was, it was nice to not be the only girl. I needed *one* good ally. The makeshift basketball court located behind our house was just a big slab of concrete, maybe a third of the size of a school gym, with a hoop on one side of the court.

Ribbing and teasing, the three of us meandered toward the court where Cade and Dusty were taking a few practice shots. Cade was dressed in gym shorts and a fitted t-shirt with a baseball hat. Before he noticed our entrance, I watched him gracefully swish a three-point shot. My eyes narrowed, instantly annoyed. A curse on all the people good in every sport. It wasn't fair. Couldn't the rest of us have a blooming chance? And did he have to look so effortlessly cool with the ball in his hand? His sport of choice was *baseball* not basketball, but he might as well be LeBron James with the way it twirled along on the tips of his fingers. Show off. His eyes met mine and he passed me the ball.

"Hey, Red."

"Cade." I caught the ball and immediately took a shot. It bounced off the rim.

"Why do you call her Red?" Dusty asked as he hustled in for the rebound and made a layup, bulldozing through a laughing Jake while he did so. Even Dusty, with his larger build and smaller height, could hold his own against the other two towering giants.

"You want to tell them, sweetheart? Or should I?" Cade stood facing me, his arms folded across his chest, a lazy grin on his dumb face.

"Nope."

"Because when we were little, she wanted me to see her underwear, so she showed me. They were bright red. I just think it's a nice little nickname so she can always remember," Cade said, smiling.

"No! He de-pantsed me in front of the entire second grade!"

"Dude," Dusty began, looking over at Cade, "you pulled her pants down?"

Cade raised his eyebrows as he looked at me. "Because..." he prompted.

"Because he's a jerk," I supplied, leaning over to stretch my legs.

"Because she barfed all over me the day before. On purpose. There are so many directions to take your barf, but she aimed right for my head. She started the war, and I answered the call. It was revenge."

"That's pretty sick, Kels," Jake said as he took a shot.

"I didn't *aim* for him. He was sitting right in front of me. It just happened. But it couldn't have happened to a better guy," I said, smiling at Cade.

He scoffed, shaking his head while I laughed.

"How long did it take to get the stink off of you?" Jake asked Cade, grinning.

"I can still smell it, even now."

"So, hold on... you guys have been going at each other since the *second grade*?" Dusty asked, incredulously.

Silence.

Jake snorted in laughter as he muttered, "Well, that will be one impressive story to tell the grandkids."

I pretended I didn't hear that last comment while Cade took the ball in for a lay-up.

"What's the bet tonight?" Tessa asked the group, while Jake grabbed the ball and swished it from the three-point-line. I shot her a look of gratitude for the change in subject.

We all looked to Jake for the answer. Though he was one of the youngest, Jake was just one of those people who always took charge of a group, by pure charisma and fun, so we usually let him. His wild ideas and bets had gotten a few of us into trouble on occasion, but he was mostly harmless. He tucked the basketball underneath one arm while the group gathered around him, awaiting our fate.

"We have uneven numbers, so we're gonna play lightning. The bet comes down to the final two battling it out. The winner gets to make the loser, or the person in second place, do one chore of their choice tomorrow."

I breathed a bit easier. One chore wasn't too bad. Jake was feeling generous tonight.

We lined up at the foul line, which was just a spot on the concrete marked with three glops of bird poop, but it looked to be about the right distance. Dusty and Jake were first, then me, then Tessa and Cade brought up the rear.

The game of lightning begins with two basketballs and everyone lining up behind the foul line. The first two people in line hold the balls. The only goal is to make a basket before the person behind you makes their basket, because as soon as the ball has left the first player's hands, the person behind them, with the second basketball, shoots as well. If the second player makes a basket before the person in front of them, the first shooter is out of the game. If the first shooter makes it before the second, they pass their ball to the third person, and then they rotate to the back of the line. If the third person makes a basket before the second player, the second player is out. It's my favorite game. Quick, intense, and perhaps occasionally in this crowd... just a *little* bit dirty.

Dusty began his shot with a swish. Jake followed suit. I grabbed the ball Dusty tossed to me and shot, groaning as it bounced off the rim. Running forward, I caught the ball just in time to see Tessa take an impressive shot that looked very much like it would be going in to put me out, until I threw my ball to block it, sending Tessa's ball flying in the other direction.

"You punk!" she yelled as she chased after her ball, while I laughed like a maniac making my shot. I tossed my ball to Cade, who immediately sunk his foul shot, putting Tessa out.

"Kelsey Marten, this is your fault!" Tessa growled good-naturedly, throwing the ball to Dusty to start the round again. Tessa was now out of the game, which put Cade directly behind me.

"Sorry, Tess!" I laughed as she glared at me and sat down on the sidelines. I didn't feel too badly, since a couple of days earlier, she had performed the same cheap shot move on me. Back in line again, I readjusted my ponytail to sit higher on my head, because my neck was beginning to sweat profusely. The night had yet to take on the chill of the evening and I was glad to have worn my joggers that hit me just below the knee.

We went a few rounds with nothing much happening. Dusty made his shot, then Jake, and I even made a couple on my first round. Cade made all of his shots as well, much to my annoyance. Then Dusty missed his shot and Jake swept in, with no mercy, putting him out, leaving only Jake, me, and Cade. In that order.

The next couple of rounds went pretty much the same—except for the one time I missed my shot. I ran after the ball, knowing full well Cade would knock me out quickly, but surprisingly, he also missed. Then he *kept* missing until I made my shot. I eyed him suspiciously as I got back into line. He followed me, leaning in close behind my ear. "Oh, I've got plans for you, Red, but not just yet. We gotta get Jake out first."

I pushed him away. "I guess I'll just have to get both of you out. I'm planning on telling my dad I want to muck out the entire north corral with a spoon tomorrow."

His grin grew even wider at my words. "That sounds a lot more fun than what I have planned for you."

That shut me up.

"You guys about ready?" Jake stood watching our exchange, an impatient look on his face.

"Jake, I'll give you twenty bucks to miss your next shot."

"What?" I flew around to look at Cade. "You can't do that."

"Twenty bucks?" Jake said, a hand on his face, mulling it over as if deep in thought. "I wouldn't miss a shot for less than thirty."

"Done."

I glowered at Cade. "If he misses, I miss. This little game will go on forever and you'll be out thirty bucks. Your only choice will be to get me out."

"We'll see."

Jake threw a ball so obnoxiously wide of the basket and lollygagged over to retrieve it, only to 'accidentally' kick it further away with his foot. "Whoops."

Shaking my head, I dropped the ball in a granny pose, holding it below my bended knees. With Cade snickering behind me, I released the ball ridiculously high, attempting to give it my best try at missing my shot to give Jake time to shoot again. If he would only quit kicking the stupid ball further away from the basket.

I failed. Miserably.

The second the ball left my hands, I knew it felt good. Too good.

Swish.

My shoulders fell. Jake was out. It was now down to me and the moron laughing behind me. Exactly what he wanted all along.

"Maybe you should shoot granny shots *all* the time." Jake laughed, tossing me the ball. Cade motioned for me to take my place just before him in line.

"You said you wouldn't do any pranks," I hissed.

He held his hand up. "This isn't a prank. It's a bet. One you signed up for."

"My money's on Cade," Jake whispered loudly from the sidelines. The three of them sat on the side of the court, the anticipation of a good show in their eyes.

"Really? With all her rage?" Dusty countered. "I'm betting on Kelsey."

"Definitely Cade," Tessa chimed in, apparently still holding a grudge for me putting her out of the game. When I gave her an affronted look, she just grinned.

"Yeah, she's too scrawny now. Look at all his muscle."

Cade grinned at me. "I'd listen to Jake and Tessa if I were you."

"You're going down."

Turning, I faced the basket. I took a deep breath and shot, exhaling when the ball went in. I grabbed the rebound and scrambled back to the foul line behind Cade. He made his shot and moved quickly behind me. We went two more rounds like that, both of us hustling, complete concentration on our faces. I missed one shot, ran in for the rebound, and threw my ball at Cade's in mid-air, on track to go in. His ball went flying in the other direction, but almost as if he had anticipated my dirty trick, he was back with the ball, making a basket, seconds after mine went in.

We walked back to the foul line, sweat dripping down our faces and breathing hard, amid cheers from the fan section.

"Accept your fate," Cade said.

"Never."

"Stubborn woman."

I turned toward the basket so he couldn't see me. I was tired, sweaty, dirty, and seriously nervous about what might lie ahead for me tomorrow, but that dang smile sneaking across my face was going to give me away if I wasn't careful.

I threw up my shot and died a little inside as it hit the rim on the left side and went flying. I scrambled after it but stopped when I heard Cade's ball hit the rim and fall into the net.

My shoulders sunk, even as the boys cheered. I turned around and saw Tessa trying to rein in her laugh and then I looked at Cade.

He held his hand out to me. I stared at it, trying to decide if the good sportsmanlike conduct was worth putting my hand in his. Finally, I lifted my hand to his and shook it, his hand gripping mine tightly. My stomach clenched.

"Good game, Red."

I took my hand out of his and found my snark buried deep down, below my shame. "So, what chores do you do around here? Feed the kittens?"

He bit his lip in a pathetic attempt to keep himself from grinning. It didn't work. "Whatever helps you sleep tonight. Meet me by the north corral tomorrow at 9 am. And don't wear your ball gown."

After high fives and good nights, Dusty and Jake hopped in their trucks to go home and Cade jogged toward the bunkhouse.

We began walking toward Tessa's car when it suddenly hit me what a horrifying predicament I was now in. Cade was an assistant to a *veterinarian*. There were countless disgusting things he could make me do tomorrow.

"What have I done?" I groaned.

"Well, maybe if you hadn't pulled such a dirty trick to get me out of the game, you wouldn't be having this problem." Tessa flung her arm around my shoulders, bumping me with her hip.

"I just get so... heated and in the zone, I block every smart thought out of my head."

"You know what you have to do now, right? To stick it to him?"

"What?"

"Whatever disgusting thing he makes you do, you have to pretend like it's the greatest day of your life."

"He'll see right through that."

Tessa nodded. "Even so. You have to."

I sighed a great, dramatic sigh. "How did he end up here again?"

"Fate."

It was all Tessa said, but I couldn't get her answer out of my head all night, among horrible nightmares full of manure, dehorning and castrating cows, and every other disgusting thing I'd ever seen on a farm.

8

Wedding Color Ideas from the Internet (circa - current)

Cinnamon Rose and Dusty Rose
Terracotta and Greenery
Pantone Rose Brown and Rose Gold

Translation according to Google:

Dark Pink and Pink
Light Brown and Green
um... Brownish gold and um... pinkish gold?

I took my time eating breakfast the next morning. Partially because I didn't want to go meet whatever doom Cade had for me, and partially because I was trying to choke down a bowl of strawberries topped with cottage cheese. The texture of the dairy product had me wanting to hurl with each bite. Parker had promised that I would see faster results if I combined fruits with a healthy protein like cottage cheese. Or white barf chunks, as I lovingly call it. Parker had taken it upon himself to give me dieting advice every evening during our phone chats. He had once been a wrestler in junior high and he knew every trick in the books to drop a few pounds. Really though, having my fiancé tell me different foods and tricks to help me cut inches off my body added a nice touch to my day and wasn't distressing or potentially damaging at all. I swallowed my last bite, forcing my body to not upchuck the correct amount of protein and carbohydrate for weight loss, changed into my rubber boots, and headed outside. Three more months and this would all be over.

I spotted two bodies in the north corral. I was disappointed to see that my being nearly ten minutes late hadn't deterred Cade. He and Stitch were standing inside the alleyway chatting easily together, their arms leaning against the fence. Standing beside them were three cows munching on grain, each of their heads locked into the manger. Cade's brown eyes lit up when he saw me approach, a hint of a smile playing on his lips, while my steps slowed, sensing danger.

"Hey there, Red. I thought you might have forgotten about our date."

My heart galloped in my chest. Maybe it was the overly innocent way Cade stared at me that heightened my senses and put me on guard. Whatever *this* was, it was going to be bad. Panicking, I grabbed the pitchfork and enthusiastically threw in a couple chunks of hay toward the cows, who grunted their appreciation. "So, what are you having me do? Should I just feed the cows?"

"Oh, that's way too easy for a ranch expert like yourself."

I skipped over Cade's amused gaze and looked to Stitch for help, the old softie who loved me deep down. "Stitch, please just tell Cade feeding cows would be more than enough for payment. Anything else you guys plan to do here is legit vet stuff and I shouldn't be a part of it."

Stitch snorted as he handed Cade a plastic glove. "You knuckle-heads need to work this out. Leave me out of it."

My eyes narrowed at the old grump who had always had it out for me. He looked at me and winked, and I immediately softened toward him again. His wife had passed away from cancer nearly ten years earlier. He had grown lonely in his home without her and one day, a few years after his wife's death, he approached my dad about hiring him as a full-time retired veterinarian. He had always been the town of Eugene's vet, including ours, but having him close by, living on our ranch, seemed a perfect solution to everyone. Stitch would be less lonely, and my parents would have an experienced vet living on their property. He had to be pushing seventy-five or so, wore a white, dusty cowboy hat everywhere he went and walked a bit more crooked these days, but man, I loved him.

Seeing him and Cade standing side-by-side was a bit of a trip, though. They both wore jeans and a loosely fitted button-down plaid shirt. Being nearly fifty years older than Cade, Stitch was much more weathered—with his hands and face like wrinkled brown leather, having spent years of his life in the sun. There was a twinkle in Stitch's eyes that could be found in Cade's as well, but for some reason, Stitch's twinkle delighted me, where Cade's made me want to punch something.

Cade nodded as he rolled up his left shirtsleeve. For the tiniest of seconds, my eyes drifted to his forearm muscle before I forced them back up again. He's a snake. Focus Kelsey.

"The deal was you had to do a chore for me, and it just so happens Stitch and I could use a hand, or excuse me, an *arm*, here this morning."

Stitch snickered the tiniest bit before the look of alarm on my face silenced him. Cade's gaze remained strong and firm on mine. Challenging, with that dang twinkle.

My breathing started coming in faster as I looked at Stitch again and the three cows they were standing by. In Cade's hand, he held a glove—a plastic glove. A *long*, plastic glove. Despair flooded my senses. Deep in my heart of hearts, I knew this was coming, even when I wouldn't allow myself to entertain the thought the night before. Tessa's idea for me to act like it was the best day of my life went out the window. Even *she* couldn't blame me; no one could have foreseen this amount of Cade's horridness.

"No."

Cade's eyebrows rose. "No?"

"I'm not doing that. Pick something else."

"This is my chore today. The rule of the bet, clearly stated by Jake, was that I could pick one chore for you to do. You want to back out of the bet?"

He said it like it was a big deal. Which, it was, kind of. If a nightly basketball bet could be considered a big deal to anybody. But it was slowly becoming a big deal to me, I realized. The basketball games were what I looked forward to every night, after Parker's phone call.

"Please, can you just not be a butthead this *one* time and pick something else?"

His eyes narrowed. "Since when did you become such a pansy?"

"I'm not a pansy, I just don't want to do that."

He stared at me a long moment, and for a second I wondered if he would take pity and pick a different chore, but he held strong. "Nope. You've grown too soft in Moscow."

My fists clenched while trying not to scream in frustration. Cade Williams was the worst. Inside though, I knew I had to do it. I wouldn't be that person who flaked out on a bet. If Dusty could eat a stink bug, I could stick my arm up a cow's butt.

Yup. You heard that right.

Dusty ate a *stink bug*.

"Give me the gloves."

"It's just *one* glove, Red."

He held out the plastic glove to me, motioning for me to roll up the sleeve of my t-shirt a bit higher. Sticking my entire arm up a cow's hind end was something I had never wished upon myself. The reasons for someone doing so were primarily for impregnating or checking cows for and during pregnancy, which was why it would be an important thing for Stitch to teach Cade. For the life of a dairy farmer or rancher or veterinarian, it was very routine, but not so much for a farmer's daughter—especially *this* farmer's daughter. I had never wanted to know an animal that personally. Figures it would be Cade to lead me to this one day.

I tried whining one last time. "Please don't make me do this."

"Just think, you can put it on your resume."

"Shut up."

I unrolled the plastic glove, watching it unfurl until it hit the ground. Aware of the men's eyes on me, I stuck my left hand inside, pulling the plastic over my wrist, past my forearm, past my elbow, past my biceps, until it rested snug between my shoulder and armpit. I crawled through the fence to stand next to Cade and Stitch, turning to face the back of the cow who stood munching on a bale of hay, oblivious to my humiliation.

Cade stepped in close, rubbing my shoulders briskly as he steered me into position behind the cow, leaving me at eye-level with my target.

I turned to look at him, sidestepping out from under his warm hands. "This feels a lot like a prank."

He scoffed at me. "What? No. It's a bet, fair and square."

My eyes narrowed as I studied him. "Wait. Are you *baiting* me so I'll retaliate and start your prank war?"

The tiniest smile touched his lips before it was gone, but I saw it. I SAW IT. That *punk*.

He leaned down and got in my face, his eyes shining merrily. "Kelsey. This was a *bet*. We've already established that we're too mature for pranks." He nodded toward the cow. "Now slide your arm inside, princess. Stitch and I have lots to do today."

Exasperated, I lifted my plastic arm. "Fine. Where am I going with this? And what do I do once I'm in there?"

"Just push your hand inside. It will feel tight and then really soft. Just keep going. It's pretty cool once you pass the gross stuff. Once your arm is in, you can feel the different parts of the cow."

"This is a bull crap chore you're making me do. I don't know how to *do* anything in there. It's a waste of a good glove."

He bit his lip, trying to hold back his smile, and giving me a rare glimpse of the elusive dimple in his left cheek. "Stitch will go in after you're done to check how far along this cow is in her pregnancy. This is just some hands-on experience for you." He nudged me with his elbow. "Come on, it'll put hair on your chest."

"I don't want hair on my..." I stopped myself just in time and met his delighted gaze. "I hate you."

"Do it."

"I won't hurt the baby inside?"

"No."

I stared at the cow's poop-encrusted behind for several long moments, imagining an eighties rock playlist as I tried to pump myself up to do it. I bounced on the balls of my feet, very much aware of Stitch most likely rolling his eyes and shifting impatiently. He wasn't one to care for drama queens, but I couldn't help it. I wasn't a freaking *vet*.

"You can do it, Red," Cade whispered.

I held my breath and squeezed my hand inside.

Don't throw up. Don't throw up. Don't throw up.

The first part was disgusting, especially as I thought about where my hand was passing through. I dry-heaved and tried backing out, but Cade's warmth at my back and light grip on my shoulder kept me moving forward. I gritted my teeth and pushed my hand further inside. The cow shifted a bit but otherwise didn't look too concerned. I was forearm deep.

"If your boyfriend could see you now," Cade mumbled.

"Shut up."

Elbow deep.

"How far in do I have to go?"

"Little further."

Cade was right. It was very squishy. Very Warm. Very Strange. *Really* gross.

And also... kind of awesome, in a 'that's disgusting, and I'll never do that again,' kind of way. But as I slid my hand out of the cow's rump, the glove covered in manure, I felt empowered. Just a *tiny* bit. I had done something hard and gross, but I had *done* it. Something that ninety-nine percent of the population would probably never do.

Although, I would have been just as proud to have still been in the 'never done it' camp, I could see it being something I could tell my grandkids about one day. Maybe not Parker, but definitely my grandkids.

However, I would *never* admit that to Cade.

NEVER.

———

"Hi, I'm looking for Kelsey Marten. This is Bev from the Blushing Lily in Salmon. I was just calling to follow up on the flowers for your wedding reception on September 12th. I spoke with my supplier and he doesn't believe he can get the Hawaiian Lily's from California. There are special restrictions on that particular flower and he's not able to transport it to a different state. I'm so sorry. I know we spoke about possibly doing the white roses instead, and I was wondering if you'd like to proceed with that order. I also need to know your wedding colors so we can provide the ribbons to match. If you could just give me a call back, that would be great. Thank you."

When the voicemail ended, I put the phone down on the porch rail and began my gentle rocking in the swing once more. After the hand-in-the-cow's-behind incident of earlier, the rest of the day had passed easily. My mom and I had just gotten home from our meeting with a decorator in town, and I had made as much progress there as I had with the florist. My mom was starting to get frustrated with me, but I couldn't help it. Indecision plagued me. The decorator had a variety of styles and colors for backdrops, table settings, napkins, sign-in tables, not to mention a warehouse full of decorations available for use, but I couldn't decide on anything. I told the decorator I needed to think about a few ideas before I could let her know.

Perhaps there were too many choices. Maybe I could convince Parker to come down and help me narrow a few things down. No. That was dumb. I could do it. I *should* do it. It was *my* wedding. Parker would not care about table settings and napkin fonts for the reception in Eugene, right? I couldn't figure out why this was all such a big deal. And the flowers... Parker's mom mentioned the white roses. I think they were going to be part of the table piece at the wedding and dinner in California. I'm sure they would look beautiful at the reception in Eugene, but would the crew from Martha Stewart's magazine be in Eugene? Or were the only photographs going to be at the California location? I needed to double-check with Parker. But when Parker called me a few minutes later, promptly at eight, I couldn't muster up the energy to bring it up.

"Babe, I wish you were here. You should come and visit. The guys at work think I've made you up. I need to show you off."

Show me off? What exactly was Parker telling them about me? With dirt in my fingernails, limp hair in a ponytail, cut-off jeans, and a residual odor along my left arm that I wasn't sure if I was imagining or not—I felt myself becoming the last person he could proudly show off to anyone.

"Believe me, I'd love to," I said as I laid across the porch swing, my feet dangling off the armrest on the other side, and closed my eyes.

"Why don't you?"

My body tensed at the question. "My dad needs the help this summer. And I've been trying to get the reception planned with my mom. And then there's the cattle drive coming up later this summer. Besides, you and your parents are still coming for the 4th, right? That's in just a few weeks."

"Yeah, we are. You're going to love it here, Kels. There's so much to do. There's a guy I work with who has connections with a news station here in town. He said he'd try to hook you up for a part-time job once you get here."

"Really? That's great. Thanks!"

"It would probably just be getting coffee for people, or whatever, but still, it's a leg in."

"That's awesome."

"Why *don't* you come?"

"What?"

"Why don't you come here? I don't understand why your mom couldn't help plan the wedding by phone. I could fly you up to Boise to do any shopping you'd want with your mom and you could visit a couple of times this summer. You keep saying you miss me, and you want to move to California, so come. My parents have a room in their house, or my sister's got a place you can stay."

I swallowed hard. A part of me did want to be in California with Parker. At the rate I was going here, planning a wedding in California would probably go much smoother. I obviously wasn't doing a great job of it in Eugene.

"Maybe we can talk about it over the fourth. I'll see how much planning we can get done here first."

The words felt wrong somehow. Even as I said them, the thought of missing out on the cattle drive broke my heart. I had missed it for the past three years and I would probably never get the opportunity again. I loved school and my degree. And my thoughts to one day become a news reporter sounded so sophisticated and big city and exactly what I had imagined for my life. With Parker's connections in California, it might become a reality. It was all so exciting, but I had a lot to do before then. I wanted to say my proper goodbyes to this ranch, and I couldn't do that if I missed the cattle drive.

The idea of talking about flowers and decorations didn't interest me at that moment, so I promised myself I'd bring it up the next day to Parker. We said goodnight and I hung up the phone, sitting up and giving the swing a gentle push with my foot.

Parker and his parents were coming in three and a half weeks. That was not much time to become a size four, convince my mom that Jennifer Harris's dress was *exactly* what I wanted, make Cade somehow stop being Cade, and get my parent's house ready for the Gillette's to visit. To get the house ready for Parker.

That evening, as I headed to bed, I made a stronger resolve to stay the course I'd planned for my life. Enjoying some time with family over the summer was good. I would always love it here and I would always be glad I gave myself one last summer at home. But come September, I would be getting married and living out my dreams in California.

With my sights once again set on Parker, I fell into a restless sleep.

9

My Daily Diet, via Parker (circa - current)

Breakfast - Apple or Green Smoothie (It's just for
    a couple of months, suck it up)
Snack - Cheese Stick and four nuts (six if I'm
    feeling especially hungry)
Lunch - Salad with Chicken, light dressing
Snack - Apple or berries
Dinner - Sniff whatever nectar from the Gods
    mom is cooking, wipe the drool off your face,
    heat up your grilled chicken and broccoli, and go
    to town.
Dessert - Always a jokester

My efforts at avoiding Cade at all costs were lost on my dad. He seemed to enjoy sticking us together to work as often as he could, no doubt for his own entertainment purposes. It wouldn't surprise me if he hid behind tractors or other farm equipment, watching Cade and me banter through picking rocks, feeding cows, and hoeing weeds together. At least he usually sent Jake and Dusty along, probably as buffers. Little good that did. Cade was setting a horrible example on this farm for two old trusty ranch hands because I was getting teased by them much more than I ever had before. True to his word though, besides the lost bet, he hadn't pulled one prank on me. Even I was impressed.

"Come over here, you two." My dad called Cade and me over from feeding the cows. We each kicked the last bit of hay into the manger and walked closer to where my dad squatted next to his loader, blowing up the front tire with air.

"Jake and Dusty are heading to Willow Creek with the horses loaded in the trailer. I need you both to take Cade's truck and meet them out there to help them check the fence. We had a couple of bad windstorms last winter and I know there are some boards knocked down and who knows what else. Each of you take a section of the fence line and fix it as best as you can. We'll work on it whenever we get a chance this summer. In a few more weeks, we'll get back out there and replace a few poles. I'm planning to put cattle out there in the fall and need it all fixed up before then."

"Yes sir," Cade said.

I tried glaring at my dad, but he refused to meet my eyes as he concentrated on his tire. I would have to talk to him about this later.

"Be nice. Both of you."

My dad's voice followed us as we walked toward his truck. With a sardonic smile, Cade stepped in front of me and opened the passenger door, motioning for me to step inside.

"Thanks, moron."

When he started the truck, he glanced over at me. "You're a little more cranky than usual, did you lose another bet or something?"

I forced myself not to roll my eyes and rolled down the window instead. "Sorry." I didn't even have an excuse for my attitude. Cade technically hadn't done anything to annoy me yet. Although, it was only 10 am.

Cade drove down the lane, the cool morning breeze filtering out the truck's smell of hay and... jerky? I leaned out the window, letting the fresh air blow across my face for a moment. I could have been cranky because I hadn't eaten anything that morning. I had meant to go grab something to eat after feeding cows, but there I was, off to fix fences for who knows how long.

"You hungry?"

I looked over at him. He met my gaze with no expression. "Maybe. What do you have?"

"There's some jerky in the glove compartment."

So it *was* jerky I smelled. I opened the latch and pulled out a half-open bag of teriyaki jerky. While it wasn't exactly on the naked diet, I had to get some calories in me before I said things I might regret.

"Thanks," I said awkwardly, taking a few pieces of jerky before offering some to Cade. I was about to close the door to the compartment when I did a double-take at the contents inside. Gasping deeply, I pulled out a can of tuna fish, complete with a can opener.

Holding the evidence out toward him, I gaped at him accusingly. "Always have a good prank at your fingertips, is that it?"

"It's my lunch."

My eyes narrowed, watching him carefully. He kept his gaze carefully averted. My voice took on a low, menacing tone. "Only a sociopath would eat plain tuna. Although, that probably checks out."

A smile lit his face, but he only looked out the window, his elbow leaning against the windowpane while his hand rested comfortably on the wheel.

I stared at the can in my hand. "Wait a minute. Or are you trying to bait *me*?"

He laughed then, my eyes trained on his and I found myself wanting to smile as well, though I held back.

"I love a can of room temperature tuna for lunch. Especially when—"

"*You* don't even believe you when you say that," I said.

"No mayo, no bread, no pickles... just plain canned fish. It's delicious."

"You are so full of crap."

We pulled up to the corral. Jake and Dusty were already inside the gate, unloading the horses from the trailer. My eyes swept across the beautiful mountain chain hugging my dad's beloved pasture.

Cade put the truck into park before the gate leading into the field. He leaned over and took the tuna fish and can opener from my hands and placed them on the dashboard, right in front of my seat.

Eye-level.

Baiting me. Practically begging me to open it and leave it hidden somewhere in his truck. Although I knew I wouldn't play his games, the sudden and intense desire to open that can is what shocked me. The twitch in my finger desperately wanted to start the war. Could it be I *missed* the pranks? No. Of course not. There were occasionally times that it had been fun. Funny. Mostly though, it was just a big, embarrassing nuisance. But the idea of repaying all the horrible smelling car pranks... No. NO, Kelsey. I had to resist. Resistance was the only way I would survive the summer planning my wedding.

"I'll get the gate." He opened the door and stepped out, but before he closed it, he poked his head back inside the cab. "Don't do anything I would do."

A smile burst across my face before I could squash it. "You're such an a—"

The door slammed shut while a laughing Cade walked over to open the gate.

———

The fresh mountain air smelled of sage and lilacs with a touch of summertime—all of which made me giddy in anticipation. Moscow, Idaho had beautiful mountains and hills, but nothing compared to the countryside of my upbringing. Maybe it was just nostalgia, but this place would always be home, even when I traded it in for the big city.

I rushed to saddle Ace with jittery hands and feet practically dancing with excitement. With a knapsack full of nails, rope, and a hammer, I climbed onto Ace's back and took a look around. Located at the base of the Willow Creek Summit, near Challis, this wide-open pasture was my favorite of all my dad's properties.

The four of us split up, each taking a section of fence. The large pastureland was corralled in by four long stretches of post and board, creating a rectangle, with nearly a mile of fence per section. The fence I chose happened to be the farthest away and I couldn't help myself as I broke Ace into a full run, racing through the field, my long hair taking flight with the wind.

With rolling green hills, tall grass, willow trees, and a creek running through the lower west corner, it was a little slice of heaven, tucked five miles from the nearest town. The image of an intimate wedding near the willows flitted through my mind before Ace snorted, shaking me from my wild thoughts.

While at home, ranching seemed so normal. At school, I spent my life chasing a degree and dating a suit coat. Swept away by grand ideas and pretty words; I had forgotten how real I felt sitting on top of a horse, riding a fence line with dirt under my nails. It had been a long while since I had ever felt this alive.

Ace slowed to a trot as we neared the start of my fence when a strange sound interrupted my daydreaming. I pulled the phone out of my pocket.

"Hey, Parker."

"Babe! How are you?"

"Good. What's up? You don't usually call during the day."

"Nothing. Just thinking about my little cowgirl. What are you up to?" he asked, the words with a thick, country-hick accent, to which I offered a polite laugh.

"I'm on Ace right now and we are about to fix a fence line."

He chuckled and I imagined him shaking his head and smiling. "Just think, you could be sitting in an air-conditioned office right now, instead of getting hot and sweaty working outside."

A hollow laugh left my throat. "How's the internship going?"

"It's going good. Busy. I sat in on a trial the other day. And the attorney I'm helping has me doing some research for a couple of cases. It's making me excited to start law school."

"I'm glad you like it," I told him. And I was. Parker had worked hard in school and I was happy to see him develop a love for his profession. He would be attending a law school near Santa Cruz in the fall.

"How's operation size four dress going?" His tone was cautious as though he knew this was a subject he should tread on lightly. It wasn't his nature to not be blunt and I appreciated his gentle broaching of a subject that caused me much anxiety even thinking about it.

I sighed. "It's going okay, I guess. It's only been a couple of weeks."

There was a pause before he cleared his throat. "My mom said she has some pills from a doctor or something like that. They're legit and all that, and they're supposed to help. If you want them. Or think you might someday. No pressure," he added quickly. "It's just if you think you might need it. Or want it."

"Why does this suddenly sound like some backwoods drug deal?"

He chuckled. "Sorry. Just passing along the info as I was told."

I opened my mouth to say something, anything, but nothing came out. Thankfully, before I could, Parker breezed past to a less awkward topic.

"Hey, speaking of my mom, she also wants to know if you were able to find a flower shop that could get the Hawaiian Lily?"

"Oh, yeah. I got a voicemail from them last night saying they wouldn't be able to get them in. What do you think about just doing white roses?"

"My mom didn't think the white roses would be fancy enough with all the decorations for the castle. I thought so too," he said.

"Oh." I swallowed my disappointment. Aren't roses the fancy flowers? "It should be okay for here though, right? Are the photographers from Martha Stewart coming to Eugene?"

"I think they're planning on it. They liked the idea of the country vibe you'll put on in Idaho."

My heart dropped. "Really? What about The Castle?"

"They'll take the main pictures there, some in Idaho too. They think it will help the dress sell better if it's photographed in a couple of different settings."

Ace jittered beneath me, either wanting me to get off his back or take off on a gallop. I brushed my hand down his mane before sliding off his back.

"So, do I need to get any specific decorations here to coordinate?" I couldn't decide if I wanted to coordinate or not. Obviously, I was having a hard time picking out things on my own, and it would probably help immensely to have some direction, but the whole idea of it kind of irritated me.

Parker paused. "I'm not sure. I'll check with my mom and let you know."

"It's hard planning a wedding so far away."

"And who's fault is that?" Parker teased lightly, but with most of his teasing, there was a slight edge in his voice.

At my silence, he added, "Listen, if you want the white roses, it's okay. It's *your* wedding, not my mom's."

"Okay, I'll think about it." What *did* I want? These decisions to be over? YES. All of a sudden, I wished I had eaten more of Cade's jerky because the beast inside of me felt ready to rip the heads off any unsuspecting passersby.

After hanging up with Parker, I was about a quarter of a mile into my fence line, slamming nail after nail into fence posts, when I determined I had picked the worst section to work. I spent more time *off* my horse, fixing and re-nailing than I spent *on* my horse. Regardless though, I refused to let my cloudy mind and hungry belly dampen this day any longer because riding Ace and checking fences was still one of my favorite things of summer.

A few minutes later, I was off my horse again, attempting to lift a section on my fence that had toppled over, and nail it back together. It was becoming quite apparent that for all my pulling and prodding, the fence wasn't going to budge.

"Need some real muscle, Red?"

Exasperated, I glanced up from my struggle to see Cade sitting atop his light brown quarter horse, Dodger, and watching me with a small smile on his face.

"Yeah, want to go get Dusty?"

Cade snorted. Sliding off Dodger, he strode over to me.

I scooted a bit to make room and after some tugging, we lifted the fence back into place. He nailed it back together while I held it upright and tried very hard not to notice the muscles and veins in his forearms shifting under his exertion.

"Are you all done with your fence?" I asked.

"Yup. Some of us are just more used to hard work, I guess."

"Funny."

We hopped back onto our horses and he reined Dodger in close to Ace. We ambled forward, our eyes casually raking over the fence, looking for weak points or flaws.

"Why does your dad have a dairy farm and a ranch? It seems like most farmers just have one or the other."

I nudged Ace alongside him. My hair had become a tangled mess in our ride, so I used the hair tie on my wrist and pulled it into a high ponytail on my head while I thought about how to answer his question. He had no mocking tone and seemed sincere in his question, which from past experience caused a few alarm bells to ring in my head.

I glanced at him to find his gaze arrested on my hair for a moment before he looked away. I cleared my throat. "My grandpa milked cows the entire time my dad was growing up. And the milking business is a steady paycheck every month where ranching is seasonal and dependent on the weather. I imagine the risk is part of his hesitation, as well as nostalgia." Cade nodded as I continued, "He always said he'd get rid of the dairy cows when I graduated." I gave him a little smile. "But he never stipulated high school or college."

Cade chuckled as he hopped off his horse to throw some nails into a sagging board. "Either way, he's a bit behind now."

I startled at his soft laugh. Cade and I had teased and pranked and laughed at each other many times growing up, but I don't recall ever making him chuckle by a conversation piece. One where I wasn't out to get him. For our style of relationship, it felt... wrong somehow, but at the same time, kind of nice.

"I think he always liked the idea of raising a family on a dairy farm," I added. "We always had a job. He taught his kids how to work alongside him."

Cade nodded as he pulled himself back onto Dodger. "Yeah, I always wished I had grown up on a farm."

Okay, that was twice now, where I had left him an opening for a joke and he didn't take it. He could have said something, anything about me skipping the lesson the day my dad taught my siblings to work. Or even just look at me with his raised eyebrows and teasing smile. I'm not saying it was a *great* opening, but the Cade I knew should have jumped at that opportunity. What was happening?

"Didn't you work on Bill Johnson's dairy a bit through high school?"

"Yeah, but it's not the same as working on one with your family."

"Well, I don't think you could handle all the early hours." If he wasn't going to take any bait, I would. Things were starting to sound a bit too much like a normal conversation for my taste.

"If I recall, I beat you out to the barn the other morning."

"That was my dad's fault."

He snorted, leaning forward to rub Dodger's neck. "Either way, every kid wants to be a cowboy growing up and go on cattle drives..." He drifted off.

I smiled and couldn't help but agree with him. Every summer growing up, we had plenty of opportunities to drive cattle from one farm or pasture to another. The biggest cattle drive, coming up a week after the Fourth of July, would take about five days total and would be filled with cowboys, roping, tents, campfires, and stargazing. It was the best week of the year and perhaps the main reason I came home this summer. It had been three years too long since my last cattle drive, and with me getting married in a couple of months, it would probably be my last. Even with Cade coming along, I couldn't help but count down the days.

"So, what are your plans after summer?" I asked.

"Vet school."

"You traded life with the minors and possibly going pro, to do eight years of vet school?"

Cade didn't say anything for a long moment, and when he did, it came out tense and guarded. "Yup."

There was an awkward silence. Dang it. I had made things weird. We had been getting on so well. I tried to steer us back. "Where are you thinking of going?"

"I've put out an application to a few different schools. I don't have much preference. Whatever one will take me."

I tried to bite my tongue, but it couldn't be helped. "Is that your motto for dating too?"

He smiled, shaking his head. "So, after the fancy wedding, what are your plans? Off to the big city?"

I didn't miss the tone in his voice at his reference to the big city, but I ignored it. "Yup. I'm moving to Santa Cruz and then I'll work toward becoming a news anchor."

He gave me a sideways glance. "Is that something you can just walk in and do?"

"Not any old baseball player, but a broadcast journalism degree helps. I interned at a station in Moscow the past three summers, so I do have some experience. I'll be starting low on the totem pole, but Parker has a few connections so it should work out eventually. How did you get onto the baseball team with your record?"

Cade grinned. "You keeping tabs on me, Red?"

I shot him an irritated look. "You wish."

"The good thing about high school is that I was a minor and everything has disappeared off my slate. So I had a really fun time and now it's like it never happened."

"What did you and your pyro friends blow up?"

"A lot more than we got in trouble for, I'll tell you that much."

I laughed and shook my head. I would never really understand boys.

"Were you being scouted to play for the majors too or just the minors?" I surprised myself with my continued probing into Cade's life after high school. A conversation with him was like taking a bite of ice cream, only to realize you wanted a big scoop.

"I was being scouted for the minors which is the next step. But I decided it wasn't what I wanted long-term, so I went with plan B."

"Which is?"

"To live on a ranch with my very best friend in the world."

"Awww... I didn't know you liked my dad's cows that much."

"Awww..." he mirrored. "Don't be so hard on yourself."

I nudged Ace closer to him so I could swat at his arm. He laughed, easily dodging my pitiful attack.

"Any chance you'd ever consider plan A again?"

He motioned between us with his hands. "But now we've bonded, and you'd miss me too much."

Our banter was friendly as we rode our horses next to each other, stopping to fix the fence as needed. I glanced at Cade as he reached up to adjust his baseball hat. If someone would have told me two months ago that I'd be fixing fences with Cade Williams this summer, I would have laughed—or probably spat in their face.

He cleared his throat. "Hey Red, I know this doesn't change anything and I really don't want it to anyway." He shot me a sly look. "But telling the boys the story of us in second grade did make me sound like a jerk, even though we both know I was the victim."

I scoffed. "I didn't mean to throw up on you and then you made my life miserable for the next twelve years. You're the exact opposite of a victim."

"I smelled your barf on me for a week after that."

I snickered under my breath.

"See? Victim." Before I could protest, he continued. "But, I am sorry for de-pantsing you. I should have thought of a better way to get you back." He raised his eyebrows suggestively. "Even though I feel like I know you pretty intimately now, Red. Well, me and the rest of the second grade."

"Your heartfelt apology has been noted."

He grinned.

Later, when we met up with Jake and Dusty, I was ready to go home. More than ready. My mind was a jumble of thoughts. I was hot, tired, and ravenous, which by all accounts in nature, was a deadly combination. There was a long stretch of fence on Dusty's section that had blown down that he couldn't fix by himself, even for all his burly muscles, so we all rode over to help. There were four connecting sections of fence that lay on the ground as we arrived. We slid from our horses, grabbing our knapsacks filled with nails and hammers. I slung mine across my shoulder as my stomach growled and ignored the boys, for the most part, concentrating on holding up my section of the board so Cade could nail it back together. The hot sun beating down on my hungry body did very little for my mood.

The conversation going on around me started trickling into my thoughts. Jake was talking about how he planned to run the rodeo circuit as long as he'd be able to while continuing to work the ranch with my dad. He and Dusty were a superb calf-roping team (at least that's what they tell me), but Jake's first love was riding broncos. He was fearless, or perhaps he just had whatever that gene was that rodeo men seem to have that made them want to risk life and limb on the back of a bucking bull or bronco. Dusty, a steer wrestler, held similar plans, although he was taking some online classes at Montana Tech. But both wanted to continue to live in and around the Eugene area.

"Way to dream big, guys," I grumbled under my breath.

There was a long pause as all the boys glanced over at me.

"What's that supposed to mean?" Dusty asked, handing a nail to Cade, his gargantuan rodeo belt buckle catching a ray of sun and nearly blinding me.

I sensed trouble brewing underneath my tornado cloud of thoughts, but of course, spoke anyway. "I'm just saying, you have the whole world in front of you and all you can talk about is coming back home and working on the ranch. Or the rodeo? Do most people make enough money riding from town to town performing tricks? What about college? Real college. Not online classes. What about traveling?

Go see the world, get some experience, and then decide if you still want to be here."

"I'd take riding a horse in the mountains over sitting in some stuffy office any day," Jake replied as he casually held the boards steady while Cade resumed his hammering. The slight stubble on his face from last week had grown fuller and darker on his slender face, making him seem older than his nineteen years. "And don't you worry, there's good money to be had in a rodeo."

"It's as good as gambling. You can't count on it. Have you ever sat in a *stuffy* office? Well, they're full of air conditioning and people to talk to and you don't break your back doing manual labor." Great. Yes. This is perfect, Kelsey. Keep talking.

"With a boss breathing down your neck, people telling you what to do, heart attacks, and no fresh air. Sounds nice," Cade interjected, giving me a warning look.

I glared at him, scooting over to help hold up the large section of fence for Dusty to hammer on the other side of me. "More money, insurance, promotions..."

"No horses, no land, no farmer's daughters."

The hairs on my neck stood up at his last statement, even though he said it in jest. "I know it's not for everybody, but there's more to life than cows and fixing fences."

"Do you wish you would have grown up in the city?" Cade asked a moment later, after piecing two sections of the fence back together. "In suburbia? With no land or horses?"

We all shuffled down the line, picking up the next part of the fence to nail together. "I love how I grew up. I'm just saying, there are other options for making a living." If these guys have never *had* an office job, how do they know they'd hate it?

"Even in an office job, you'll have days that suck, just like anywhere." Dusty countered, motioning for me to hand him a nail. "If you love your job, you still have to deal with crap, just like anywhere else."

"Yes, but there can be more money in city jobs. And security. Living on a ranch is so dependent on the weather..." My voice trailed off. At that point, I was just talking. I was annoyed, hungry, cranky, hot, ready to go home, and not sure why I was trying so desperately to prove this point I wasn't even sure I completely agreed with. So of course, I kept talking.

"If everybody worked in the city, what would people eat?" Jake asked. "Some of us are born to work the land."

I motioned around me at the mountains and field glistening in the sun. "But how do you know that for sure if you haven't tried anything else? Sure, it's beautiful here, but have you ever been to California? The Oregon Coast? The East Coast? All I'm saying is that it's a big world out there, and it's not a bad idea to explore a bit before you settle on something just because it's what you already know and are comfortable with."

Jake shook his head, exasperated. "Listen, girl, I know who I am already. I know what makes me happy. I'm fine with going to college, but I don't need to work some city job to find out I'd hate it. You worry about yourself. You're the only one here who seems confused."

Sweet Dusty changed the subject just then, but the heart of our camaraderie had disappeared, and it was my fault. We finished the fence and rode back to the trailer in uncomfortable silence. I could tell by the way Cade refused to look at me, and the stiff, unbending way he yanked the saddle off Dodger, that he was still in the middle of our conversation, and by the look of it, I was not winning the argument.

The two of us got back into his truck for the ride home and my stomach tangled into knots waiting for him to say something. I didn't have to wait long. He reached across the cab, his hand brushing against my knee as he opened the glove compartment and flung the bag of jerky in my lap. "Here, eat something."

Before I could say anything, he started right where we left off. "Your dad raised you on a farm. Do you think he should have moved to the city?"

"Cade, I didn't mean for that conversation to get blown out of proportion."

He ignored my remark and waited for me to answer his question.

I sighed and tore off a piece of jerky, taking a bite. "No. I enjoyed growing up here, but he could have made more money and been much less stressed with a different job. I wasn't talking about me; all I was saying was—"

"You were definitely talking about you. Isn't that exactly what *you're* doing? Getting married to a rich, city kid, so now you think you've set some sort of *example* for the rest of us. Is money that important to you?"

My face burned as his words infiltrated my heart, but I wasn't done fighting yet. "You're going to go there?"

"Is money that important to you?" he pressed again.

"It comes in pretty handy."

"Sure it does. But tell me something, that boulder I saw on your finger the other day, did your boyfriend pay for that?"

"Yes."

Cade looked at me incredulously. "*He* paid for it? With money *he's* earned? Did he have a big fancy job while going to school?"

"How is this any of your business?"

"It's not. Did he have a job?"

His eyes bore into mine. I stared at him for a moment before answering slowly. "No. Not during school."

"So did he save up to buy it then? By the looks of that thing, that's not something a normal guy could buy on a whim."

"Oh, so him proposing to me had to have been a whim? Is that it?"

"Nope. I mean there's no way he could have bought it without a job, so he either went into some crazy debt to put some bling on the trophy wife, or daddy paid for it."

Trophy wife? "Just shut up, okay."

"You've changed."

"That's generally the idea."

"Not for the better."

"I can't imagine that I was high on your list of favorites to begin with."

"You used to be fun. Whenever I pranked you, you'd give it right back. Now you act like you're too good for everybody here. You never used to talk to people the way you just did."

"What's that supposed to mean? Because I gave two guys some advice to try a few things before they settle on what they already know?"

He turned to face me. "Maybe some people don't need the whole world. Maybe some people are satisfied with a good honest life, making a good honest living."

I barked out a laugh. "And you're an expert on making a good honest life, huh? You wanted to throw a ball for a living."

He ignored my jab. "Your dad raised you working eighteen-hour days. He put food in your belly and clothes on your back. He sent you to college on the money he worked hard to make, only to have you come back a spoiled brat."

His words cut deep, but I tried hard not to show it as I gritted my teeth. My words came out chipped and brittle. "I love my dad. I love this ranch. I never said I didn't appreciate it. I just don't want that life for myself."

"Why?"

"Every reason I just told you."

"Every reason you just told me sounded like it came from someone else. Not from you." He held my gaze for a moment as he turned the truck onto my parent's lane. "Last time I checked, you sure seemed to love being home and riding that horse of yours. Today even, you looked like you were one step away from heaven. Maybe it's *you* who needs to think about what you might really want."

I searched for another angle. Another argument. Nothing came. My body was shutting down. The only thing I could think about was asking Parker how he could afford the ring and then wondering if I wanted to know.

I avoided Cade for a few days while I licked my wounds. As much as I would have liked to write off everything he said, I couldn't get his words out of my head. I hadn't been nice to the boys, especially Jake, and my words pricked at my conscience. Don't get me wrong, I had a few things to think about and I did apologize to Jake and Dusty, but

Cade's self-righteous attitude was enough to make my blood boil, even if he was right about a few things.

Most things.

And like some sort of weird, adrenaline addict, my hands twitched for some sort of... retaliation.

10

Journal Entry (circa - high school)

Tessa and I stood down the hallway today and watched as an unsuspecting Cade opened his locker to find a squirrel inside. The second the door opened, that thing bailed, jumping onto Cade's shoulder, and took off down the hall. I was a bit disappointed by the whole thing. To think it took two days for us to trap the little bugger. Next time I'm going with a snake.

"Hi, Kelsey. It's Bev calling from The Blushing Lily again. I was just wondering if you needed me to order those white roses and whether you've picked your colors yet. Anyway, just give me a call back when you know. Thank you."

I threw my phone down on my bed while I lay back on the pillows. The voicemail notification from Bev had been on my phone for three days before I worked up the motivation to listen to it. I had known what she would ask, and I already knew what my answer would be. Nothing—because I had no answers. So naturally, I avoided her and her voicemail.

I lay there on the twin bed in my childhood bedroom for about ten more minutes, surrounded by posters and faces from the movie High School Musical. The room still looked like it was ripped straight out of my junior high yearbook. Pictures of Tessa and me and my family were scattered and taped in clusters around my floor-length mirror. Thankfully, the pink walls of my childhood had been buried under a soft, inviting blue-gray color, but little else had changed. My bed sat against the wall in the center of the room, and on the far wall was a large window facing the back pastures.

My dad had given me the morning off. Tractor work in the fields had begun, so there were no wheel lines to move. Jake, Dusty, and Cade were doing the milking and feeding. I had been excited for a morning off, but now, alone with my thoughts, I felt I'd rather be working. I picked up my journal laying on the nightstand next to my bed and thumbed through it for a minute before snapping it shut. Too many lists and pranks and the name Cade scattered throughout the book.

My mind went unwillingly to the conversation I'd had with Parker over the phone the night before. Though I tried to forget Cade's accusation that he hadn't been the one to pay for the ring, I couldn't. I wasn't sure I wanted to know his answer, but I forced myself to ask anyway.

"Parker. How did you pay for my ring? Did you take out a loan or something?"

There was a pause, and I could hear his stilled breath through the phone. "What? Why?"

"I'm just curious." I held up the ring in front of my face, the striking diamond catching the light. "It's an impressive ring, I just want to make sure you didn't go into some crazy amount of debt."

He laughed. "You scared I'm in the poor house now?"

"No... I'm just... I just want to know."

"Well, rest assured, I'm still plenty rich. And handsome." I imagined him grinning his arrogant grin into the phone as he said this, and I rolled my eyes.

"I never doubted that. But seriously, how did you pay for it? You didn't have a job."

He groaned. "Ugh, babe. It's fine. My dad and I had an arrangement in place. It's paid for. Don't worry about it."

It's not that I didn't think parents could help their kids out from time to time, if their circumstances permitted, but the ring was just the beginning. What else in Parker's life did he get handed to him? I had worked hard on the farm, putting money in a savings account labeled 'college' that I wasn't allowed to touch. Hours of sweat, milking cows, moving wheel lines, and driving tractors paid for my college, and by the time I got ready to enroll, I was able to pay for my tuition in full. Every year. It was at *that* moment I became grateful to my parents for ripping the cold hard cash from my grubby hands every month and forcing me to deposit most of it into a bank.

My mom called me for breakfast, so I heaved myself out of bed and headed toward the door when I stopped in front of the large mirror on the wall. I lifted my tank top just below my breasts. Flexing my stomach muscles, I turned from side to side, trying to spot any difference in my body for all the bird food I had been eating lately. I pulled down my running shorts and examined the same with my hips because I already knew *that* would be the problem area. My body felt leaner, but it was hard to tell. The night before, I had tried on my tightest pair of size six jeans, which now felt more relaxed, but jeans and form-fitted dresses made for a celebrity were very different. To say I was terrified for the fourth of July to get here was an understatement, which was a real shame because it was my favorite holiday.

We were two weeks into June, which meant for the next three weeks, I needed to push myself. Though Tessa was on board for a few extra runs each week, she was a surprisingly hard sell, and only agreed if I finished out the softball season. Thankfully, we only had one more game against Cade's team. I just might have to be sick that day.

The kitchen and dining room shared the same space as our large family room. Separate spaces, but one cohesive unit. When I walked into the dining room a few moments later, I was surprised to see Stitch and Cade sitting at the table chatting with Dad, and Mom stirring something on the stove. Mom's eyebrows immediately rose as she took in my short shorts and tank top. I refused to be embarrassed. Obviously, I would have put on more clothes if she had come upstairs and told me we had a couple of breakfast crashers. I had been planning on choking back a green smoothie (another of Parker's helpful suggestions) while sitting next to my mom, helping her do her crossword puzzle, per usual. This wasn't my fault.

She directed me to bring a large pot of oatmeal to the table, followed by milk and several things that make the oatmeal tolerable, like sugar, nuts, berries, chocolate chips, cranberries, and honey. My skin prickled a bit and I glanced over at Cade, expecting to see him watching me, but he seemed engrossed in the dry conversation of milk prices between my dad and Stitch, almost as if he were intent on ignoring me. We hadn't spoken much since our fight in the truck, but thankfully, there had been little opportunity.

I took my seat across from Cade, and after a quick grace, the table became alive in a flurry of hunger. I took a small spoonful of the carb-laden breakfast, partially because I didn't want to offend my mom, but mainly because I didn't want weird looks or observations as to why I was drinking a tall glass of green sludge instead of eating oatmeal. This was the wrong crowd for that. I added a pile of strawberries on top but regretfully refrained from adding any sugar. Although, my eyes followed the rapidly dwindling sugar bowl as it made its way around the table. When it made its last stop in front of Cade, it was empty. Mom, ever the conscientious hostess, noticed right away.

"Kelsey, will you go refill the sugar bowl for Cade?"

The conversation of hay, grain prices, and the clanking of the silverware around the table dulled to a low volume in my ears as I zeroed in on the empty sugar bowl. My eyes automatically lifted to Cade's and found him already watching me. I held his gaze and watched as a small, imperceptible smirk began to form on his mouth. He motioned with his head toward the kitchen, essentially telling me with his eyes to go get him some sugar. A flash of unexpected tingles shot through my body. I sprung from my seat, my chair scraping the hardwood floor behind me loud enough to pause the conversation. Stitch and my dad glanced over, but I only smiled tightly to the table before turning to walk into the kitchen, my face ablaze.

It felt as though I were moving in slow motion—my brain buzzing with possibilities.

No. Play it straight. You don't have time for this.

I stopped at the cabinet holding the canister of sugar and pulled it out. Sugar was the safe choice. The choice I had time for. Starting a war was not an option. I still had lots to do this summer. Should it come up, I'd never be able to explain it away to Parker. It had only been just over two weeks since I'd arrived home, and I did not want an 'I told you so' from Tessa.

But that itch was... itchy.

The cards had been dealt and I had the makings of a royal flush. It was too late to fold. I was all in. Ever so slowly, I put the sugar canister back into the cabinet. My heartbeat was blasting in my eardrums. My heart was pounding with a newfound adrenaline rush, as I reached for the salt, carefully keeping myself out of view of the table.

I didn't look at Cade once, but when I set the bowl in front of him, I felt his gaze burning a hole in my skin. I busied myself in my pot of berries, stirring and feigning interest in the conversation down the table. From under my lashes, I detected a slight hesitation in Cade, before he dumped two large spoonfuls into his oatmeal and stirred. He took a bite.

Not able to help myself, I looked at him then. He had removed his hat at the table and for a second I was arrested at the sight of his rumpled hair, brushed back impatiently. It hung just past his ears, but it was the bit in the back that refused to lay down that had a smile on my face threatening to break. It gave his strong, confident face a boyish appearance and I couldn't look away. He was *not* looking at me. He chewed slowly, his brow furrowing as he stared into his bowl. He glanced across the table as if to see if anyone else seemed to be having the same trouble before he took another tentative bite.

Slowly, he turned his head to look at me. Accusation danced in his gleaming eyes, and I watched his mouth curve into a dangerous smile. His head shook slowly as his eyes burned into mine. There was no going back now. The fire racing up my veins had me ready to tear the walls down in both eagerness and dread.

Cade took another bite as if he'd forgotten, and then gave a small cough, which was my undoing. A grin burst across my face in all the glory of someone who had just executed the perfect prank. I had to tamp down the laugh bubbling up my throat that threatened to expose us both. He reached for the honey, drowning his oatmeal in it before topping it off with a heaping pile of chocolate chips and nuts. He then proceeded to eat the entire bowl, smiling at me, until the last bite. I tried several times to stop looking at him or to at least stop smiling like a lunatic, but even biting my lips couldn't get the job done. Both of us were locked in this strange game, while the world around us went on, oblivious.

Call it an apology or stupidity, or both, but either way—without my saying a word, I had just entered the prank war.

"Cade, pass the sugar, would you please?" Stitch's low voice broke across the table.

I froze. My mouth fell open while Cade grinned at me and handed the bowl over to Stitch.

Dang it.

He just tied the score up.

K elsey — I'm gonna need some prank help. STAT.
      Tessa — I KNEW it. You lasted longer than I thought,
but you were definitely going to cave.
      Kelsey — Calm down and help me think!
      Tessa — I'll be right over.

C ade wasted no time executing plans he had probably been
      dreaming of since he got here. The next morning, I stumbled
into the garage with sleep-crusted eyes to pull on my boots to help
my dad milk cows, you know, like a good employee, when I stepped
into a boot filled with manure. He had made himself scarce, bailing
hay and driving a tractor all day, although, he did also find the time to
somehow SNEAK INTO MY ROOM and hide an open can of rotting
salmon under my bed, which I regretfully did not find until two days
later. Now, I kept the window from my room barricaded by my
dresser whenever I was gone.

The prank life was a stressful life.

I had never been afraid of mice. They were always running wild
around the barn and burrowed inside the hay all around the farm.
Granted, I would jump out of my skin every time they darted in and
out because they startled me. It would be a different story if I found
them inside my home, but out in the barn, I enjoyed watching them.

Catching the mice was the tricky part. It took three days and seven
homemade traps, but ultimately, I caught three. Placing the mice
exactly where I wanted them... well... that was the fun part.

After overhearing Cade tell the boys he was heading into town
that evening, I waited for the perfect time to set my plan into motion.
Literally. It turned out my old friend the birch tree was a great
lookout point to watch it all unfold. And this time, I made sure that I
wasn't wearing a stitch of red.

At last, the object of my summer angst strode out of the
bunkhouse, dressed in jeans and a fitted polo shirt. His baseball cap
was nowhere in sight. I didn't care about where he was going, but I

did wonder what occasion warranted him to go without his beloved baseball hat? Just as he opened the door to his truck, Dusty and Jake called out to him from behind. Turning toward them, he laughed at something they'd said. I had already forgotten how uncomfortable the tree was until I was dangling from a branch and forced to wait. The binoculars in my hands, however, were a great addition.

Cade climbed into his truck and tossed a wave out the window, backing up slowly. In an instant, his door burst open, and he launched himself outside. I could only assume at that point he had knocked over the random bucket sitting upside down on his front seat and sent three scared little mice running wild all over the cab. It was hard to tell because the truck was still moving. He had been so startled that he'd failed to put it in park. I snickered silently and watched the delightfully gratifying scene unfold.

Seeing a commotion, the boys came running over. Cade, having wised up to what happened, jumped into the pickup and shifted it into park while the boys flung the passenger side door open. I couldn't help but feel proud of my efforts. There I sat, laughing, tucked safely away in my tree, behind a pair of binoculars, and wishing I would have thought to record it all for blackmail purposes.

Once they seemed certain all the mice had been released back into the wild, Cade pulled both boys in close by the shoulders, their heads touching as they discussed something. I peered closer, on edge... waiting. The nerves in my body began to tighten as a bad feeling came over me. Perhaps I should have picked a different hiding spot. Or at the very least, a different tree. Specifically, somewhere Cade had never seen me hide—which would have been, basically, anywhere else on the farm.

The next second, all three boys broke from the huddle, and bolted toward my tree, with Cade in the middle, running the fastest.

Before my survival mode kicked in, I sat in stunned alarm while watching him gracefully hurdle a fence. Squealing, I dropped the binoculars and scrambled out of the tree. I wasted no more time and took off running. Dusty and Jake were taking a curved approach, one on each side, but angled toward me in such a way it left me only one direction to go.

The farm has an irrigation pond just south of my parent's home, about a quarter of a mile. It was really just a ditch, but wide enough that we called it a pond. Growing up, it was full of fun memories of swimming and skipping rocks with my dad and siblings. However, I had nothing but bad things to say about it now as I came upon it with a pair of revenge-filled boots rapidly closing in on me.

Call it adrenaline, or perhaps the effect of a good joke perfectly executed, but I was laughing hysterically when Cade caught me in his arms. Pulling me close, he whispered in my ear, "Hope you enjoyed that, Red, cause it's my turn now."

I refused to give any thought to the way my body reacted with each puff of his breath in my ear. It was just reflexes. Spinning me around, he grabbed my legs and flung me over his shoulder like a sack of flour. By this time, Dusty and Jake had caught up to us, both of them panting with laughter. I tried to fight but was howling too hard to be much of a disturbance.

My affection for Jake and Dusty went down a few notches as we reached the edge of the pond. They each grabbed a leg while Cade took hold of my arms. My feet left the ground as they began swinging me back and forth.

"Any last words, Red?"

I shook my head at the two cowboys looking quite pleased with themselves. "Really, you two? After all of our history together, you do this to me after a few weeks working with him?"

Dusty had the presence of mind to look a little chagrined trying to hold back a laugh. Jake just smiled. "Yup. We never had a good enough reason to mess with you until he showed up." He nodded his head toward Cade.

I glared at them before issuing a warning to Cade. Which admittedly, would have seemed more threatening had I not been being swung like an upside-down turtle. "You better be watching your back from here on out."

He raised his eyebrows. "I'm terrified. But I believe your little prank is about to be canceled out."

They let go on three, plunging me into the pond. I came up for air, gasping for breath, but it must have looked refreshing enough because Jake and Dusty joined me immediately, splashing and laughing.

I scooted closer to the edge and held my hand up expectantly toward Cade.

He studied me for a moment before crouching down to the edge and extended his hand out toward mine. The tiniest whiff of his cologne permeated the air between us. I must have been hungry because the word 'delicious' was the only way my boggled brain could describe what I was smelling. I was missing Parker. That was the problem. It had been too long since I had smelled something so masculine and sexy.

Just before I could grab at his hand, he yanked it away and grinned at me. For a slight second, I was taken aback by the sheer rugged attractiveness of his smile. Blinking, I forced my gaze upward into a pair of knowing eyes. "You didn't think I'd fall for the oldest trick in the book, did you, Red? Not a bad job with the mice, but I have to say, I think the end of this prank was the best part." Reaching down, he patted my cheek twice before standing up. "See you kids later."

"Have fun on your date, lover boy!" Jake called.

Cade threw a quick wave over his shoulder as he walked back toward his truck. Cade was going on a date. That explained the dress shirt and no hat. Of course, he would be dating this summer. Why wouldn't he? Some people (not me) might find him attractive. I couldn't expect him to never leave the ranch.

I yelped as I felt myself being lifted in the air only to be dunked again. I came up sputtering. Shouting threats, I jumped on Dusty's back, trying to throw him off balance. Soon we were just a group of kids laughing and playing together.

Extracting myself from the fray for a moment, I paused to look around. The sound of a cricket nearby had me searching the pond banks for the belching insect. I remembered so many summer evenings of my childhood playing in the pond and falling asleep at night to the sounds of the sprinklers and crickets outside my window. The spray of the sprinklers always kept perfect timing to the chirp of the crickets. There's a certain amount of comfort in a rhythm, always knowing what to expect and what you can count on. At school, I thrived on routine and following a plan. Surprises left too much to chance. And now, with being apart from Parker for the summer, the dress, and Cade's antics—my first month home had thrown me through a few loops.

But there was a rhythm on the farm that spoke deep into my soul and soothed my clattering mind. The evening was now blessed with the happy sounds of laughter and taunting as a water fight broke out all around me. I smiled as Dusty body-slammed Jake into the water, and I knew I would have picked the same tree to hide out in if it would bring me back to this moment.

In a surprising plot twist, however, I realized there was only one thing missing from this scene, and currently, he was driving down my parent's lane, headed into town to pick up his mystery date.

The next morning in the barn, I did a double-take at the old chalkboard behind the door leading into the milk tank room. Before cell phones and note apps, the chalkboard had been used as a tally system for my siblings and me to keep track of the hours we worked each day for my dad. It hadn't been used in years but was now covered with fresh writing. I moved closer to inspect and much to my dismay and utter delight, the names Red and Cade were scrawled across the top of the chalkboard, with a line separating us. *Prank War* was scrawled across the top and Cade had three notches underneath his name. The most recent was for last night's dunking and I assumed the other two were for the manure and salmon. With nobody there to see, there was no need to hide the smile spreading across my face. I grabbed the chalk sitting on top of the board and scratched two notches under my name as well—for the salty oatmeal and the mice.

Tessa was right. This summer just got a whole lot more interesting.

11

Reasons Cade Williams is the worst
(circa junior high - current)

77. Cow's butt
78. Manure in boot
79. Another freaking can of fish.

"Kels, honey, are you out here?"

Mom poked her head out of the front door a few nights later to find me draped across my parent's porch swing, listening to the crickets work their magical relaxation spells. I was enjoying the last of my dwindling endorphins from my run with Tessa earlier that evening. The boys had softball practice, so there were no basketball games to be played. Tessa had driven home immediately after our run. I had only made it as far as the porch swing.

Mom stepped out onto the porch, a ratty, pink apron tied around her ample waist. "I just got a voicemail from Bev at The Blushing Lily. Have you decided on what flowers you want yet?"

My face fell, annoyed. For all the love that was holy, Bev didn't quit. It was only June. My wedding wasn't until September. I groaned, leaning my head back and putting an arm over my eyes. "Not yet."

There was silence for a moment before I heard my mom move closer. "Kels, we need to talk about wedding stuff for a minute."

"Okay." I knew this was coming, but I still wasn't prepared. I had been creatively avoiding this conversation for the past three weeks. The award for worst daughter ever goes to... Kelsey Marten.

"Karen, the woman taking care of all the decorations for the reception needs to know your wedding colors. She said she'll order the tablecloths and the napkins in the exact colors you want if she doesn't already have them, we just need to let her know." Perhaps it was my unresponsive attitude lying like a limp, dead fish on the swing that had her continuing in a more sympathetic tone. "I know it can seem overwhelming, but there are just a few things, like colors and flowers, that once you decide, will help make the rest of your decisions easier."

I pulled myself into a sitting position. My mom joined me on the swing and together we swayed gently.

"Isn't there an old country song that talks about rocking to the rhythm of the crickets or something?" I asked. "I think Tessa and I danced to it in elementary school."

Mom laughed, "I'm pretty sure it's called *Rocking to the Rhythm of the Rain* by the Judds."

"Oh yeah. That sounds right."

"That was a good song," she added.

We sat for a moment in silence before she spoke again. "Is there a reason you always change the subject or act like you're dying when I try to talk to you about wedding stuff?"

I twisted the ring on my finger. It wasn't that I didn't want to plan a wedding, it was just that... things were... hard here. It was hard to think and to get inspired by what Parker and I would both love, then take those different tastes and create something worthy of Martha freaking Stewart.

"Not really. I just didn't think I'd be so uninterested in all the details. I had always heard how much fun it was to plan a wedding, but if I have to make any more decisions about font sizes, or napkin colors, flowers, or invitations, I may kill someone."

"But if you'd just pick your colors or make a few decisions, it will be easier, I promise. Even just *one* little thing."

"I'll look again tonight and let you know in the morning."

Nudging me in the arm, my mom said, "Try not to make it sound like I just assigned you some horrible school assignment."

I smiled. "Sorry."

The crickets were soon joined in their song by a frog. The loud belching sound was horribly off-key, making us giggle.

"That's quite the chorus they have going on out there," Mom said as she leaned her head back against the swing, one of her purple fuzzy house slippers tucked under her legs, while the other kept us in motion.

It was quiet between us for a moment as we listened to the squeak of the swing. What I needed to say, had to say, and *loathed* to say, was beating in my ears so loudly, I knew it was time.

"Mom, I need to tell you something."

The swing stopped rocking as my mom looked at me with a wide-eyed expression on her face. "What?"

"Parker found me a dress for my wedding. It's free for us. It was Jennifer Harris's custom wedding dress, but she's not getting married anymore."

My mom threw her hand up to her chest and burst out a sigh like she'd been holding back a dam full of water. "Oh, good grief. You aren't hurt? Or pregnant? Or moving to Timbuktu??"

I gave my mom a questioning look, surprised at her outburst. "What? No? Why would you think that?"

She laughed slightly. "Oh my heavens, by your tone of voice, I thought it was doomsday. Now. Tell me about this dress. And how and why and what?"

I laughed and told her the details, relieved she seemed in a contrite mood.

"Jennifer Harris, the actress?"

"Yeah."

"That's crazy. Kind of exciting, though. Have you seen the dress?"

"Parker sent me a picture of it. It's gorgeous. I'll show you when we go back inside. He said it's even better in person."

She nodded her head slowly. "Can't wait to see it, but I thought you wanted to go dress shopping and pick out one yourself?"

"I did. But this just came up and I think it will be kind of cool. A fun story to tell the grandkids," I said, repeating Parker's words back to her.

The swing groaned a bit as Mom leaned back next to me once again. She patted my knee. "There can be lots of stories to tell the grandkids. I just want you to make sure it's *your* story."

I swallowed. "Mom, I still would like to go shopping in Boise for dresses, but maybe just for bridesmaid dresses instead."

"Are the bridesmaids still going to be just Amanda and Tessa?"

"Yeah." My best friend and sister were the two logical choices, even though Amanda was already married and lived with her husband and son in Washington. I had other friends home this summer, but if I chose one of them, I'd have to choose them all. It just got too complicated.

"Alright. I can't wait to see the dress."

"Parker and his mom are bringing it on the fourth." Which was now exactly one week from today. Mercy, this summer was flying by.

The swing continued in motion and the weight I had been packing on my back, dropped to the ground. I didn't figure I was out of the woods completely, especially once my mom realized just what she would be missing out on, but at least the truth was now between us.

"Mom, what was it like for you when you and dad were engaged? Did you have fun planning the wedding?"

"I didn't mind it. Like you, I didn't care about all the minor details, other than dress shopping, picking colors, and taking pictures together, but it was all so fun and exciting." She glanced over at me wryly and added, "If I had known that would be the last time I'd get your dad in a suit, I would have tortured him even longer with it all. But I also had my fiancé in the same town as me, so it was easier to go over ideas we both liked. He didn't care too deeply about specifics, but every once in a while, he'd have some input."

I smiled as I tried to imagine my tough-as-nails, overall-wearing farmer dad picking out wedding colors and having an opinion on dresses.

"Has Parker been helping with ideas much?"

The question made me laugh as I nodded. "He'd plan the wedding himself if I said the word. He and his mom have lots of ideas and they want it really fancy. His family seems to be a big name in California with a lot of connections and people they're inviting. It's just..."

I paused, waiting, not sure what exactly was fixing to come blurting out of my mouth, but knowing it probably wouldn't come out filtered.

"It's just?" Mom prodded.

"I just... sometimes... I feel like I'm two different people," I said. "At school, I was Parker's type. I dressed nicely. I was always studying and driven toward finishing my degree. He took me to fancy dinners and plays and everything we did was... big. Over the top, even. And it was fun. But then I come home and... none of those things are a part of me here, but this is who I am too. I guess I'm just confused about what my tastes really are. Even down to the idea of planning a wedding. I don't know what my colors are. I know the colors Kelsey of Moscow would pick and I know the colors Kelsey of Eugene would pick and they're... different."

Mom was quiet for a moment as I slunk down lower onto the swing and leaned my head against her shoulder. Already my thundering heart had slowed to a dull knocking. There was something about unloading all my burdens on my mom that made me feel better. I needed to remember to do it more often. I was so grateful for my parents. I couldn't imagine losing one of them. Without asking me, my mind thought of Cade and having to say goodbye to his dad in high school as he passed away. I wondered who he talked about things with. His mom? Stitch? Maybe nobody?

"I know one thing," Mom began quietly as we rocked into the night. "You could have gone to California with Parker for the summer. He could have easily gotten you a job with his connections and you could have planned your wedding with him. But you're here. You came *home* instead of being with your fiancé. I'm not saying that decision was good or bad, but for some reason, it felt like the right choice for you. You just need to figure out why. And I know you will. So don't worry about getting me the colors right away. We have time." With a quick kiss on my cheek, she squeezed my shoulder and went back inside, leaving me alone, surrounded by my thoughts and a tone-deaf frog.

The Fourth of July was an important holiday for Eugene, starting with a big parade that lined the streets. The town clubs, churches, and businesses all sponsored a hometown float, and candy littered the streets. But in my mind, the parade was all smoke and mirrors, because the real party started back at Tessa's family's home later that afternoon. Since the dawn of time, or at least as long as I could remember, our parents had been hosting a large pot-luck-style barbecue for family, friends, and the neighborhood. 'Neighborhood' was a subjective term in the country—it basically meant anybody we knew within twenty miles of us.

The entire rest of the day would be busy with eating, slip and slides, gun competitions, basketball games, dancing, and fireworks. It was my favorite holiday, hands down, and I was ecstatic to be here this year. For the past three years, I had either celebrated in Moscow with Parker or traveled to California over the fourth to spend time with his family. Obviously, I was in love and wanted to be where my boyfriend was, but now that I was back home gearing up for the big event, I couldn't believe I had so casually sacrificed my favorite day of the year.

The week leading up to the fourth was busy for everybody. My dad and the boys were working hard to get the chores and tractor work to line up just right so that the workload on our nation's birthday would be light. My mom spent the day beforehand cleaning the house, getting Logan's room ready for him to visit for the weekend, baking pies, making salads, and preparing her famous baked beans.

As for me, when I wasn't helping either of my parents, I was trying to get their house ready for Parker and his parents. Secretly. For lack of a better term, I was in the middle of Parker-proofing my parent's home. On the sly.

Which was exactly why, the morning of July third, I did NOT need Cade messing with me.

My parents were currently in the town of Mackay, an hour away, to pick up a tractor part. I had just gotten through feeding the cows and was running inside to take advantage of the precious time I had in the house by myself. There was a mountain of frames with embarrassing photos inside that needed some attention STAT. Dusty and Jake were off raking hay in a field somewhere. Cade was... who knows where, which in hindsight, should have alarmed me. When I passed by the large haystack near the barn, something caught my eye. I slowed, then I stopped short. Then I gaped.

Then I cursed Cade.

And then after cursing Cade, I cursed myself for not being able to resist the stupid salt, and I even cursed my sweet mother who was kind enough to still do my laundry but refused to use a clothes dryer.

Speckled across the entire haystack, for the whole world to see was my entire load of laundry. Earlier that morning, it had been hanging discreetly on the clothesline behind our house, now it was tacked against the haystack. Upon closer inspection, he had even tagged outfits together. My skimpy shorts and tank top were pinned together, my short skirt and see-through shawl were scandalously paired together amid t-shirts, gym shorts, socks, and two pairs of jeans sprinkled across the expanse of the haystack. Thank goodness my underwear hadn't been out on the line this morning.

But wait.

A bra. My black, lacy bra—which I hardly wore—hung stretched out at the highest point on the haystack. Dead center. I hadn't worn it in months and I had no idea how it got there.

It was a pretty gutsy prank considering I was the boss's daughter. He must have only had the guts because my parents were out of town at that moment.

"Out of quarters, Red?"

I stiffened as footsteps fell behind me. Turning, I lifted my eyes to his, severely. "Tampering with my clothes is a big line you're crossing. You sure you're ready for the consequences?"

He looked intrigued. "Are you threatening to rifle through my underwear drawer?"

I shot him an annoyed look as I jumped up onto the bale of hay, and began gathering up my things. "Stop it. Or I'll have my fiancé take you down."

He laughed. "Your California fiancé? I think I'll be okay." Stepping up onto the hay bale next to mine, he began collecting the t-shirt and jeans, throwing them over his shoulder as he helped clean up his mess. I gave him a side-eye, anticipating him doing something atrocious, but he held up one hand as a white flag. "I'm just helping you."

"In a hurry to get these down before my dad sees?" I paused, my hand in mid-air. "Maybe I should keep them up."

He smiled, reaching for the black bra. "Fine by me."

I slapped his hand away and grabbed the incriminating garment. "I'm not even going to ask how you got ahold of this because I know for a fact it was *not* on the clothesline this morning."

He just laughed and dropped his hand, jumping down from the bale. "I don't spill my secrets."

"But if I find out you snuck into my room and went through my underwear drawer, there will be hell to pay!" I threatened, my voice taking on a psychotic tone. "There have to be *some* boundaries this summer."

"Noted. I'll see you later, Red. I've got to go put another notch under my name." He handed me the clothes he had picked up and saluted me, not even trying to keep the grin off his face, and began walking toward the bunkhouse.

My eyes unwittingly focused in on the way his jeans hung low on his hips as he strode away and my face betrayed me as it warmed considerably. Irritated at myself, I yanked the rest of my clothes down from the haystack before storming to the house.

How in the *crap* did he get a hold of my bra?

12

Reasons Cade Williams is the Worst
(circa junior high - current)

80. Black Bra

The walls in our home had not been updated in years. My mom hadn't been much of a decorator in terms of style, but she had been an avid picture-taker while her children were growing up. What we lacked in trend, we made up for in picture frames. Those old-fashioned oak collage style frames that could fit twenty or so pictures together, to be more specific. You know the type. They were everywhere. Mine and my siblings' pubescent faces were plastered in every room in the house. Pictures of me participating in dance recitals, sporting events, ranch and school photos, dating back to when I was a baby. My mom seemed to love the junior high years, which meant that the chubby face of my adolescence stared back at me everywhere I went. I was determined it would not do so to Parker.

Parker and his parents were set to arrive at five that afternoon, and my parents would be back within the hour, which meant I had to hurry. I wanted to make subtle improvements, small enough that my mom might not notice right away, but enough to get all the incriminating photos of me out of plain sight. Especially the picture of me bearing a wide metallic grin, showing off my night headgear. Another photo from the awkward middle school years that had no business frightening some poor visitor in our family room.

While I hadn't the time or expense to get rid of all the oak frames completely, I was going to drastically reduce their number. I aimed to replace a few key photos while rearranging the collages on the wall in a more pleasing manner. I grabbed a flathead screwdriver and the stack of pictures I'd been collecting for weeks. Most were baby pictures when everybody was cute, a few of me in grade school where I was nothing but skin and bones, and I did have to add a handful from junior high, but only the pictures which hid half of my body, or were at some blessedly good angle.

I was kneeling in the family room, bent over a frame in concentration when I heard footsteps in the kitchen.

"Red?"

I froze. Why? Why was he in my house? Why didn't he knock? I stayed still, hoping he wouldn't walk the few steps further to investigate.

Who am I kidding? Of course he would walk a few steps further to investigate. His eyebrows raised as he took me in, curiously. "What are you doing?"

"Nothing. What are you doing?" Go away. Go away. Go away.

He sauntered closer and to my utter horror, the headgear picture I had just broken free was face up on the ground next to me. A corner of his mouth lifted as he picked up the picture. "You're taking this one down? It's my favorite."

I jumped to my feet, holding my hand out to grab it. "Shut up. Give it back."

He stepped back and held it just out of my reach. "No, I'm serious. Was this a night headgear?"

"Yeah." I no longer reached for the picture, but I watched him carefully, waiting for him to tease me, but he only stared at it, a small smile on his face.

"Gotta love junior high. I had one too."

"You did?"

"Yup." He flashed his teeth at me in a toothy grin. "You think these are all-natural?"

I breathed a laugh before I lunged for the picture, yanking it out of his grasp. "Okay, now go away."

Instead of moving, he crouched down and began leafing through all the old pictures I had removed from their frames.

"Are you trying to torture me?"

He held out another picture toward me. "This was the year we were on the same soccer team in city league."

I removed my face from behind my hands and glanced at the picture. "I remember. You used to tie my shoelaces together during the timeout huddles."

"You kicked me in the shins for that."

"I'm always playing defense."

He snorted as he finished thumbing through the pictures and stood back up, facing me once again. "Why are you replacing all of these?"

"It's time. Did you need something?"

His gaze clung to mine a few seconds too long before he pulled my pink running shorts out of his back pocket. "You left these outside."

"Oh, you mean, like on the clothesline?"

He grinned. "Yup."

I took them from him, tossing them onto the couch behind me, and turned back to my pictures. "Thanks."

He turned to go, but not before calling over his shoulder. "You should keep the headgear one."

No stinking way.

The Gillette's waltzed into my parent's home the way they did everything—with a grand flourish, obnoxiously so. I knew my parents' modest home on a dusty ranch was a far cry from their gated community mansion with a pool. They had to be masking their judgments behind gracious hugs and hellos. I had met Parker's parents several times before. Twice, when they came to visit him at school and three or four times when I traveled back to visit them in California with Parker. They were always courteous and kind but had a way about them that gave the impression that they were always so very busy. They seemed graciously put-upon every time Parker and I would visit, and always made a note to tell us how much work they were missing because we were there. It was done in subtle ways, so small you might not notice, but whenever I was speaking or answering a question, I always felt I needed to rush so as not to take up too much of their time.

In Moscow, I was 'school Kelsey.' Busy, busy, busy. That Kelsey fit into their world perfectly, right down to my tailored jeans and expensive shoes. Which was why today, I had donned my designer blouse and name-brand skinny jeans for the occasion. Farm Kelsey, with her cut-off jeans and t-shirts, was much more confusing.

"Hello, dear." Mrs. Gillette pulled me into a hug that was nothing but bones and elbows. My face was suddenly pressed against her chest where her flowery perfume caused my eyes to burn. "It's lovely to see you. I have a son who has been driving us crazy with how much he misses you."

I laughed, but my breath caught as Parker stepped into the entryway behind his father. My eyes drank him in. He was wearing a fitted blue polo t-shirt and dark jeans. His sandy blonde hair was perfectly styled. He smiled happily at me, dimples for days, but waited patiently for his turn to greet me.

Mr. Gillette smirked as I held my hand out to shake his and instead, he pulled me into a hug. "Let's drag this out and see how long we can make him wait."

I had always liked Parker's dad. He had a lean build, salt and pepper hair, looked the most comfortable in a suit and tie, and was nothing but a smooth politician. But he had a natural, friendly manner with people that put me at ease—especially when compared to his wife's suffocating presence in a room.

"That's enough, old man," Parker stated, sternly.

His dad laughed and moved to follow the trail of his wife's scent to greet my parents.

"Hey, babe," Parker whispered. He pulled me close and breathed me in. "You smell good."

Thank goodness. After feeding cows, tearing through the house all morning making improvements, and an afternoon stint for my dad that involved spraying weeds with heavy-duty chemicals, I made sure to shower and use all my best smelling lotions afterward. The double life I was leading was exhausting. I smiled and snuggled into his embrace. "Thanks. I'm glad you're finally here."

He pulled back and did a full-body scan, taking in every inch, before pulling at the waist of my jeans. "Your pants are looking bigger." He waggled his eyes at mine, excitedly. "Those green smoothies doing the trick, like I told you?"

He waited expectantly for my reply, but I was too gobsmacked at the turn our conversation had taken. My happy heart of two minutes earlier took a steep plummet when I was suddenly reduced to nothing but weights and measures. I blinked and tried to smile at him. He hadn't meant to be rude, he was just curious to see a differ-ence, like I was. Parker was never one to beat around the bush, so this shouldn't have surprised me, and it shouldn't have offended me. Before I could say anything, we were pulled into the kitchen.

Parker hugged my mom and shook my dad's hand. I knew Dad was a bit miffed to be missing work in the middle of the afternoon to entertain guests he didn't want, but I was proud of the good face he put on. I'm sure it helped to know all the boys were taking care of the chores for the festivities tomorrow.

Mom ushered everybody into the family room, just past the kitchen. "Sit down, please. I'm sure you're all tired after your flight and your long drive." The Gillettes claimed the couch, my parents took the love seat, while Parker and I sank down on the two steps leading into the sunken family room. For a moment, everybody was quiet.

"We didn't realize how far Eugene is from Boise," Mrs. Gillette said. She had perched herself, in her brown, designer trousers and her soft, cream short-sleeved ruffle top that looked amazing, if not a bit young for her, on the old brown sofa my parents had been given for a wedding gift. I mentally did the math. Twenty-five years ago. Parker's parents were sitting on a couch older than me. Why hadn't we sat in the formal living room, located just off the entry hall? Why did we traipse everybody past the kitchen and into the family room stuffed with the mismatched furniture?

"Yes, it's quite a drive. Pretty though, isn't it?" Mom said, cordially, the pink of her cardigan giving her warm features a lovely glow. "I've always thought Idaho was the nation's best-kept secret."

Diana Gillette's painted eyebrows put up an honorable fight to lift upward on their own, but essentially there was just too much botox for her to raise *only* her brows, and had to get her entire forehead involved. So her face lifted the slightest bit before she agreed to Mom's statement, politely. She fooled nobody. I noticed Dad watching her curiously, as though he had never seen anything quite like this leathery skinned, cosmetically enhanced woman in all his life. He probably hadn't. The room seemed to shrink in her presence, though she said very little. I felt every movement and my eye was continually drawn back to her, watching, like dodging eggshells on the floor. I didn't want to say the wrong thing or worse, not be prepared should she ask me a question. Parker grabbed my hand. I turned to him and smiled gratefully.

Thankfully, Mr. Gillette slipped into politician mode and started asking my dad a bunch of questions about the ranch. My mom and Mrs. Gillette began quietly discussing wedding things and I molded myself against Parker's body with a sigh.

"You really are looking good," Parker said in my ear, apparently not going to leave the topic alone for a blasted minute. "Is this a size four body yet?" His hands squeezed my waist gently as he brushed a quick kiss against my cheek.

I swallowed my annoyance and glared at him while he only laughed and pulled me closer. He was only teasing, making light of our situation. It was fine. He had to be a little worried about the dress fitting, same as me, but the past few years, I had finally gotten to a good place where my body was concerned and now it seemed it still wasn't good enough. I was probably just hungry. The cowboys, aware now of my quick temper when hungry, had started packing apples in their lunches when we were out working somewhere to have something to feed me when I got grumpy, but by now, I was sick of apples. I wanted cake.

Parker continued, unaware of my private angst. "We brought the dress for you to try on. I think you're going to like it. My mom wants to make sure it's going to fit. Or at least that it's close enough that it should be easy to slip on in a month and a half. And off," he whispered, raising his eyebrows suggestively. I'm happy to report that *his* eyebrows rose upward just fine. Very natural.

"Kelsey, dear," Mrs. Gillette's voice purred from across the room. "I thought we'd leave the men here to talk about men's things, while we women run down the hall to help you try on the dress. How does that sound? I can't wait to see how stunning you're going to look." She gave Parker an exaggerated glance. "But Parker is banned from your bedroom. He can't see you in the dress until you're walking down the aisle."

Parker huffed theatrically but stood and pulled me up with him. "Just don't be gone too long. Your dad might make me put on my work boots."

My dad laughed, but the light didn't quite reach his eyes. "That's not a bad idea, young man. Do you have any?"

Then I was whisked away.

While Mrs. Gillette ran out to the car to grab the dress, my mom and I stood waiting in my bedroom. Once I eyed my childish things and posters surrounding my wall, I immediately thought to move us to the bathroom, but it was no good. The guest bathroom was tiny. Before I could do anything, Mom pulled me into a hug. "Are you alright?"

I smiled at her, inhaling her natural scent of lavender and lemons. "Yeah. I'm good."

"Do you realize you haven't said more than two sentences the entire time they've been here?"

I opened my mouth to say something, but Mrs. Gillette breezed into the room and gently set the gown, stuffed into a white zippered dress protector, on the bed as if it were full of diamonds. At least her eyes were only on the dress, so perhaps she didn't notice that at my parents' home, I still slept on a twin bed.

"It took Hendrix over seven weeks to finalize the design of this gown specifically to Jennifer's liking. Then it took a team of ten over two weeks to complete the dress," she spoke in a hushed tone as she slowly unzipped the protector.

"Who's Hendrix?" My mom asked.

"The designer," I replied. Three sentences now.

"The floral work alone was so fine it took hours and hours to intricately hand weave." Mrs. Gillette went on as if we hadn't spoken at all. "Hundreds of bridal shops along the California coast were in an all-out bidding war to get this dress, but Hendrix gave it to me."

I was tempted to ask if she'd like a minute alone with the dress until finally, she pulled the gown out of the bag and held it up for us to see.

Um.... hi.

My mom and I both gasped. I threw my hands over my mouth as I stared. The most elegant dress I had ever seen was being held in front of my face. The picture Parker had texted me had nowhere near given the impression of a gown *this* stunning, and the picture had looked wonderful. Jennifer Harris had excellent taste.

The color was a soft, milky white. The dress was long with a form-fitted, light mermaid tail. I hadn't been able to see from the picture, but a delicate, shimmering overlay of embroidered flowers and lace wrapped around the dress. No matter how intricate and beautiful the design, however, the crowning and the most intimidating jewel was that plunging V neckline. Upon closer inspection, I realized the bottom of the V would be about an inch above my navel. Mrs. Gillette turned the dress so we could see the open V-shape in the back, tapering off at the lowest point on my back.

"Go ahead, you can touch it." She motioned me toward her. The beadwork along the back and the sides was incredible and so detailed, but I couldn't stop thinking about the neckline. I glanced down at my chest and tried to imagine how that would work. After losing twenty pounds in college, what little I had before in the chest definitely shrunk before the rest of me did. It wasn't fair that the first place a woman loses weight is her chest.

Mrs. Gillette eyed my form critically. "The beauty of a dress like this is that no matter what bust size you have, this will be a flattering look. Much more so than if you were trying to fill a cup size."

Her eyes rested for a second on my modest cup and embarrassment rose inside of me before I could squash it. Well, it was good news either way, and she probably hadn't meant any offense. Relieved, I pushed away visions of me at the altar with the tissues I'd stuffed into my bra slipping up and out of my dress.

"Should we try it on?" Mrs. Gillette looked at me, expectantly. I wondered if I had a choice. How it would look if I shooed everybody out of the room and tried it on alone? There was nothing like having an audience to witness the humiliation of squeezing into a dress that was too small.

My mom eyed the slender curves of the dress. "We should probably help you. It looks a bit delicate."

I breathed a nervous laugh. "Should I take out an insurance policy?" Four sentences.

Nobody laughed and I refused to look Mrs. Gillette in the eye when I began removing my shoes and pants. The shirt came next. I could feel the heat rising to my cheeks when I forced myself to remember that I had lost the weight and didn't have anything to worry about. The tiny stretch marks that marred my skin from the excess weight were barely visible. I raised my arms high as both women held the dress over my head. Silky, satin material cascaded onto my shoulders and down my back. So smooth, like it wasn't even there.

The skirt fell over my head and body with ease, it nestled past my shoulders and bust, but when it came time to put the narrow-wasted material over my hips, there was a snag. As in, my hips. My hips were the snag.

They were too big.

Frowning, Mrs. Gillette tried inching the fabric a millimeter at a time past my waist, but when the delicate fabric started to bulge, she stopped. Her eyes flicked up to meet mine.

"How close are you to a size four, dear?"

My mom drew a sharp breath. "This is a size four?"

Mrs. Gillette ignored her and held my gaze, waiting for an answer. Shame and mortification, and every other horrible emotion you could imagine, filled my body. My breathing started coming in shallow breaths.

Mom stood next to me and fingered the dress bunched at my shoulders. "Hold on, this is a size four? Kelsey isn't a size four. The designer will have to take it out a bit."

"I'm afraid Hendrix can't do that. The moment he messes with the dress, it loses all of its Jennifer Harris credibility to be sold later. Kelsey told Parker it wouldn't be a problem, so I just assumed..."

To be honest, I don't remember telling Parker it 'wouldn't be a problem.' I remember thinking it might be a big problem. However, I did tell Parker I could do it. And I would get it done. Mom's gaze lifted to my face and this time I met her eyes. I could see the puzzle pieces fitting into place. Running with Tessa, the refusal to eat breakfast, the apples, no carbs, the trip to Salmon with no milkshake—all of it, but the worst part was the hurt in her eyes. I hadn't told her. But I was in the middle of this thing now. I said I would and now I had to.

I turned to Mrs. Gillette. "I'm close. I'm between a four and a six right now, but this dress is a bit tighter than the pants I've been measuring against, but I'll get it done. Now I know where the problem is." My hips. Looks like more torturous running was in the cards for me. Ugh. And squats. Tessa was going to love this.

She didn't look too impressed. Her eyes shifted to my mom while her hand went to her throat, coughing weakly. "Peggy, is there any chance I could get a glass of water? This dry air is wreaking havoc on my throat."

My mom stilled and glanced at my face. She didn't want to leave me. The way my stomach tightened at the thought of being alone with Diana Gillette, I didn't want her to leave me either. Good manners won out, however, and my mom left to fulfill her summons.

The second she was gone, Mrs. Gillette got down to business. "If you don't mind me asking, what is your weight loss regime?"

Regime? Was I in the army or getting married? Suddenly I was wishing my dear fiancé and his family a thousand miles away. "Eating healthy foods, little to no carbs, apples, chicken… that sort of thing."

Her head nodded. "And exercise?"

I wanted to melt into a puddle on the floor, but to my shame, I answered her, trying (somewhat unsuccessfully) to keep the defensiveness out of my tone. "I run three to four miles a day, sometimes twice." Okay, Tessa and I had run twice exactly *one* time. It all just sucked too badly, even for Tessa. I was stretching the truth, but I didn't care. My humiliation meter was officially maxed out.

She nodded, reaching a hand and smoothing my hair, coming to stand behind me. "You have such beautiful hair. I was a brunette once." Our eyes met through the mirror and she gave me a weak smile before continuing brightly, "I think you're almost there. Just another inch or so on the hips and it should be perfect. I am so appreciative of you being willing to wear this dress." She breathed out a laugh. "Although, I don't think it's much of a sacrifice." Her fingers brushed the material on my arm. "I knew the moment Hendrix offered it to me that it would be perfect for you. Once we got everything to fit just right. Not to worry, every woman has trouble spots, it's just finding the right way to take care of them." She was still playing with my hair, lovingly twisting and pulling it up in a multitude of half-do's and watching the effect in the mirror as she continued to speak, her voice low and soft, but at the same time, giving me cause to shiver. "And really, what a better reward for losing weight than getting to wear one of the most exquisite dresses ever made. And I've been in the business a long time."

My mom returned to the room just then, holding a glass of ice water. The tension in the room was so thick between us it could be cut with a knife.

"Thank you, Peggy." She was all smiles as she dropped my hair and took a step away from me, taking the drink offered to her, her manners impeccable. "What a beautiful necklace." She motioned toward the small silver pendant hanging from my mom's neck.

The two women stood conversing stiffly while I stood in front of the mirror still reeling over Diana's words, my breath coming in shallow. My body felt heavy with... weight? Perhaps it was the wedding dress stuck halfway on my body or maybe it was indeed my hips, but my shoulders seemed to carry the brunt of it all. I was too dazed to move. Lifting my eyes, I studied the two women in front of me for a moment. The grandmothers of my future children. The differences between the two women could not have been more evident. Where my mom was soft colors, curves, and rounded edges, Diana was straight with sharp lines and harsh angles. My mom wore little makeup beyond mascara and blush, with a little lipstick on Sunday. Diana's face was a mask of paint with strokes of bold colors encased under a platinum blonde bob. Even under the makeup, her beauty was evident, but there had been a price to pay.

Forcing a bright smile to her face, Diana turned toward me and began lifting the dress off of my body, while telling me about weight loss pills and special wraps we could order that were magically designed to shrink any particular area on a person's body. And wasn't it always that way, she continued. Men never had to worry as much about their figures as women had to. The price for beauty. On and on until the dress had been removed from my body and zipped with great care back into the protective case. Mom shifted beside me, watching my face, clearly uncomfortable with Mrs. Gillette's approach, but not sure of the proper way to deal with this shiny and polished, snake-like guest in her home.

"Only if things get desperate," Diana added.

I stood there calmly, fighting back tears, as my wedding day loomed closer.

13

Health Benefits of Big Booties
(circa - current)

1. Built-in padding for riding a bike
2. My own seat on a bus
3. No sagging jeans
4. The ability to dance most excellently to the song, 'Baby Got Back'
5. Boys love a little junk in the trunk (at least some do)

The Gillettes stayed until 9:30 that evening. I had to hand it to them, that was about three hours longer than I had expected them to stay. At least for Parker's parents. Our house had been filled with semi-stiff chatting while trading stories about our childhood antics. I laughed when I was supposed to laugh and I gave Parker reassurances when his dad tried to embarrass him with tales, but my mind was far away in a foggy, emotionless haze. I felt exhausted and like I wanted to run a marathon all at once.

At the end of the evening, my mom served them each a piece of her famous fresh strawberry pie with homemade whipped cream. Good manners required Mrs. Gillette to have a piece, although she begged only a small one. I wondered if she was the type of person to eat pie. Of course, I wasn't the type of person to eat pie these days either, but I pretended I didn't feel the weight of my future mother-in-law's eyes on me before I declined politely. My mom frowned but moved on to serve my dad and Parker a large piece. Parker gave me a sympathetic pat on the back as he took his first bite, trying to make me feel better. I felt nothing but aggravation.

When the guests were saying their goodbyes by the front door, Parker took me aside and offered to drop his parents off at their hotel and come back to hang out with me longer, but I begged off, claiming exhaustion.

"I'm sorry," I said. "I can hardly keep my eyes open right now. We've been pulling long hours trying to get ready for the Fourth." I pulled him in for a hug. "I promise I'll be better company tomorrow."

The Gillettes would be spending the entire day with us tomorrow, before leaving for California the next morning. I would have one more day with my fiancé, and with the way I was feeling at that moment, it seemed like plenty of time.

He put on a pretend pouty face before he smiled and pulled me close for a kiss.

A few moments later, we pulled apart amid numerous throat clearings and laughter. We smiled sheepishly, shook hands, and hugged everybody goodbye, and then finally... *finally*... the door closed.

My mom gave me a look that said she wanted to talk, my dad sighed with the relief of an introvert forced into entertaining guests for four hours, before walking back into the living room to turn on the TV, and I, suddenly feeling energized for the first time in hours, ran down the hall to change into my running clothes.

"Kelsey." Mom folded her arms, trailing after me down the hallway. "Can we talk for a few minutes?"

"Can we talk later? I want to go for a run before it gets any darker."

"You're going for a run now? It's so late."

"Once I get to the road, the streetlights stay on until eleven." By that time, I'd made it into my room and began yanking off my (apparently not skinny enough) skinny jeans and floral top like they were on fire. The only thing I wanted in this entire world was to be alone with my thoughts. No Mrs. Gillette, no Mom, no Parker. Just me in blessed silence.

Mom stopped outside the doorway to my room. "I don't think it's safe to go this late. I'll worry."

I pulled on my running shorts, grabbed the first tank top I could find and slipped it on. "I do it all the time. I've got some pepper spray. I'll take that if it'll make you feel better."

"If you're not back by 10:30 at the latest, I'm sending a search party."

"Fine."

The yellow July moon hung big and low across the horizon as I stretched my legs by the tree on our lawn. While the glow made running down the lane more feasible, it cast eerie, long shadows from rocks and trees. I shivered a bit as I stretched my calves. The darkness didn't *really* scare me, but if I thought about it too long, I'd freak myself out. Once I ran past our half-mile lane, the streetlamps on the paved county road eased my mind. Not running wasn't an option. I had so much emotion clogging my brain at that moment that I needed a release, and other than eating the entire frozen treat section in my mom's freezer, running was the only way I could find that.

I was about to start my run when I heard gravel crunching behind me. On instinct, I stepped into the shadow of the tree, peering out behind it. Cade rounded the bend by the barn. He was coming from the bunkhouse and dressed in basketball shorts and a tank top. He moved closer toward me as he absentmindedly stuck his headphones in his ears and scrolled through his phone. Toward the lane. Toward me.

Crap.

Crap. Crap. CRAP.

Nooooo.

I needed peace and quiet and what was walking toward me was the exact opposite of that.

I debated my options. I could either hide or wait for him to go ahead before I ran after him, but then we would have to pass each other eventually on the way back home. And it just felt creepy. In my mental state, not going for a run tonight was not an option. It left me with only one more choice.

Make him go away.

I knelt and found a couple of rocks in the bed of the tree and inched my way further into the darkness before I flung it in Cade's direction. I missed. Which ended up being even better because it landed with a thud on the road just to the side of Cade. He startled and stopped walking, peering out into the darkness. A smile crept across my face. I flung another. This time a loud clank shot through the quiet night as my rock rattled jarringly into a piece of metal farm equipment parked on the side of the road. Cade swore as he jumped backward, his head whirling in all directions.

I tried to keep it silent, I really did, but the way he kept swinging around in confusion was too much for me. I covered my mouth with both hands, but not before a mix between a laugh and a snort filtered out into the darkness.

He stopped, his head snapping toward my direction.

"Red?"

I stilled, adrenaline pumping through my veins.

"Red." He growled my name and took a couple of steps toward my hiding spot in the shadows. "You're going to pay for that."

I still didn't move.

"Do you want me to come over there and find you?"

The mild threat caused my breath to hitch. He moved toward the tree once more before I stepped out into the moonlight. The joke was over. His dark eyes widened as he took in my scantily-clad body.

"Did I forget about our late-night rendezvous?"

"I'm going for a run. What are you doing?" I knew the answer, but it was best I took charge here.

He smiled, walking toward me. "This ought to be fun. So am I."

"No, you're not."

He raised his eyebrows. "Oh, but I am."

"This is my house. I call dibs. You'll have to go in the morning."

He stared at me for a long moment as a competitive gleam etched itself onto his face. "You can't call dibs on a road."

"I was here first."

"That's debatable. For all I know you were watching for my sweet hiney out your window all night."

I scoffed. "It's *my* road."

That gleam had turned into a full-out grin now. "Face the facts, Red. All your wildest dreams have come true. You and I now share the same mailbox."

My shoulders slumped, defeated.

"If you'd prefer, you're more than welcome to run on ahead of me." He motioned with his arms for me to go ahead of him and lowered his gaze to my butt with a teasing smile.

Heat flamed in the back of my eyes at his words, and I looked away quickly. With my raw emotions, his out-of-bounds flirting felt like a big hug from a friend, which was crazy because Cade wasn't really my friend.

"Or," he said, "since we're both determined to go running tonight, how about we call a truce. We run together, but not make it weird. I'll listen to my *good* music, you can listen to your Justin Bieber, and protect me from all the bad guys in the dark."

I eyed him carefully. "No pranks?"

He gave me a pointed look as he swept his arm behind him, indicating the rocks I just threw at him.

"That wasn't a prank," I protested. "That was an... opportunity. But I will be marking it on the chalkboard later."

He folded his arms across his chest, waiting me out.

"Fiiiiine," I drawled. "But don't feel like you have to keep up if you get too tired."

"I think I'll be okay."

I had definitely upped my running game the past couple of years. Two to three miles were fairly easy. Four miles with Tessa had stretched me, but I could do it. I hadn't wanted to attempt much more, but Cade's confidence made me remember just whom I was dealing with. A highly trained collegiate athlete who could probably run ten miles in his sleep. I really hoped he wasn't in a long-distance running mood because, thanks to my big mouth, I was in this thing until the last bitter, gasping breath.

We started at a semi-comfortable pace. True to his word, he left me alone, which gave me time to think, and after a while even forget about who was running next to me. The darkness made me more nervous than I thought, and I appreciated having Cade next to me. Of course, I'd take *that* secret to the grave. When we turned off my lane and onto the county road, he switched sides with me, putting himself between me and whatever cars we might pass. He gave no sideways glance, no teasing smile, and he seemed so focused on his running, I wasn't even sure if he knew he had done it.

His legs were longer so I had to push harder than usual to match his stride, and though I would have died if he admitted it, I suspected he held back a bit to keep pace with me. Soon the pain in my legs turned numb and my mind drew back onto Parker and his mother. And the dress. The stunning, mind-blowing dress that I would be tempted to loathe if it wasn't so beautiful.

An inch and a half.

One and a half more inches off of my hips in less than two months. Three-quarters of an inch every three weeks. During the past few weeks of dieting, I'd felt my body get leaner and harder. At school, I had lifted weights, adding depth and tone to my weight loss, but I was so scared to add muscle to my body this time. So I was living on a strict diet of dried leather and rabbit food, otherwise known as lean meats, veggies, and apples. And in the summer of fresh fruit, family breakfasts, pies, ice cream, and barbecues, I became aware of my sacrifice every minute of every blooming day. Then I'd wake up in the night with cold sweat on my face after another nightmare of not fitting into my dress the morning of my wedding, and I'd do it all again the next day.

Then there was earlier that evening. My skin still crawled thinking about my conversation with Diana. Or rather, her conversation with me. It was all so confusing. I didn't know what to think. I knew what I *felt*—guilt, embarrassment, anger, among other things. My problem was that I didn't understand how I *should* feel. I had signed up for this. Even after I found out the dress was a size four. Even after I knew what it might take to make it work, I had agreed. But was humiliation and shame part of the deal? What if my body didn't go that small? Did I want it to? I felt strong and healthy between a six and an eight. What would I feel like as a four?

Then there was Parker and a nagging thought in the back of my head that wouldn't go away. In every glance, in every touch, and every look Parker gave me that night, it stayed with me—itching at me until I had to scratch it. He had *known* what it would take for me to wear that dress when he asked me, and though he seemed to sympathize, he never argued.

He didn't offer me one bite of his pie tonight. With his mother's shrewd eyes focused on me, I would have declined anyway, but it was the gesture I needed. The gesture would have made me forget. Attempting to fit into the dress that wasn't designed for my body wouldn't have bothered me so badly if we were a team. If, deep down, I knew for a fact that he liked me no matter what size dress I wore. No matter *whose* dress I wore. Instead, I felt like a lab rat. Running myself in circles while everybody watched and waited—judging and critiquing.

The doubt and anger of the evening pushed me onward, matching Cade step for step until we hit the stop sign a mile onto the county road. A lone car sputtered toward the intersection. As if by mutual agreement, we slowed down to a walk and bent over, leaning our palms on our knees as we worked to control our breathing while we waited for the car to pass.

"What are you listening to?" he asked, yanking an earbud out of my ear before I could stop him. "And if I hear the Biebs, I will broadcast it to everyone I know." Confusion marred his face when his quest came up empty because my air pods were playing static. White noise.

"I'm *not* listening to you huffing and puffing, old man."

His head cocked to the side. "Oh really? Bring it on, Red." He turned around and began running backward, facing me, keeping to the exact pace we had been running before. I lurched forward and caught up to him, though it took me much longer than it should have. The universe hated me. The guy hardly looked winded.

So, I did the most mature thing and pushed him.

Oh my gosh, was that *all* muscle?

Laughing, he slowed and turned back around, giving me back my earbud. "Why no music?"

"It helps me think."

"So why do you have something in your ear at all?"

"It quiets my distractions so I can focus."

"Are you saying I'm a distraction?"

"I'm saying you're annoying. Now be quiet. I usually go another mile and then head back."

He sighed. "I guess I'll cut my run short tonight."

I glared at him, but he just winked at me and turned his music back on.

I stumbled over my feet. Tingles shot up my body and pooled in my belly. I righted myself before he noticed. Where did *that* come from? That wasn't part of our code.

We were just rounding the turn back onto my lane when my

vision started to dance with spotted circles of black. Panicked, I slowed to a stop and leaned over, resting my hands on my thighs. No. No. No. I ran back through everything I ate that day and to my shame, I couldn't come up with much. An apple for breakfast and then I had been so busy rearranging my mom's house, I had forgotten to eat lunch. Dinner was with the Gillette's and because my emotions had been so jumbled, I could only eat a few bites of chicken and broccoli. It took a few moments for Cade to realize I had stopped and was now doubled back toward me. I squeezed my eyes shut, willing the blackness to dissipate and my running companion to disappear. My body had the strange sensation of starting to float before I quickly sat down, trying to prevent myself from fainting.

Cade arrived just in time for me to pull my knees up to my chest and sink my head into my lap. The feeling like I was going to pass out had gone away, but I would need to sit for a few minutes before moving again.

"You alright?"

If he only knew. "I'm fine. Go ahead. I'll be right behind you."

"So you can stare at my backside like I'm a piece of meat? No thank you. I've got more self-respect than that."

I scoffed loudly but said nothing. He studied me a moment before sitting down beside me on the road, the heat from his body radiating into mine.

"What's going on, Red?"

If he thought I would be spilling my guts to him, he had another thing coming.

"I just felt lightheaded for a sec. I'll be fine now." I started to stand before flashes of darkness appeared in my eyes and forced me to crouch down again.

Cade's hand shot out to steady me for a fraction of a second, before releasing his grip and standing up. "When's the last time you ate something?"

Though I didn't look up at him, the suspicion in his voice confirmed what he had already guessed.

"Dinner."

"What did you have?"

When I didn't answer, he squatted down to my eye level, waiting until I looked at him. "Hey."

I was surprised to see skepticism... mixed with something else in his eyes. Was that concern? "Why are you running right now instead of spending time with your boyfriend?"

"What?" I fought off my urge to stand up and walk away. Probably because I might faint if I tried, but honestly, playing out of left field tonight, baseball boy?

"You heard me."

"It's late!"

"It's 10:00, grandma. Didn't he come all the way from California to see you? So it's only 9:00 to him."

"We hung out and then he took his parents back to their hotel. I'm going to see him all day tomorrow." Ugh. Kelsey, stop. Stop explaining things to him.

"Why aren't you eating?"

I stood up slowly, willing myself not to blackout. After standing for a few seconds, I took a couple of tentative steps. So far so good.

"Kelsey."

My real name on his lips brought my gaze up to his. His brown eyes were furrowed deeply as he waited for me to give him an explanation. I gave him nothing. Finally, he sighed. "Do you want me to go grab my truck and come get you?"

"No. I can walk. Go ahead." I motioned him forward. "I promise I will not be looking at your butt."

He snorted as he moved to walk beside me. "You wouldn't be able to help yourself."

"I'm serious, I'll be fine. You should finish your run."

"And then who will protect me from all the wild animals?"

A cow bellowed in the distance at that exact moment. He looked at me. "See?"

Cade grinned and a laugh bubbled out of me before I could stop it. We walked a few hundred yards in companionable silence before the need to black out had me bending over and taking deep breaths.

When I righted myself once more, Cade put his arm around my waist and pulled me to his side before I could stop him.

"What are you doing?"

"Not what you're thinking. I just want to get home and if I have to half carry you, then so be it."

I thought about struggling out of his grasp but instead found it to be quite comfortable. It was nice to have something to lean against. *Someone* to lean against. After a minute, I wrapped my left arm around Cade's waist. I told myself I'd straighten up in a few minutes, but he was warm, and after a zealous three-and-a-half-mile run, Cade still smelled surprisingly good.

"Why are you running this late?" he asked as we walked.

"Why are you running?" I repeated back to him, desperate to keep the conversation away from myself.

"I always run at night. Don't you and Tessa usually run around seven or so?"

"You keeping tabs on me, Williams?" I asked.

"Always."

My cheeks warmed while I lightly poked him with my finger. "Stop."

He poked me back. "Your turn. Why are you running?"

I blew out a breath. "How did we even get here?"

"What? A moonlit hobble down a country road?"

"No. Talking to each other like normal people."

"I know. It's terrible. I promise I'll be back to my adorable self tomorrow. Now answer."

Rolling my eyes, I said, "I'm running to be healthy. I've got a dress I need to fit into for my wedding and I'm working on that."

"Don't you buy a dress to fit you?"

"Usually. Not this time." Thanks to an actress that I now hated with a passion. Yup. It had been decided. I hated her.

"And you're not eating for the same reason?"

"I eat. Today was just a crazy day and I accidentally ate a lot less than usual."

"Does your boyfriend know you're not eating?"

It was like I wasn't even talking anyway, so I pinched him and ignored his last question. We were coming up on the last bend in the lane next to the house. Despite a few lukewarm efforts to get away I still found myself tucked against Cade's side. When he finally released me, the evening chill against my damp, sweaty clothes, had me sucking in my breath. I did *not* miss his arm. Not at all. It had just been his body heat I liked. It had nothing at all to do with being pressed against a muscly, good-smelling, boy body. It had nothing at all to do with Cade. I was sure of it. Like, ninety-five percent, absolutely, almost without any doubt, sure.

"The things you do to try and put the moves on me, Red. It's embarrassing."

"You wish," I responded as I made my way toward the house.

"Don't let this romantic night go to your head. I still plan on owning that chalkboard by the end of this summer," he called after me.

I shook my head, laughing in spite of myself. "It's on."

I was on the top step about to open the door to my house when I stopped and called out, "Cade."

He turned around at the sound of my voice.

"Thanks."

He threw me a wave and disappeared into the night.

14

Checklist for the 4th of July (circa - current)

1. Greet Mrs. Gillette kindly at the town breakfast ✓
2. Eat the fruit bowl, like Mrs. Gillette, instead of stuffing my face in pancakes and syrup like everybody else ✓
3. Don't be mad at Parker when he doesn't offer me one bite of his sugar-laden carb-fest breakfast
4. No candy at the parade, except for that tootsie roll I might accidentally shove into my mouth when nobody is looking ✓
5. No hamburger
6. I'm serious. NO HAMBURGER

My brother Logan arrived home just before the town breakfast. He had graduated from high school four years ahead of me and was already pretending to be an adult, working in construction in Boise. We had fought like cats and dogs growing up, but once he left home for college, the rare occasions and holidays I would see him had helped our relationship so much. He had grown to appreciate my adorableness. I guess, in some cases, distance did make the heart grow fonder. Or at least fonder in a way that he stopped giving me swirlies in the toilet and farting on my face. Brothers. Either way, I was glad to see him walk through the front door.

"Hey, fuzzball," he said, affectionately pulling me in for a hug. He looked around, nose wrinkled. "Where's the boy toy?"

"We're meeting him and his parents at the town breakfast." I stepped back to look at him. "Wow, a half a bottle of cologne isn't doing it these days? You have to pour on the whole bottle to get rid of the smell?"

He grinned. "I don't hear any complaints from the ladies."

He flung his bag onto the dining table and looked around the room. "Are Amanda and Spence coming this weekend?"

"No. Mom said they had some big meeting this week and couldn't make it over." My workaholic sister and her husband lived in downtown Seattle and were both cut from the same corporate cloth.

I eyed Logan critically. His hair was cropped short and stylishly combed. His clothes were new with very few wrinkles. He had that look of a guy who... had a girl. "Who is she?"

He shot me a confused look. "What?"

"Who is she? You are looking too self-assured for Eugene."

He walked over to the kitchen and yanked open the fridge, peering inside. "I always look this good."

I watched him carefully. He was dating someone. Which honestly wasn't surprising, because he usually had a girl, sometimes several. "Do I know her?"

Reaching into the fridge, he pulled out a Tupperware container, opened the lid, and sniffed it. He looked at me. "Any idea what this is and how long it's been here?"

"Orange chicken. Mom made it a couple of nights ago."

"Good enough for me." He plopped it on the counter and grabbed a fork.

"You know we're eating breakfast in about ten minutes," I said, trying hard not to be jealous of the deep fat fried chicken balls slathered in sugar he was inhaling. I had eaten grilled chicken and asparagus during that particular dinner.

"I'm just warming up my stomach."

"Who is she?" I pressed again, arms folded, being every bit the annoying sister I used to be.

Exasperation poured from his eyes. Bingo. I had him now. "You remember Courtney Hill? I think she was a year or two older than you."

My brow furrowed. "Yes."

"She moved to Boise and I ran into her at a concert last week. We're meeting up at the barbecue tonight."

Courtney Hill. The cheerleader who dated everybody in Eugene and three towns to the north? Who also had the reputation to back it up? Awesome. To my brother, I said, "Wow. Ran all the way to Boise and Courtney Hill was your best option?"

His eyes narrowed. "Easy. I kind of like her, so be careful what you say."

We stared at each other until I gave in. "Fine. You're right. Sorry."

He nodded. "And how's Prince Charming?"

If he would have asked me any other day, I might have brightened appropriately. Instead, I had to work on my facial expression. "He's great. We had a fun chat with his parents last night."

"Sorry to have missed *that*."

I smiled at him. "We'll be hanging out with them all day, so you'll have lots of chances to catch up."

After sweating our guts out at the parade, my parents, Logan, Parker, and I arrived at Tessa's parent's house for the potluck—each of us armed with side dishes, salads, and more of my mom's strawberry pie. As soon as our car was in park and I saw Tessa's backyard, the first real smile of the day swept across my face. Tessa's parents own a large orchard. They harvest apples, cherries, and peaches, and a variety of vegetables. Their white, two-story farmhouse with a wrap-around-porch sat in the center of their sprawling lawn, interspersed with maple trees. Twinkle lights were strung from the porch to the trees and underneath the lights were long, serving tables, waiting to be filled with food. Scattered across the lawn were round tables with chairs and stacks of blankets piled on the ground to be used for picnic-style dining. I stood staring at the magical scene and hated myself for missing it all the past three years.

Parker's parents hadn't made it yet. They had wanted to run to their hotel to get their things packed since they would be leaving early the next morning. Of course, we all knew that meant they were hiding out for a bit before having to put on their 'people' faces. Okay, it was possible that my less than positive interactions with Parker's mother might have been tilting my viewpoint. I promised myself I'd try to keep an open mind the rest of the day.

Family and friends I had known my entire life began showing up. I laughed and hugged and talked about the weather, and introduced my fiancé to the little old town ladies like the best of them. And I loved every second. Parker's parents even arrived sooner than I had anticipated, so I had to give them a little credit.

Parker, for the most part, had taken the role of the upbeat, positive fiancé. Shaking everybody's hand, making small talk, and laughing vivaciously at jokes that weren't that funny. The gesture was sweet. I was happy he was trying to fit in, but something about it felt forced, like he was some overly smooth politician trying to win over America's heartland. Ugh. My whole thought process was out of whack. It had to be. I blamed it on the dress and all the wedding stress. I had never had these thoughts about Parker before now.

Tessa asked if I could help her with the food, so I left Parker alone, pretending to be interested in the pros and cons of bull riding versus bronc riding with Jake and Dusty. I smiled at him, ignoring his slightly alarmed face at my departure.

"Sorry to pull you away," Tessa said as we hurried to the food table. "But my mom has been overrun by casseroles and jello salads and needed more hands."

I laughed. "Well, it wouldn't be the fourth without Betsy May's green jello salad." Betsy May was in her eighties, lived down the road from my parents, had been widowed for over twenty years, always had lipstick on her teeth, and usually forgot to take out a curler or two from her hair. She was frail, but feisty, even in her old age. And every year, bless her sweet heart, she brought the biggest bowl of green jello salad packed with everything from julienned carrots, raisins, pineapple, marshmallows, and shredded cheese. Because we loved her, Tessa and I took a heaping spoonful every year and then secretly played a game to see who could eat it all in one bite.

"Mom told me to put this somewhere." Tessa and I turned to find Logan standing behind us, looking confused and holding a sheet pan full of brownies.

Before we could say anything, his eyes fell on Tessa's and widened appreciatively. "Oh, hey there, Tess. I'm sorry, I probably put on too many clothes for you." He looked down at his clothes and started to lift the hem of his shirt upward. "Should I take my shirt off? To make you more comfortable?"

First, Tessa glared at me, while I looked away, laughing silently. Then she smiled sardonically at my brother, taking the pan of brownies from his hands and setting it on the table behind her. "Go ahead and keep it on. We wouldn't want you scaring away all the children."

He grinned. "Are you sure? I remember hearing a while back that you preferred me with my shirt off."

She blushed but covered it all up with her laughter. "No, you misunderstood me. I said I preferred you with your mouth shut." She pushed a delighted Logan away from the table. "Now, go away."

Logan laughed and headed back toward his friends.

"You just *had* to tell him about my tiny crush in high school."

"If I recall, he overheard YOU telling me you liked him better with his shirt off. But my confirmation of it was pure revenge after you and Cade became friends."

"We had *one* class. Okay? One. The teacher made us sit by each other. We were friends by association."

I shook my head, smiling.

"Where is Cade? Is he here?" Tessa asked, looking up to scan the new arrivals.

I pretended to glance around the lawn as well, even though I could have told her that Cade was across the yard from me, talking with Pete Jones and Robin Miller.

"Is there something going on with your brother and the town skank?"

I followed Tessa's gaze to where Logan joined Courtney at a table, watching her as she leaned into him, laughing obnoxiously at something he said. Ugh. I know for a fact Logan isn't that funny. "I don't know. They met up in Boise once and they're bringing it here for everybody to enjoy, I guess."

Tessa was quiet for a moment, rearranging the salads on the table to make more room.

"You don't still like him, do you?"

"No."

I waited, but she refused to meet my eyes. "Tessa..."

Her eyes darted to mine, frantically. "No. It was all a long time ago. But could you please talk a little louder? I'm not sure Betsy May heard you all the way over there."

I gasped. "You do like him."

She looked at me, exasperated. "No! But he already overheard one embarrassing conversation years ago, he doesn't need this one to boost his ego."

That was true. "Good. Keep looking. You're much better than him." My friend was a blonde, athletic bombshell. She had dated some stellar guys in Moscow, and it was beyond my comprehension that she still could have the hots for my confirmed bachelor, play-the-fields, flirt with anybody wearing a skirt, idiot brother (whom I happened to love dearly, but still... an idiot).

For a while, we kept busy placing and rearranging all the food coming in onto the tables. I plopped serving spoons in the bowls and took in the dizzying array of smells only a neighborhood barbecue and potluck could produce. My dad and Tessa's dad manned the barbecue grill, cooking up a mountain of hamburger patties and hotdogs. All around me friends were laughing, children were running wild and playing chase, and everything seemed right in the world.

Once the food lines began to form, I situated Parker and his parents next to Logan and Courtney and scurried inside the kitchen to help Tessa's mom, ignoring Logan's glare in my direction. Too bad, big brother. Parker needed a place to sit and there was no way I would be able to eat a thing sitting next to Diana Gillette.

A giant hamburger fell out of nowhere and landed on my sorry-looking plate filled with raw veggies and watermelon. The weight of the burger caused my pile of rabbit food to jump off my plate and land on the grass.

I whirled around to find Cade staring at me with his arms folded. "What are you doing?"

I had been hiding out, off to the side of Tessa's house, shoving my salad fixings into my mouth. I had been too embarrassed to eat my plate at a table in front of people. I wanted to avoid the questions and the looks I would no doubt get when I plopped my obnoxiously healthy plate down in front of a bunch of women on the Fourth of July holiday. So, I had kept myself busy helping Tessa's mom in the kitchen and keeping the food stocked and supplied with tongs and serving spoons while everybody lined up with empty plates at the food tables. The plan worked great until she shooed me out of the house to go eat with everyone. That's when I discreetly made myself a plate and took off for some privacy.

"Eat it."

"What? Why?"

"Because you almost fainted last night and you've hardly eaten anything all day long."

"You've been watching me?" My initial reaction brought a flutter to my stomach, but anger soon took its place. The last thing I needed was another person watching what I ate.

"Can you blame me, Red?" His smile was roguish and completely out of line.

A sudden fury snarled at my insides. Not wanting to cause a scene, I pushed at his chest and edged him further toward the side of Tessa's house. "Stop. Stop watching me. Stop with the flirting. I'm engaged, okay. Just stop, Cade."

"Eat the hamburger and I'll leave right now."

"I don't care what you do as long as you stay away from me. What I eat is none of your business."

He brought his face closer to mine. "It is my business when you almost pass out on my watch and I have to half-carry your bony butt all the way home."

My chest rose up and down in indignation, but I had no defense.

"Why are you hiding? And why doesn't your boyfriend care that you're not eating?" He jabbed a finger past my shoulder, and I turned, spotting Parker and his mom speaking quietly by the drink station.

"He doesn't... he cares..." The words jumbled in my throat.

How could I explain Parker's part in this food equation? It wasn't really his fault. I had agreed to it. But the truth was, he did care what I ate at the moment. He cared one and a half inches worth of what I ate. And after being in his family's company the past two days, I had confirmed what I had begun to suspect long ago... he was scared of his mother. That was the real bottom line. But I owed the man standing before me no real explanation. Other than being at the wrong place at the wrong time, he wouldn't have cared either.

"What's going on?" Tessa peered around the side of the house, breaking into the tension between us. Her eyebrows raised as Cade took a step back from me.

He turned to Tessa. "Did you know she's starving herself?"

Her face fell as she looked at me, "What?"

I glared at Cade before meeting Tessa's eyes. "I'm not starving myself. I'm watching what I eat so I can fit into my dress in two months."

Cade mumbled something, yanking off his hat to run his fingers through his hair.

Tessa stepped closer to us and lowered her voice. "Doesn't it fit you?"

"Look, do we have to do this now?"

"Yes," they both said simultaneously.

Crossing my arms, I sighed, annoyed at both of them. "Jennifer Harris is a size four."

Tessa gasped, her hands flying up to her mouth. "What? Can't they just alter it? Why didn't you tell me?"

Cade scratched his head. "Wait. The actress?"

I shot a venomous look in Cade's direction. "It wasn't anybody's business."

"Why can't they alter it?" Tessa asked again.

"Once they change it in any way, it loses the Jennifer Harris appeal."

Tessa covered her mouth with her hands. "What?"

"What in the sam hill does Jennifer Harris have to do with anything?" Cade interjected, throwing his hands up in the air.

Tessa filled him in while I leaned back against the railing of the wrap-around porch. A bead of hot July sweat trickled out from my hairline above my temple, sliding down the side of my face and catching momentum down to my neck, where it disappeared into my shirt. There had been too many people discussing me—in front of me, around me, about me, that all at once, I became numb to it all. I was a turtle in my shell, blocking out the world. Tessa and Cade became background noise. I didn't care anymore. Dress sizes. Jennifer Harris. Parker. Fainting. Shout it from the rooftops.

Exhaustion clamored up my limbs, tempered my heart, and settled into that little place in my brain called willpower, which was located next to the part formally known as self-control. At that moment, I was an alcoholic and that hamburger on my plate was a big neon sign. And even though I still felt annoyed with him, I had to give Cade some credit because he knew how to make a hungry girl a hamburger. Two thick slabs of bacon, lettuce, a juicy red tomato, pickles, and a slice of cheddar cheese oozing out the sides, all pressed between a soft, white, carb-infested bun. I swallowed the excess moisture in my mouth as all my other senses went completely off the grid. I grasped the hamburger tightly in my hands and let the plate fall to the grass.

The first bite felt like Christmas morning. That specific moment as a child when I opened the very first present but knew I still had piles of gifts left. The excitement. The wonder. The magic. It felt just like that. Warm and meaty and bursting with flavor. And the bread. Oh, the bread. The second bite felt like a lazy dive in the pool on a hot summer's day. Carefree and glorious. The third bite tasted like a funnel cake at the fair. The fourth bite felt like my toes in the sand from an afternoon lounging on a sunny beach. Somewhere in the middle of the beach and the top of a roller coaster, I realized both Cade and Tessa had stopped talking and stood watching me.

"What's going on?"

I blinked. My thoughts seemed a bit fuzzy, so I looked to Cade in question. His eyes narrowed on me while he folded his arms and leaned against the house, clearly intent on staying where he was. Then I knew... the voice coming through the fog in my brain was Parker's.

15

Things I will eat on my Honeymoon (circa - current)

1. Cheeseburger. Extra cheese, grilled onions, bacon. Extra mustard
2. All the cakes. Cheesecake. Chocolate cake. Vanilla cake. I hate bananas, but throw one in a cake and I'll eat that one too
3. Six or ten loaves of French bread
4. Let's throw in a large sausage and pineapple pizza
5. I plan to become intimate friends with a Pepsi fountain. Regular. Not the diet kind
6. ~~Chicken and veggies~~

"Hey, Parker," Tessa said. "We were just talking. How are you? Are your parents having a nice time?" Her bumbling intention to iron out any friction seemed to backfire because Tessa was rarely friendly to Parker and it only served to make it seem like we were all hiding something. The way Parker plodded closer and ignored Tessa's questions gave me good insight that he was thinking the same thing.

I turned toward him and smiled. His eyes dropped to the three bites I had left of my hamburger and back up again, his eyebrows raised.

"Babe."

The food in my hand felt like it weighed a hundred pounds. I looked down at the bits of mauled hamburger. Somewhere in the middle of my caveman engorgement, mustard had dripped all down the side of my hand. I bent low to grab the plate I'd dropped and handed it to Tessa.

Cade yanked the plate from her hands and thrust it back toward me. "Wait a minute. You're not done."

Glaring at him, I muttered, "I'm full."

He turned and looked at Parker like he was the lowest form of life he'd ever seen. "Did she tell you she almost fainted the other night cause she's not eating enough?"

"Just leave it alone," I pleaded with Cade, sending silent and murderous thoughts his way.

"Who's this?" Parker looked at me, pasting a tight smile on his face as he nodded toward Cade. "A cousin?"

"Nope."

Cade's abrupt answer made me squirm. I threw him a dirty look. How much trouble could he get me into in one day?

Still ignoring Cade, Parker looked at me expectantly, the way a teacher might look at a student who had some explaining to do. As if the fact that Cade standing in my space at that moment was my fault. As if I ate that hamburger to be a naughty, disobedient child. That was my breaking point. I was not a child. I was his girlfriend—his fiancé at a holiday barbecue, and I ate a hamburger. Nobody died. I didn't gain ten pounds. I felt better than I had in weeks.

"No, Cade is... he works for my dad."

This time Cade leaned in closer and stuck his hand out. "Cade Williams. Kelsey and I live on the ranch together."

"Alright, that's enough," I said as I pushed Cade's hand away before grabbing Parker's arm and pulling him away from the side of the house. No matter what phase of life I found myself in, Cade always seemed to be lurking somewhere, ready to do damage at a moment's notice. Tonight, I would give him a piece of my mind, but not now. Not in front of Parker.

"I need to talk to you." Parker's voice scratched at my nerves.

"Fine."

"Can we go somewhere private?"

I walked him toward the apple orchard across the driveway. Tessa and I had spent many days wandering the rows of trees, playing made-up games of princesses and pirates. It didn't feel right to sully those memories with a bad conversation, but Tessa's lawn was still full of party-goers.

"Are you okay?" he asked.

No. I was a jumbled, emotional, hungry mess, but I wasn't sure how to explain all of it to Parker without insulting him or his mother.

"Next question."

He sighed. "Look, I know it's been hard for you. And I'm sorry. But I need to know you're in this thing. Mom said you've still got a ways to go before the dress fits. What are you going to do on our wedding day if you can't get it on?"

"I went for a run yesterday and almost fainted. I only had a bowl of strawberries and a few bites of dinner in me. I'm weak, grouchy, and now, apparently, I run the risk of fainting. And I'm so glad your mother is giving you updates on my body."

He ran a frustrated hand through his hair. "Babe, I don't want you to make yourself sick over this. You need to eat, but you just need to watch the type and amount of calories you consume."

He must not have noticed the look on my face, because he kept talking. "You know I hate to put you through all of this. I know how much it stinks, but my mom is counting on this now. The dress will put her shop on the map. The designer's our good friend and he deserves credit for the amazing dress. The photographer's on board.

Martha Stewart Wedding is going to put a four-page spread in their November issue."

"What if I change my mind?"

Panic seized Parker's face as his eyes shot to mine. "About what?"

"The dress."

He blew out an exasperated breath. "Over a hamburger?"

"No. I just..."

"Kels, I get it. You needed a cheat meal. It's probably fine, but just watch your calories from here on out and it should be okay."

I stiffened. Did he actually mention calories again, to my face? It seemed so easy for him to sit back and watch me run in circles as long as it kept him in good graces with his mother. "I don't want to do it anymore."

Wild with alarm, he took a step closer to me. "Babe, you already gave your word. You gave my mom your word. Does that not mean anything to you?"

"Don't play lawyer with me," I snapped. "If I recall, I gave you my word *before* you told me about the dress size." I turned my back toward him, covering my face with my hands, and took a deep breath. Where had this all come from? Parker and I had never fought before. Ever. In our entire relationship, I had never spoken to him like that.

His voice was quiet when he spoke again. "Look. If I could go back and bag the whole thing I would, but for now, everybody is lined up and on board because *you* signed on for this." The heat of his body closed in behind me as his arms encircled my waist. His breath tickled my ear as he spoke. "I'm sorry this is hard on you. I *promise* I wouldn't have asked it if I thought it would be like this."

My heart softened the tiniest bit. With the way I wanted to stuff my face in Tessa's chocolate cake she just put on the table, it was obvious I was some sort of unhealthy emotional eater. Perhaps a couple more months of resistance would be good for me. I had over-reacted. My hormones and appetite had been all over the map the past couple of days and all it took was one hamburger to derail me. Thanks, Cade. Another checkmark for him.

Parker was still talking in my ear. "Just think, it's just two more months. That's it. After that, it's smooth sailing. You and me on a private yacht in the Bahamas. No dress. No photographer. All the food you can eat."

I felt myself relaxing in his embrace. Two months and I was done. Certainly, there would be harder things in my life than this. I had given my word and apparently, if I was going to fit into this family of lawyers, I would have to keep it. I turned around in his arms and looked up at him.

"Are you still on board?" he whispered.

"Yes." I tried to smile. "Sorry I freaked out."

"Understandable. Holidays are hard. I'm sorry for my part in that."

His eyes locked onto something past my head. "One more question. Was there any other reason you wanted to come home for the summer?"

"What?"

"Was planning the wedding with your mom the only reason you came home?"

If air quotes were a thing, I mentally attached them to his sentence. I refrained from pointing out that he and his mother seemed to be taking care of the bulk of the planning without me and instead muttered, "Basically, why?"

"I just want to make sure that the cowboy living with you had nothing to do with your decision." His words spat out with a bitter undertone and hints of accusation.

Following his gaze, I found Cade helping Tessa's mom pack away the folding tables to make room for the dancing. "I had no idea my dad hired him until I was already home."

"How come you never mentioned him before?"

"Because I didn't think it was worth mentioning." Um, had I never mentioned Cade? How do I even explain him? "He's a... friend. Kind of. And a really annoying one at that. Nothing more."

"He seems pretty defensive of you. He's been watching you the whole time you've been talking with me."

The knowledge of Cade watching out for me, even though I

wanted to gouge out his eyeballs, did funny things to my stomach—
but that could also be the greasy hamburger rolling around down
there. Outwardly, I rolled my eyes. "He's just worried I'm not eating
enough. He helped me home after I almost fainted."

I had been trying to think of a redeeming quality in Cade's character when Parker's eagle eyes shot to mine. Then I realized my
mistake.

"I thought you said you almost fainted while you were out
running?"

"I did." Crap.

"I thought you ran with Tessa."

Crap. Crap. Crap. "I usually do."

"But you were running with *him*? Alone together?"

I had nothing to hide. Nothing happened. Our run together came
about very innocently, if not maddeningly, but it would take some
major effort to convince Parker. I took ahold of his face, forcing him
to stop looking at Cade. "Parker, it's not what it sounds like. It was late
last night, I walked out to go running and Cade walked out from the
bunkhouse to go running at the same time." I tried to go with a
different approach. "I was glad he was there by the end because he
helped me get home. I could have been alone and fainted on the road
in the dark."

He stiffened and drew back from me, and my effort to plead to his
sensitive side missed the mark. "Last night?" His cold tone filled me
with dread. "You sent me away to my hotel because you told me you
were tired. And then you went running with him?"

I moved my hands up to cover my face and eyes, wanting to
scream and strangle him at the same time. Blowing out a breath of
frustration, I said calmly, "Listen, it was a fluke thing. We've never run
together before, and it will never happen again. But it was a serious
blessing in disguise that he was there." Even now I can admit that.
The thought of waking up, passed out on the side of the road by
myself made my body shudder. "I was tired last night, but still needed
to run. I'm sorry it all got so messed up, but I really want to stop
talking about this."

He seethed, and I could tell he had more to say to me when Tessa's mom pierced the night air with her famous two-fingered whistle.

"What the..." Parker mumbled as he turned around to find the source of the sound.

"Dancing's about to start," I replied, pulling his arm along with me as I walked toward the crowd gathering on the lawn. I wanted to be done talking about stupid things on my favorite holiday in the world.

The rest of the evening passed by without major incident. Parker and I danced around all subjects of food, dresses, and Cade Williams the rest of the night. But the elephants in the room were all around us. Literally. Every elephant except Jennifer Harris's dress hanging in my closet. Yet it was still there... in everything I didn't eat. In every glance Parker and his mother gave me. Every time I passed up anything remotely delicious at the food table. Cade kept his distance for the most part, but the one time he thought about coming closer to me, I gave him a look that essentially said, if he took one more step, I would rip his body apart and then sell each piece on the black market. He raised his hands in the air and backed away slowly, holding my gaze. I refused to let my mouth give in to the smile that was threatening to show itself. It would just give him more ammo and I was still peeved.

All around me, there was movement as old friends laughed and danced together. We stood in large groups reminiscing about the good old days—telling stories and catching up on old classmate gossip. The conflict with Parker earlier that evening was pushed aside and I laughed easily with Margo and Holli and my old friends, even knowing Parker hated every minute. Or maybe *because* he hated every minute.

He stood next to me but had lost his need-to-please zest from earlier. I noticed him glancing at his phone every twenty minutes and fidgeting with his feet. He was polite when called upon, but did not engage any further. His mom, who had fussed and fawned over all the details of the party when she arrived, was now sitting stiffly in a lawn chair next to my mom and some friends from town, feigning interest and sneaking a yawn every so often. Parker's dad had been on his phone most of the night. My eyes scanned through the fading sunset and saw him in the orchard, on his phone with his hands gesturing animatedly.

I tried to look at the visit from Parker's angle. He knew nobody besides me and Tessa and his limited acquaintance with my family. The same for his parents. He ran into the party on full steam. It was only natural that he fizzled out at the end. I wondered if he would remember anything once he left. I wondered if he would remember the stories told or memories shared that night. Was it all just an act? A front? Would I be on edge the entire time we came home to visit once we were married? Obsessing about whether or not he was enjoying himself? If he liked my friends? Or would we come home much at all?

Something else had bothered me—perhaps more than the hamburger or the accusations or the body shaming. Maybe it was a combination of everything coming to a head tonight. It was something I knew in Moscow, and somewhere along the way I had convinced myself that I didn't care. That it would be fine. That once we were married everything would magically work itself out. But now that I was home, it didn't feel fine.

Parker didn't fit here.

And it all felt... wrong.

16

Qualities I want in a Husband
(circa junior high - revisited)

~ Handsome
~ Dark hair preferable, but will settle for blonde if there are dimples
~ ~~Makes me laugh until I can't breath~~
~ Rich
~ Be a good dad (play with kids) - (No conclusive data yet)
~ Helps me wash dishes
~ Loves to cook
~ Treats me nice
~ ~~Feeds me when hungry~~
~ ~~Knows how to ride bareback~~
~ Does not like to prank

Parker and his family planned to leave after breakfast the next morning. A full night's sleep seemed to be the refreshment everyone needed. His parents were charming and charismatic once again. Our mothers sat at the kitchen table together going over the last few details of the wedding. Parker's parents insisted they would be happy to pay for everything, but my parents bristled at the thought. While Mrs. Gillette waved away any help at paying for the lavish event they were planning in California, she benevolently backed off her insistence on helping to pay for the small reception planned for Eugene. She seemed to understand that my parents, while not wealthy, had enough pride to pay their part in their daughter's wedding. Since the Gillette's had no real part in this reception, other than showing up, she relented.

I sat at the table next to the women, quietly pushing lone bits of apples and oranges around the bottom of my bowl of fruit. Though it was technically my wedding, it had begun to feel less and less so and I was happy to keep to myself while the women discussed the particulars. My mom attempted to involve me but backed off at my disinterested attitude. Parker sat with my dad and Mr. Gillette in the living room, adjacent to the kitchen table. The sound of Sports Center mumbled quietly from the room, as the two dads watched TV and spoke casually about the latest golf game. Parker's eyes flitted to mine when he caught me staring. He stood up and walked over to where I sat.

"Wanna go for a walk?"

I nodded, grabbing my bowl and depositing it in the sink before meeting him at the door where we both slipped on our shoes. The morning air was starting to lose its chill and the smell of freshly cut hay calmed my anxious heart. The smell of home.

"Any objections to canceling all the plans and just do a quick courthouse wedding with a backyard barbecue after?" I said the words to tease him as we meandered our way down my parents' half-mile lane. A way to ease the last bit of tension between us, but I felt surprised at how perfect the whole idea sounded.

Parker chuckled lightly, without much humor. "We've got to get you back to the city. All this country air is mucking up your brain." He ruffled my hair for a moment before setting his arm across my shoulders. I wrapped my arm around his waist and nestled closer to his side. I sunk down a bit to fit more snugly under his arm. He was barely two inches taller than me, and I always had to crouch.

We walked in silence for a few paces, listening to the birds in the trees above us.

Clearing his throat, Parker spoke. "So, we're good with the dress still, right? You'll still plan to wear it?"

"Yes. I told you I would."

He nodded. "Okay. I just..."

"What?"

"I just want you to promise me that you'll do what you need to do to fit into it." He stumbled over his words as if the whole topic was uncomfortable for him. I swallowed the anger that rose in my chest. Most of it.

"Yup. I'll make sure to eat just enough so that I'll faint every time I go for a run," I said, pulling away from him.

"That's not what I meant. You need to eat. I don't want you to get sick or hurt. I..." He brushed his hand through his hair in frustration. "I had to lose a bunch of weight in wrestling in junior high. I had two days to lose eight pounds and I did it. I ate the bare minimum and worked out as much as I could. It sucked, but it was only for two days. That's what I mean. This will be hard, but it will be over in two months."

He stopped our walk and turned toward me, cupping his hands on my face as he waited for me to look at him. "I wish I had never agreed to the dress. I can promise you that. But everything is in motion now. We have to do it. We gave our word and now people are counting on us. They're counting on you."

"Who?" I asked. "*Who* are these people so invested in whether or not I wear this dress?"

He looked surprised at my outburst. "My mom for one. A big spread in Martha Stewart Weddings will drive a lot of business to her store. Needed business. Wedding shops in Santa Cruz are ultra-competitive. My mom would never say anything, but her sales have been down lately, so she is my number one concern. Not only her, but we also have the photographer booked, and now Hendrix is counting on you. I know it's just a dress, but it's really not. It's Jennifer Harris's dress and that makes it a commodity."

His words banged around in my thoughts as we continued our walk in a tentative silence. The quiet only lasted a moment before my fiancé laid down his next topic as if the previous matter had been resolved.

"I want you to stay away from that farm kid."

"Who?" I asked, playing dumb.

"You know who."

"We work together. I'll see him around."

He shook his head before looking at me. "Just don't be alone with him. That guy wants you and I don't trust him. You shouldn't either."

I barked out a laugh. "Cade? No. That's not possible. If you only knew our history."

"History is history. I know what I saw. If you want us to work out, you have to stay away from him."

"*If* I want us to work out?" I repeated incredulously, my voice rising. "I'm wearing your ring. We're getting married in California. I'm exercising constantly and eating like a bird to fit into your dress in two months. I got weight loss advice from your mother. Doesn't that mean we've already worked out?"

"Allegedly."

There was a long pause as I stared at him. "What's that supposed to mean?"

"You haven't worn the dress yet."

A second ticked by. Then another. Fury clawed its way like fire through my insides, leaving singed ashes in its wake, even as the back of my eyes filled with tears. I turned away from him, using all my concentration to keep the tears from falling. There were so many things to say, but I couldn't get a word out. It turned out, I didn't have to.

Parker sighed heavily. "Babe. I'm sorry. I shouldn't have said that. I just... I feel like all we've done is fight this whole visit. You're different here. We never used to fight like this at school. I can't help but think once we're married, things will get better. The dress thing will be over. Things will be back to normal."

The heat from his chest pressed against my back as he leaned in and nuzzled my ear. I flinched and stepped forward, pulling myself away from him and out of his arms.

He made an impatient sound and stepped toward me again. "It's just all this stress. I didn't mean it. You know I love your body. My mom appreciates you being willing to wear the dress. The publicity for her and her shop will really help her out."

I closed my eyes and tried to let his soft words soothe my fractured heart. If Parker were only a boyfriend, his words might have ended us. But he wasn't. He was going to be my husband. And as my future husband, didn't that deserve some grace? We had committed to each other and I understood the stress that he spoke of. I still didn't trust myself to speak, but I allowed him to wrap his arms around me and pull me closer, though I remained stiff and unbendable.

"Love you, babe," he whispered in my ear. "I'm sorry." I could give him nothing more than a tight smile. That seemed to be enough for him and he grabbed my hand and slowly began leading us back to the house. "We better go. I'm sure my parents are ready to hit the road."

It was an unfortunate turn of events that on July 5, the evening after the Fourth of July megaflop fest, the Tramps and the Pitches played against each other. It was also an unfortunate event that my car overheated four miles into my ten-mile drive to the baseball fields south of Eugene. I usually rode with Tessa, but she had been running errands for her parents in Mackay that afternoon and would be coming from the other direction just in time for the game.

I had spent an afternoon in quiet contemplation. Thankfully, I had been in the tractor most of the day, so I didn't have to speak with anybody. Thoughts of the dress and Parker and even Cade had been rolling around in my head. The excitement I had for my wedding when I had first arrived in Eugene had been tainted from fights with my fiancé, his mother, not enough food, and a dress that didn't fit.

I pulled my car to the edge of the two-lane road and killed the engine. Smoke oozed out from underneath the hood in front of me. I climbed out of my car and popped the trunk. No water.

Heaving a sigh, I climbed back into the front seat and reached for the phone inside my purse. Reached, moved, shoved, and frantically pushed all the while resolving to get a smaller purse as I discovered one more unfortunate fact to ruin my night.

I forgot my cell phone.

In my scramble to leave the house on time, I went through the motions of brushing my teeth in exactly five seconds before running down the hall, grabbing my keys, and flying out the door. I could picture exactly where my cell phone was sitting on the bathroom counter.

I nearly laughed when, five minutes later, Cade's truck slowed to a stop on the road next to mine. Of course, it would be Cade who rescued me. It didn't matter that nearly four thousand people were living in and around Eugene when not one car, not *one*, drove by in my time of distress. Well, that wasn't true. Sweet old Betsy May drove by, waving to me on the side of the road, her big eyes bugging out of her thick-rimmed glasses and pink lipstick smeared all over her teeth, but I had heard she recently had her license taken away and I would not be risking it.

Cade rolled his passenger window down. "Hey, Red. Headed to the game?"

I paused in my shuffle to grab my purse and backpack. To the passerby, his voice was kind, friendly even. But there was an edge to it —a bite of fake innocence that had me turning to face him.

We locked eyes in a battle of wills. I refused to crack first.

"Oh no, did your car break down?"

I stared at him. Not in the mood.

"Shoot. It looks like you're stuck here for a while. Unless..."

"Cade." My voice was a warning signal for him to proceed with caution. Too bad Cade never heeded warning signs.

He looked at me with a gleam in his eye that was entirely too smug. I still couldn't bring myself to ask. And I wouldn't grovel. I'd rather miss the game and walk back into town.

When I didn't say anything, he sighed and patted the seat next to him. "Well, I have an extra seat in my truck right here. So if you need a ride, just let me know."

When there was still annoyed silence on my end, he revved his engine like he was getting ready to leave. Forcing my hand. Forcing me to *ask* him for a ride.

Fine. With a smile sugary enough to take the color right off a sucker, I said, "Sweet, Cade, could I get a ride with you in your ah... nice... truck?"

His eyes narrowed as I coughed out the word 'nice.'

"No."

"Cade!"

"Say it like you mean it."

"How about I promise not to swing the bat into your head during the game if you give me a ride?"

"Nope. I've seen you bat. You can't promise that. I've made it a habit to scoot back a whole foot when you're up."

I resisted the urge to stomp my foot. "Cade. I'm not in the mood. Please give me a ride. We're both going to be late now."

"Tell me something you like about me."

With that, I scoffed, slamming my door shut and flinging my backpack into the bed of his truck. I was attempting to hoist myself into the back when suddenly he was next to me. His hand clutched at my forearm, pushing me toward the truck door.

"Hey," I protested as he pressed me against the passenger window. His arms were folded, and he stood, glowering at me. For reasons I could not define, my two-timing heart raced at his nearness.

"Tell me something you like about me. And mean it. Or start walking."

"Why?"

"Because deep down, you're a big faker. And today, I'm tired of it. Clock's ticking."

Although I had a bucket full of sarcastic things I could have told him, the way he was looking at me, he wouldn't have accepted those answers. And he was right, the clock was ticking. Our game would be starting in seven minutes. The question didn't feel strange, although it probably should have. We *didn't* say nice things to each other. But perhaps that was his whole point. The tiniest thrill shot through me as I contemplated my answer. I thought about how horrible the last few days had felt, but even amid the teasing, when I was in Cade's presence, I had felt accepted. Appreciated. Pretty, even.

That was it. While I couldn't measure up to my fiancé's standards, or his mother's, or even my own, Cade made cheap passes at me that hinted at something bigger. Something kinder. Something I had needed just then. I had always known I never really hated Cade. He drove me crazy, yes. He was the cause of countless embarrassing days of my childhood. Sure. But still, underneath it all, he had a good heart. Whether or not it was always directed toward me, was a different story.

So I mumbled my answer that really hadn't been difficult to come up with. "You make people feel good about themselves."

He watched me for a moment before a crooked smile swept across his face. At least, I think that's what my peripheral vision picked up on. My eyes were intensely focused on an interesting patch of sagebrush just past his right shoulder.

Was this far enough away from the farm kid to please Parker?

My breath caught as his hands landed on my shoulders, moving me over a few inches so he could yank open the passenger door behind me. "And you're fun." Leaning closer, he added, "And smoking hot."

My eyes shot to his in surprise, but he just smiled and motioned for me to climb into his truck. And I did so, in a blush-induced daze of befuddlement.

Most of that ride to the game with Cade passed by in a blur. A foggy, warm, cozy blur. It was a mixture of trying to hold back a smile that wanted to burst from ear to ear, to willing myself not to cry from... relief. And appreciation of a compliment that would end up meaning more to my fractured heart than I'd ever be able to express. I remember laughing a lot, despite myself. I remember teasing him and watching proudly as his ready laughter filled the space between us. I remembered we were both careful not to bring up Parker or anything that happened the day before. And I remember feeling disappointed when we pulled up to the baseball fields.

Fun.

How long had it been since somebody had accused me of being fun? Tessa mentions all the fun times we had back in high school. We had *fun* on our softball team, *fun* playing pranks on Cade, *fun* times sitting next to each other in science lab, and *fun* sneaking out of our gym class. But I don't think I had been accused of being fun at any time in the past four years at college. Studious? Yes. Friendly? Sure. Responsible? Of course. But *fun*? Never fun.

It thrilled me as much as it confused me.

How could I be one thing to somebody, and something so completely different to another?

The Sons of Pitches led one of the biggest upsets of the season that night. The most notable play happened between me and Cade. I was on third base with my team up to bat. The bases were loaded. Holli hit a line drive toward third base. The baseman snagged the ball and threw it to home plate where Cade stood waiting for me as I collided with him. When we disentangled our limbs, jostling and teasing, his glove had come up empty.

He had dropped the ball.

An average build, five foot six, one hundred and thirty-five-pound woman caused this nearly professional college baseball catcher to drop the ball, leading The Pitches to a victory of 3-2.

Yeah. I didn't buy it either.

17

Cattle Drive Checklist (circa - current)

1. Sweatshirt
2. Gun
3. Earplugs for dad's snoring
4. Tampons (This is going to be fun.)
5. Sunscreen
6. ~~Ring~~
7. Baseball hat
8. Cowboy hat
9. Sugar cubes and carrots for Ace
10. Water gun (just in case)

The week between the Fourth of July and the cattle drive was a busy one. After my uncomfortable parting with Parker, our phone calls had decreased in number as we both nursed our battle wounds. I wasn't sure what wounds I had inflicted upon him, but either way, the silence was welcome. I still focused on eating healthy and exercising, but I made sure to eat the proper amount of calories for my body. The wedding dress in my room got pushed to the back of my closet so I didn't have to stare at it every day. My body went on autopilot because my mind was entirely consumed with pranks.

Whether he had meant to or not, Cade's confession of me being fun sparked a new breath of life inside of me. I went out of my way to tease and prank him and even got Stitch and the boys in on it in the process. I was constantly looking over my shoulder for signs of Cade. A sixth sense had begun to develop inside of me, and I could feel in an instant when something didn't seem right. I was reeling over the latest joke Cade had played on me, so when I watched him leave in a truck with Dusty to feed cows, I made my move.

Walking into the bunkhouse, I found Stitch sitting in a chair, sipping his coffee, a newspaper sprawled out over the table in front of him. Glancing around the dim interior, I discovered the place had changed very little since Stitch had moved in a few years ago. There was a bed in the corner, an old black and white television on a makeshift shelf, and a refrigerator in the cramped kitchenette complete with a tiny stove, located near the entrance. A round oak table, along with three rickety chairs, sat in the middle of the room. The only clue to life in the bunkhouse was the picture of Stitch's wife on his nightstand. A rickety staircase, located next to the front door, led to Cade's bed on the second-floor loft.

"Stitch, can you help me with something?"

He eyed me warily.

I held up the horrifying black mask that Tessa and I found at a thrift store earlier that week. "I want to hide this mask on the bathroom mirror, so when Cade walks in he'll scream, but he'll never tell me if it scared him, so I'm hoping you'll be here to keep him honest."

Stitch shook his head as he drained the last sip of his coffee. "Girl, what are you doing?"

"What?"

"Why are you doing all this?"

"Because he put a mouse in the tractor which then proceeded to crawl UP MY LEG. That's why. Your grandson hates me."

Stitch muttered something under his breath as he stood up and plunked his cup into the sink.

"What?"

"I said there's a fine line between love and hate."

"What do you mean?" I hesitated before asking but found I was curious about Stitch's take on things.

"It means you wouldn't be puttin' forth so much effort towards hating someone if, deep down, they didn't mean somethin' to you. All the teasing, all the pranks..." he fluttered his hand through the air as he trailed off. "Just makes an old codger like me think something's... off."

I shook my head. "I don't hate Cade. He doesn't hate me either, but it's not love. He lives to torture me."

Stitch guffawed. "You both couldn't leave each other alone the second he got here."

"*Me*? I tried to play nice, but he wasn't having any of it."

Shaking his head, he added, "If you knuckleheads spent half as much time being nice, instead of dreaming up yer next stunt, you might be singing a different tune right now."

I had been feeling much nicer toward Cade lately, but to Stitch, I said, "Without pranks, we're nothing. Besides, I've got Parker, remember?"

"Do you?"

I stared at him for a long moment before my gaze dropped low when I found his to be too intrusive.

I cleared my throat. "Well, I'm not looking for love. But I am looking for revenge." Biting my lower lip, I put my palms together in a prayer pose, bringing them up near my face, silently pleading with Stitch.

His eyes twinkled but his stoic face never even twitched. "Did that mouse really run up your leg?"

I nodded, somberly. "It was halfway up my shin before I felt it."

Rolling his eyes with an exasperated sigh, he motioned for me to pass by him. "Oh fine."

I grinned and ran into the bathroom to hang up the monstrosity.

After a confirmation from Stitch that Cade had squealed like a little girl upon discovering the mask, I headed to bed that evening on top of the world. Okay, he didn't actually squeal, but Stitch did report that he "startled a bit," which was all the leverage I needed for another notch under my name.

After the two of us took part in a very epic but disastrous water fight in the barn a day earlier, my dad had since banned the two of us from milking cows together. It was epic because I started the fight and got the last spray on Cade before my dad walked in and broke it up, so I counted that for a win. Unfortunately, it was the dang white t-shirt I was wearing that had my dad sending me directly into the house to change, but not before Cade winked at me as he scrawled a notch under his name as well.

So, naturally, tonight I took satisfaction in the fact that he watched me mark my point.

I was just this side of sleep, cozied up in my twin bed when an unnatural scratching sound alerted my senses. I rolled over. Probably just a cat. *Scratch.* My eyes popped open as my body tensed, listening for the sound. There it was again. A faint scratch at my window. It sounded almost like a tree branch scraping against the glass, except there was no tree next to my window.

Brushing aside my first impulse to throw myself under the covers and hide, I willed myself calm and inched my way out of bed. The red light on my alarm clock glowed an ugly eleven-thirty.

Another scratch.

Desperately hoping it wasn't what I suspected, I pulled back the curtains. Gasping, I stumbled backward, tripping on the corner of my bed and landing on the floor with a hard thump. I peered closer, clutching my heart as I stood and investigated again. The mask I had scared Cade with, hung suspended in mid-air, wearing a long, dark robe, which gave an eerie, ghost-like impression. The rope wrapped around the neck was cinched tight and complete with fake blood dripping off the mask.

Holy crap.

Opening my window, I ripped the dead ghost down. I swore in surprise as Cade suddenly appeared behind the mask with a delighted grin on his face.

"You are sick!"

"Was the blood too much? That was Jake's idea."

"You are so gonna get it," I threatened through clenched teeth while my heart ricocheted around in my chest.

His laughing subsided as he lingered a moment longer, his gaze casually traveling down my body and back up again. The chill of the night air caused goosebumps to break out on my legs and arms. Or was it something else? Glancing down, I flushed. My simple blue tank top with gym shorts hitting my upper thigh was comfortable for sleeping, but I was anything but relaxed now. When Cade's eyes met mine again, the gleam of triumph had softened and a small smile grazed his lips as he simply said, "Can't wait."

He tugged his baseball hat down low on his head and turned toward the bunkhouse.

"Sleep tight, Red," he called to me over his shoulder.

I stood there a moment longer, watching him go, before crawling back into bed. Surprisingly, I had no nightmares; the demented creature had been all but forgotten. I did, however, have a hard time blocking out a pair of brown eyes as they drank me in with a gaze that could only be described as... heated.

Dad called off all pranks for the entire cattle drive. Worried we might get out of hand, spook the cattle, or come home with broken bones, he forced us into a truce. Fine by me. Our pranks were starting to feel different anyhow.

In the wee hours of the morning, the entire crew gathered in the stables, saddling and packing our horses to prepare to leave. Three yellow light bulbs hung low across the stables, casting a warm glow throughout the drafty room. Inside the stable, to the left, were eight stalls, each filled with horses. Opposite of the horses was a large section of the room piled with hay and extra feed. A small hallway divided the two sections leading to a doorway near the back end of the stables which housed the tack and saddle room. Stitch stood in the stall next to me, brushing down his horse along with a pack mule standing nearby. While each of us carried our personal items on our horses, Stitch's pack mule carried most of our food, water, cooking supplies, as well as the first aid kit. Most cowboys need a lighter pack, so if we ever ran into trouble or had to chase after a cow, we could do so easily.

I shivered, dancing lightly on the balls of my feet to keep warm while I brushed down Ace inside his stall. Pulling an extra sweatshirt out of my pack, I pulled it on, not caring if it made me look like a puffy snowman. I found myself jealous of the sun, who still had another hour of sleep before showing his face. With the exception of my dad, the rest of the gang were not cheery risers. So, we all went about our business, not saying much, but my silence was mostly because I was so engrossed in my thoughts.

I told Parker last night that I would be unavailable for the next week. The reception would be spotty on the trail and I was leaving my phone at home. With it already near mid-July, the summer was flying by and the pressure was mounting. Which in turn, somehow gave me the strongest desire to bury my head in the sand and block out everything. The only thing I wanted was to go off the grid for five whole days. It sounded like heaven. Though I felt Cade's presence in the stable next to me, saddling Dodger, I kept my focus on the task at hand. My thoughts were taking me on a much different course than they ever had before. My attitude toward Cade wasn't an all-consuming need for revenge or war like it always had been. Our relationship felt... lighthearted. Fun. There was that word again. Something had changed and I'm pretty sure the night before, outside my window, had something to do with it.

We had a great first day on the trail, meandering through sagebrush and small hills. The towering mountains before us and the smell of sage and mountain air provided a breathtaking day at the office. The cows were always slow to move on the first day, but they soon got into a rhythm by mid-afternoon, picking up speed and dust. My dad and I rode most of the day in front of the cattle, leading the pack, and we ended the day riding tail behind the herd and getting fed a cloudy diet of dirt—but I wasn't complaining. My soul felt alive and invigorated in the saddle. My body, however, was still out for review.

That evening, we found a nice spot to camp for the night near a stream for the animals and with plenty of trees for shade. I pulled to a stop and attempted to climb off Ace after the first full day in the saddle. Three pathetic tries later and there was still no way my leg was going to arch high enough to slide over the horn. Sinking my head low onto Ace's neck, I decided that this would be my bed for the night—and quite possibly my deathbed.

Stitch, at hearing my pitiful moaning, ambled over to assist my dismount. Once my feet hit the ground, I doubled over for a moment as my legs tightened and seized under the pressure. Riding horses occasionally was one thing but riding a twelve-hour day with only a few breaks felt much different. No matter how many cattle drives I'd been a part of, the pain of that first day always seemed to fail my memory.

Straightening up, I took the bandana down from my face and brushed my clothing in an attempt to rid myself of one layer of filth.

"You all dusted off, princess?" Dad teased as he passed me with a load of cooking supplies.

"I could use a hot shower. Did you pack one of those?"

"You wish," he threw back over his shoulder.

The smoke from the fire Stitch was tending drew me toward the camp. With movement all around me, I paused for a moment, enjoying the peaceful scene. The cattle surrounded us, grazing quietly in the pasture after filling their bellies with water from the stream. The cowboys were busy unpacking their tents and bedrolls. Most people in the world will probably never know the joy and contentment at the end of a hard day's ride, but as much as I loved the day, the nights were my favorite. There were no cell phones. No distractions. Just a gang of tired cowboys sitting around the campfire eating and telling stories. Laughter rang out across the crisp, clear evening—a long day of work behind us. There was something so satisfying about this simple, but beautiful way of life. School and deadlines and Parker had pulled my dreams in all directions, but here, out in the middle of nowhere, my head was clear, and my direction was certain.

I realized something else as well, something that stopped me in my tracks and gave me much reflection throughout the rest of the night. I discovered that the sweetest memories in my life were not in the classroom or a big city, they were not in a fancy car or an expensive theater, but sitting tired and dirty, out on the range, in the middle of nowhere, surrounded by the people I loved.

18

Journal Entry (circa - grade school)

When I grow up, I want to work with animals. I think it would be fun. I can always get Tessa's dog to come to me when she won't go to anybody else. I think I have a special gift. Animals just really love me.

The sounds of pots and pans clanging together while Stitch endeavored to fix breakfast on the portable grill became my alarm clock the next morning. Rummaging around in my tent for my sweatshirt, I noticed Dad had already packed up his sleeping bag.

Goodness, I must have slept like the dead.

Once dressed, I hobbled my stiff body to the fire and filled my cup with hot water. Not much of a coffee drinker, I rummaged through a couple of the food bags and found the packets of hot chocolate Stitch always throws in for me.

"She moves. Slowly," Dad teased as he moved behind me, grabbing a package of bacon out of the cooler. "I'm surprised to see you up so early."

I smiled. "Yeah, it's a shocker because Stitch is about as quiet as a stampede."

Stitch looked at my dad from where he stood whipping up his pancake mix and said, "We'll see if she's still whining when her belly's full of my famous hotcakes."

Hotcakes. I hadn't heard pancakes described like that since my grandparents were alive. They always served us hotcakes when we stayed overnight. My heart wanted to burst with sudden delight for some reason. The word brought to mind visions of home and family and warm memories filled with hugs from my grandparents, and maple syrup slathered on fresh, steaming hotcakes.

I plodded over to Stitch and gave him a kiss on his weathered cheek. He reddened and turned away while I laughed, grabbing myself an apple from the box. I brought a bag of apples on this trip, mostly to make me feel like I was trying, but mark my words, I was going to eat Stitch's hotcakes. I was going to eat whatever the cowboys were eating. When I told Parker I was going off the grid, I meant it in every way possible, size four dress be hanged. Besides, I would not be the high maintenance princess that lugged an entire box of healthy food to eat on a *cattle drive*. A real farm girl had her limits, and the cattle drive was mine.

Glancing up while stirring the chocolate mixture in my cup, I was surprised to find Cade's eyes on me as he sat on a log near the fire. He didn't look away or even stop staring. He just watched me. My fingers immediately went to my hair. I had slept with it down and hadn't thought to check my crazy mop before leaving the tent. It felt a little messy, but not too bad. Glancing discreetly at my yoga pants and sweatshirt, everything seemed to be in place. The hair on my neck stood up as I glanced at Dusty and Jake, packing up their tent, looking innocent enough. I looked back at Cade again. This time, a slow, reckless smile grew on his face, his eyes challenging me.

He mouthed, "Nervous?"

My hands balled into fists. That little... My dad had said no pranks, but in his twisted way, he was trying to make me paranoid.

Stalking over to him, I plowed into his shoulder on my way past, causing him to fall off his log. I guess the joke was still on me though because he kept right on laughing.

Over a breakfast of half-burnt pancakes, bacon, and leftover beans from the night before (Stitch was nothing if not thrifty), my dad divided out the assignments for the day's ride. On a cattle drive, the position of each cowboy was important. We had to lead the herd, keep stragglers from falling behind, as well as keep the cattle from spreading out too much. Throughout the day, we switched up positions so that everyone could take turns doing something different, but it was mostly to keep one person from being stuck eating dust, riding tail for too long.

"Dusty and Jake will take the lead, Kels and Cade will be riding flank, and me and Stitch will take the first-round riding tail. We'll switch things up after lunch."

At those words, we broke camp, packed up, saddled our horses, and moved out with a chorus of *"hi-ya's and giddy-ups."* Out of all the positions on a cattle drive, riding flank was my favorite. As a flank rider, I stay about a half to two-thirds of the way behind the cows on one side, keeping the herd moving forward without spreading out too far. Rarely did cows get out of formation, so my job was just riding with the group and I loved it. This would keep me at a safe distance from Cade as well, as he would be across the cattle pathway from me, doing the same thing on the other side.

Sweat dripped down my face. The breeze that circulated the air yesterday had been absent all morning, leaving instead a dry heat with a fog of dust that settled deep in my lungs. I tied my handkerchief around my face to help me breathe. A glance across the way at Cade told me he had covered his face as well.

A couple of hours into the drive, my dad rode up next to me. "You all right?"

"Yeah," my muffled voice choked out.

"I'm gonna have Dusty switch with you for a while."

"No, I'm okay." I didn't need any ammunition for the guys to tease me about. It had been three years and I wanted to prove my worth as a cowboy this trip.

He peered closer to me. "You sure? It's getting hard to breathe. The boys won't mind switching for a bit."

I nodded again. "No, I'm okay. Really. You have it worse than I do."

"Yeah, but I'm a lot tougher than you," Dad teased.

"You wish, old man," I said. "We should be getting close to stopping for lunch anyway, right?"

He nodded. "Yeah, probably in another hour or so. We'll stop at the little creek just on the other side of the ridge."

"I can make it."

Shaking his head, he muttered, "Stubborn woman." His eyes crinkled and I imagined his smirk underneath his bandana, but I also saw a flash of admiration. And excitement. My dad loved the cattle drives more than anyone. "If it gets too much for you, wave at me and I'll have Dusty switch you."

"Alright. Stubborn dad." He laughed as he turned his horse around sharply and rode back to his post behind the cattle with Stitch.

All my fake bravado aside, I was very glad to see the creek in my view a long seventy-two minutes later. The cattle were excited as well as they stumbled into the water, drinking greedily. I hopped off Ace and led him down to drink while I splashed my face and neck with the cold water. *Heaven,* I thought, as I inhaled my first breath of fresh air in four hours.

With my eyes still closed, I felt a warm body move in next to mine. Glancing over, I saw Cade kneeling on the bank. He stripped off his shirt before dousing his head into the water, face first. Sitting back on his knees, he kept his eyes closed, rubbing water briskly all over his face and neck. Swallowing hard, my gaze followed a drip of water moving slowly down his neck, before trailing across his very chiseled chest. He knelt over again to repeat his actions, revealing a tight and muscular back. My face warmed, but I could not look away. His arms were... perfect—toned and muscular, strong, but not overkill. My goodness, he was nearly perfect.

"See something you like, Red?"

Snapping out of my Cade-induced trance, I discovered that somewhere in the middle of my wolfish examination of his body, he had finished washing at the creek and was now sitting back on his haunches, watching me. Reluctantly, I pulled my gaze higher and met a pair of raised eyebrows and laughing eyes. Feeling very much like a child caught eating a forbidden cookie, my brain refused to come up with an answer to save me.

"Nope." Clearing my throat, I stood up, slowly dying inside as Cade's grin grew wider.

"That's too bad."

I heard his words but pretended I didn't as I fled back to camp.

Mortally embarrassed, I avoided Cade the rest of the day, although I felt his gaze on me several times. After the noon meal, we loaded up again, this time with my dad and me in the front, leading the herd. We had followed the stream the rest of the afternoon, stopping just at the base of the mountains. The sun sat low in the sky by the time we pulled into camp, our stomachs rumbling. It was a testament to how hungry we were when Stitch's 'famous' campfire beans had our mouths watering. While the boys led the animals to the creek, I admired my view for a moment. With the pastureland behind us and the mountains towering before us, it was the best of both worlds.

A newborn calf, born a day earlier, stumbled away from the main herd and meandered toward a mountain trail. Hesitating only a moment, I grabbed my rope from my knapsack and set out after the calf. I'd be back before the boys missed me.

The trail grew dense and thick as I rode into the forest pathway. My eyes roamed over every fallen log or tree branch, searching for signs of life. The calf couldn't have wandered far.

An eerie feeling settled over me as I led Ace down the darkening trail. Goosebumps appeared on my arms. As if he could also sense something amiss, Ace pulled against his bit, prancing around as his ears stood at attention. When we came around a small bend, a soft bellow sounded up the road and I jerked Ace to a halt.

The calf's head poked out from behind a fallen log, looking as if his leg was stuck. Feeling the eyes of the forest on us, Ace and I inched forward, with pounding hearts and quivering hands and hooves. Twenty yards in front of the calf, my trusty horse stubbornly refused to push onward.

"Come on, Ace," I mumbled as I slid to the ground. Without Ace beneath me, a vulnerable feeling overtook me and I hesitated. The calf cried out once more. I took a step forward.

A low purr reached my ears. I froze and peered into the brush at my side. A loud snort behind me told me Ace was now running back toward camp. Out of the trees, something tan and furry flew out in front of me, landing directly on top of the calf. Before my eyes could process any more a horrifying shriek pierced the air. My mouth gaped and I watched helplessly as the mountain lion ripped into the tender flesh of the newborn calf, blood spilling everywhere.

My breath came in sputters and my body started to shake while my feet felt paralyzed, frozen to the ground. The urge to retch rose from my stomach, but I couldn't look away. I stared in fear at the remains of the innocent calf I had seen alive only moments earlier. Feeling the danger and knowing it was now or never, I forced my stiff legs in motion and I took a step backward.

A twig cracked under my foot.

The ears of the mountain lion stood erect as he snapped his head toward the sound. Toward me. His steely eyes found focus squarely on mine. After assessing each other for a few seconds, without breaking eye contact, I took another step backward. With little effort, he stepped over the dead calf, staring at me, his eyes carnal and hungry. I stopped. Stopped moving. Stopped breathing. Stopped wondering what Stitch was fixing for dinner.

I was dinner tonight.

He crept toward me, his long tail curled up high, his predatory stare fixed on me. My body bubbled over with panic. I wasn't supposed to die this way. I didn't want to be a statistic on the morning news. All I could hear was the sound of the calf's neck-snapping as vicious teeth tore into tender flesh. All I could see was the blood pouring out of the calf's neck, staining the lion's mouth a savage red.

With rapid breaths, I danced backward with him, step for step, but still, he was faster. Gaining on me. Was I supposed to make myself bigger? Or play dead? Loud or quiet? Suddenly, all my lessons on wild animal training (which honestly hadn't been much) blended together. My brain couldn't think past the pounding blood drumming in my ears. Blood I imagined oozing out onto the forest floor at any moment. With the predator gaining on its prey and no other option in sight, I screamed. The sound shattered through the eerie stillness of the trees which stood in anticipated silence. The lion startled a bit and slowed his prowl. Ten yards from me now. Crouching his hind legs and tail low to the ground, he sat on high alert... poised... watching me. Numbness in every sense of the word consumed me.

And then... he moved.

The lion leaped through the air toward me. Flying. In one last-ditch effort to live, I dove sideways toward a tree a couple of yards away.

A loud shot boomed through the forest.

The lion jerked backward into the air landing on his back. He flailed about wildly, whimpering as blood oozed from his chest before he laid his head down on the trail and closed his eyes. A few more twitches and gurgles, then all was quiet.

Crashing footsteps thundered through the forest floor. I turned my head and saw Cade rushing toward me with his rifle in his hand.

"Holy crap, Red. Are you okay? Did he get you anywhere?" Suddenly, I was yanked to my feet as he pulled my arms up and turned my body, frantically inspecting my sides for any injuries.

He shook me gently, probing me with questions, trying to find a spark somewhere in my glazed eyes. He turned my face toward him, forcing me to peel my focus away from the dead lion. His touch and anxious scrutiny nearly did me in, but it was the concern in his eyes that unlatched the floodgates, and my overwrought tears broke the surface.

The enormity of what just happened and what *could* have happened overwhelmed me, turning me into a sobbing mess of a disaster. Visions of a mutilated calf and the mountain lion jumping toward me filled my head. My mind played the scene on repeat like some horror show rerun, and I buried my face behind my hands.

The moment I found myself too weak to stand, Cade, pulled me to him. He crushed my head against his chest while our heartbeats thrashed about wildly together. It was then I realized the arms that held me so tight were shaking. The forest sat strangely silent in sharp contrast to my weeping. There were no birds chirping, no buzzing or humming of insects. It was as if all the creatures had been reminded of their spot on the food chain and humbly retreated.

Cade sank to the ground, using a tree trunk as his backrest while he cradled me. My legs sprawled out over the top of his right thigh as I curled into his chest. The emotional wave that first engulfed me had begun to pass—lulled to calm by Cade's soothing touch. Except for the occasional gasp in breath, the salty tears sliding down my face and soaking his shirt were now silent. Exhaustion pierced every limb of my body. It was a heavy load to carry, this brush with death, and I found myself missing the innocence of just minutes earlier. We could have sat there for one minute or thirty, I had no way of comprehending anything but

Cade's arms around me and the gentle rhythm of his fingers caressing my skin.

Cade had grown even warmer as he held me. Instinctively craving contact, I nestled closer, placing my hand on his chest. He radiated heat and comfort. Safety. His body held everything I needed. When I lifted my head, I was surprised at how close his face was to mine. His eyes were soft as his hand found my cheek. My gaze found his lips. My body on autopilot now. He bent toward me. I lifted my face to meet his—our lips a whisper away.

"Kelsey!"

We jerked apart. He released my face almost immediately as we turned toward the voice, which startled us back into reality. Dad and the boys were riding full speed toward us on their horses. I blinked in a daze, my body and mind were slowly returning to their original harrowed state. I felt self-conscious sitting on Cade's lap, although mere moments earlier I hadn't minded a bit. By the time Dad had reached us, Cade and I were standing a respectful distance apart and I was immediately swept into my dad's arms.

"Holy freak, that's a big cat!" Jake called out as he and Dusty investigated the dead carcass.

"You shot him clean through the heart." Dusty looked back at Cade proudly.

"It's a good thing, cause I only had one shot to get it right," Cade mumbled as he walked over to where Dusty and Jake crouched around the mountain lion.

"What happened?" Dad asked me.

At the risk of getting chewed out for leaving without a gun and without telling anyone, I told the story anyway. And while I did get a minor talking to, my dad was just grateful it ended the way it did.

Walking over to Cade, my dad shook his hand, then pulled him in for a hug. "Son, thank you. You saved my girl's life here today."

Cade shuffled uncomfortably at his words. "I'm just glad I came when I did."

"How did you know to come?" he asked. "We heard her scream, but you were way ahead of us."

"I saw her take off with her horse and I figured she went out after that calf. I followed her to see if she needed a hand. Just as I rounded the bend in the road, I heard her scream and saw him about to pounce."

His eyes bore into mine—both of us lost, reliving a time that had passed only moments ago. The men resumed talking about me like I wasn't there, but I didn't care. I *wasn't* there. My mind was over-wrought with visions of the mountain lion's eyes on mine, the gunshot, and Cade's warm embrace. My dad slipped his arm around my waist as I felt my body get weaker. The adrenaline rush had evap-orated, leaving my limbs and head dense and heavy. As my dad lifted me onto his horse to take me back to camp, to my utter shame, my thoughts were no longer of a dead calf or a mountain lion, or even my fiancé, but of the missed opportunity of a kiss.

19

Journal Entry (circa - high school)

Cade william's dad died last week. Today was his viewing.
My parents asked if I wanted to go and I told them
yes. Everybody knew Mr. williams. He was one of the
best teachers ever. If any kids were acting up in his
class, he'd arm-wrestle them. If they won, they didn't
get detention. If they lost, well, it was usually best out
of three. He was in a car accident. Anyway, at the
funeral, I told cade how sorry I was about his dad and
he didn't say anything, but he hugged me tightly. I
didn't know what else to say or do, we're not really
friends, but I hugged him back just as hard.

I forgot to thank him for saving my life.
   I forgot to *thank* him for saving my *LIFE*.
   My thoughts pushed sleep aside as I lay in the two-man tent my
dad and I shared. Dad had fallen asleep long ago, as was evidenced

by the turbulent snores hurling into my left ear. As hard as I tried, sleep was far from my thoughts. Every time I closed my eyes, I relived the moment the lion sprang toward me, the gunshot, and finally, my time spent wrapped in Cade's protective embrace. Until I remembered, to my complete horror, that I had never once uttered a thank you to my rescuer. The one whose quick-thinking, skill and kindness left me alive and comforted. It was that awful feeling of something left unfinished. A gift wrapped, but not delivered. A thank you card written, but never sent.

And it was eating me alive.

All things considered, at the time, I had been too much in shock to relay anything too heartfelt, but still... he needed to know. And I needed to tell him. Something had changed in the woods. Our relationship had been constructed from taunting and pranks, but tonight, the wall dividing us had cracked, and the feel of his arms tight around me and his breath on my neck warmed me still.

I sat up. I was never going to get any sleep until I talked to Cade. Or at least Stitch. He was always up later than the rest of us, tending to the fire, drinking coffee, and listening to the sounds of the night. Stitch wasn't a talker, so by default, he made the best listener. My sweatshirt felt soft against my skin as I pulled it over my head. I slipped on my shoes and crept out of the tent as quietly as a loud zipper ripping through the night could be, but my dad's snoring didn't change a beat.

A lone figure sat around the campfire, staring into the smoke. Rubbing my bleary eyes, I walked into the camp, stopping short when I realized it was Cade sitting there, with Stitch nowhere to be found.

He sat on a large log next to the fire, his forearms resting on his thighs, looking every bit the modern cowboy that I had come to expect from him. He turned his head to watch me as I forced myself into my continued approach.

Telling myself it was because I didn't want to wake the entire camp with our conversation, I sat next to him on his log. Just big enough for two.

I put my feet on the ring of the fire pit, my leg brushing against Cade's thigh.

"I can't stop thinking about it."

Cade nodded slowly as he stared into the fire. We sat quietly for a moment, an air of peace between us.

"I've been lying in bed thinking about how much your aim's improved. I almost had to do a double-take to make sure it wasn't Dusty shooting that rifle." Curse my stupid mouth. Why was this so hard? Why couldn't I just be nice and grateful to him? Perhaps it's because we've had so few normal conversations and I wasn't sure how to go about it.

Cade snorted. "You were thinking about me in bed? Dang Red, what was I wearing?"

That's why. Because it was hard for Cade too.

I bumped him with my shoulder. "Don't let it go to your head. For some reason, I'm feeling inclined to be nice to you tonight."

He chuckled lightly and the comfortable silence settled back down around us. We sat, hypnotized by what was left of the fire, the bright, orange flames of earlier reduced to white ash and embers. Rubbing my hands briskly across my thighs to ward off the chill, I took a deep breath. I had been toeing the line between us long enough. It was time to cross it.

"With all the craziness of tonight, I forgot to thank you, Cade. You saved my life and I just wanted to tell you thank you. It doesn't seem much in comparison to what you did, but I don't know how else to tell you."

He stilled, turning to look at me for the first time since I sat by him. My heart pounded as his eyes studied my face, grazing my lips before he looked back toward the fire.

"Red, you don't owe me anything. I would have done the same for anybody here."

I swallowed my disappointment with his blanket statement.

"Don't take that the wrong way. I'm glad I was there in time. You scared the crap out of me." He nudged me with his shoulder as he winked at me, our tone friendly and light once more.

Other than Cade, I couldn't remember a time anyone under the age of 65 had ever winked at me. Especially not someone my age, but according to the big puddle of mush that was now my body, I seemed to enjoy it.

I cleared my throat. "I noticed the bullet didn't go through the lion's heart *quite* dead center; it was a bit to the left. I wondered if you need me to give you a few tips."

"I'm sure that would be very informative."

I grinned. "Have your people call my people and we'll set something up." I breathed easier now. *This* was the relationship I was comfortable with. The teasing. The back and forth. Too much tenderness left me feeling vulnerable. This was normal. Safe.

I stood to go, awkwardly. Not because I wanted to, but because I didn't know what to stay for. I had said what I came to say.

"Wait."

Pausing, I turned back to him as he stood to face me.

He was quiet for several moments before he spoke. His voice seemed far away, but there was a fire in his eyes. "We go the rounds, you and me, hiding behind all the pranks. But underneath all the jokes... I think you're still all talk."

"What?"

"You're still all *talk*." He spoke slower and firmly, his chin tilted upward, his eyes gleaming, his voice challenging, daring, goading... always baiting. "But today was real. You were real. I was real. And I liked that."

I stopped breathing—confusion and elation surged throughout my body. I opened my mouth to speak, but no words came out. I wasn't sure what he was asking me or what he wanted, but the moment between us in the woods still simmered in my mind. When his eyes flickered ever so slightly to my lips, I took a step back. "I'm not... going to kiss you. I'm engaged."

"I'm not asking you to." His words were soft, but his eyes were liquid heat.

I had to get out of there. Say something. The tension had to break or else I would snap, but my words had left me. I turned to go, but before I could take a step, his fingers clasped my arm, staying me. Turning back, I gave him a questioning glance before he pulled me closer into his body. Before I could protest or think about Parker or pranks or walls or boundaries, my head found his chest, and all other thoughts were silenced. His heartbeat was strong and steady, and perhaps, a little faster than normal. Parker's face briefly entered my mind, leaving almost as quick. Friends could hug. Startled, I wondered when I had begun to think of Cade and me as friends, but that thought, and all others, vanished when I felt his arms surround my body and pull me against him.

The fire snapped and all at once, I knew exactly what he meant about me being all talk. I understood what he wanted me to give. That real part of myself I kept guarded and tucked away from all the world. That vulnerable part, deep down, beneath the false confidence. The part buried by the jokes and the teasing. The part filled with fears and doubts that even Parker had no access to. Cade had a taste of it tonight... that raw vulnerability. But instead of feeling embarrassed or ashamed, he tucked my worry beneath his arms, soothed my fears with his touch, and chased away the nightmare.

A slow burn spread through my veins. It traveled through every nook, touching every limb, finally settling like fire near my heart. My arms encircled his waist, feeling the softness of his shirt and the strength of his back. He was warm and smelled of campfire and pine trees, so masculine, and so like him. His cheek rested against my head while his arms pulled me even tighter against him. Our bodies molded together, bending and obliging. For several long moments, we stood, speaking only through embrace and whispered breaths. The walls between us reduced to rubble now.

All at once, he stood tall and gently released me from his arms. The chill of the mountain air seeped between us as he moved away, only to stop and face me once more. "Red, when I saw the mountain lion ready to pounce on you, I..." He shook his head, as his words trailed off. "Just don't go anywhere else by yourself. Or at least without a gun."

"That could have happened to anybody."

He nodded slowly. "I know. But you're not just anybody. Not to me. And I'm discovering... that I kind of like having you around."

With those words, he doused out the smoke from the waning fire and walked over to the tent he shared with Dusty and Jake. "Sleep tight, Red." I watched him unzip his tent and step inside, leaving me alone in a cloudy haze of words, both said, and unsaid.

We returned to the ranch two days later, tired and dirty. Once our cattle had been delivered to our destination, it only took a day and a half of riding to make it home. The trail went much quicker without any cattle to push and prod along. My legs had grown accustomed to the week in the saddle, but as I trudged into the house that afternoon, the stiff muscles made it difficult to walk. I hugged my mom and then immediately excused myself for a hot shower, and some time alone with the roaring feelings billowing inside of me.

Though I wore a hat and tried to keep the sunblock at the ready, the sun had colored my skin a rosy pink. The freckles scattered across my cheeks and nose had turned a shade darker. I turned the faucet on and let the water run for a minute to heat up while I undressed and studied myself in the mirror. My long ponytail, with bits of straw dangling from the ends, had loosened from the ride and hung wild and unkempt down my back. I pulled out the elastic and shook my hair. Steam billowed out of the tub by the time I stepped inside, my body immediately relaxing on contact. I took a deep, warm breath, allowing the moisture from the hot air to coat my lungs before exhaling. The shower began to soothe my clamoring heart, lulling my body into giving rise to the torrent of thoughts I had tried so desperately to push away on the cattle drive. Now, stripped down from watching eyes and expectations, I began to sob —letting the water take my tears—and wondering how I had let myself go so far down this path. Once the well had dried and after a long soak and a strong scrubbing, I turned off the water. I wrapped myself up in a towel, peeked out into the hallway to make sure nobody was around, and sprinted into my room, locking the door behind me.

I wanted to shut out all the feelings except the decision-making part of my brain. That part wanted to go ahead and pick the colors the Kelsey of Moscow would approve of and rattle off the information to Parker and my mother. That part was desperate to call my fiancé and discuss our future. The plans we had so carefully made. That part of myself wanted nothing more than to get back on track. To be efficient. Smart. Logical. She would fit perfectly molded to a big city lawyer. She didn't like disappointing people, or changing plans, or causing upheaval. She didn't like gossip.

I *wanted* to shut everything else out because those feelings would be so much easier. It's easier to keep things the way they've always been.

But I could not.

That part was clear to me now. The past couple of months, the Kelsey from Moscow and the Kelsey from Eugene had begun to collide, shattering walls and rebuilding with the best parts of both, and I wasn't quite sure which world this new Kelsey belonged in.

I pulled on a pair of clean underwear and opened my closet door. Shuffling past the hangers, I pulled out Jennifer Harris's dress. After all this time, I still hadn't thought of it as mine. It pulled so heavy on the hanger, it nearly snapped. I scooped up the bottom half of the dress and draped it over my bed. It slipped easily off the hanger, but I doubted it would slip as easily over my curves. I found the bottom of the dress and tugged it over my head. It had only been two weeks since the fourth (and a week of Stitch's hotcakes), but I was curious to try again—this time with no judgmental eyes adding weight to my shoulders. Or hips.

Just as it did before, the dress glided on easily past the shoulders, slid past my stomach, and came to a screeching halt at my hips. Ever so gently, I tugged the material down my body inch by inch, willing my great-grandmother's birthing hips to toss me a bone. After a few minutes of microscopic progress, the dress made it past my hips, and finally, blessedly, touching the floor.

I gasped and looked in the mirror. A wide, disbelieving smile shone on my face. I had done it. All the sacrifices, all the healthy food, the running... I had done it. It was still too tight, obviously, and I didn't dare sit or bend a millimeter, but I could see the possibility. A tidal wave of satisfied relief passed through me. I shuffled closer toward the mirror, not wanting to tear or split a seam, and examined myself. The front V-neck dipped low across my stomach, stopping an inch above my belly button. Mrs. Gillette had been right. The dress was flattering for any cup size, with just a hint of breast peeking through. The effect led the eye to my naked collarbone, where a stunning diamond necklace would make the perfect finishing touch.

I swished back and forth, watching my reflection. The part of my dress suctioned to my hips didn't budge, but the gathering of satin at my calves and feet felt perfect. Hendrix had designed one of the most beautiful dresses I had ever laid eyes upon. I could imagine somebody walking down the aisle wearing this gown. No. Not walking... floating. This was a dress a woman floats in. I turned and eyed it from the side. My curves had been pressed and molded into something so tight and flattering. Every detail down to the tiny beads and flower overlay was utter perfection. This dress would make somebody very happy.

But that someone was not me.

After the initial excitement of stuffing myself into the dress, it all deflated. The balloon had popped. I now knew, with certainty, what my heart had been hinting at for a while. It didn't matter that I could fit into this dress. Even if I had inches to spare on my wedding day, even if I had the boobs to make this thing pop, it wasn't me. It wasn't mine. It wasn't *me*.

I had tried so hard to fit into my life with Parker. Just like with the dress, I had almost succeeded, but it would have all been a lie. Not until coming home did I realize how much I had changed. How much I had let go of.

Some change was good. I left for college ready to be different. I spent my high school years being the target of pranks and jokes. Many that I instigated, but often, many that I had not. I always returned the favor, but toward the end of my senior year, I wanted to be taken more seriously. Then prom night happened, leaving me irritated and completely fine with high tailing it out of Eugene.

At the university, Tessa and I immersed ourselves into college life —attending classes and study groups, and the occasional party. I wanted to shed my entire identity from high school, so I lost the extra twenty pounds (made much easier when I was no longer surrounded by my mom's rich, calorie-packed foods), bought expensive clothes, and formed myself into the person I always imagined I'd be. This change was a slow process at first as I came back home to the ranch the summer after my freshman year, but then I stopped coming home. I yearned to be different. A smart, stylish woman headed toward a big life—an impressive life. I enjoyed my communications class in college and soon began tinkering with the idea of broadcast journalism.

I met Parker soon after the first semester of my sophomore year and fell in love with his big dreams and easy assurance of where his life was going. Success dripped from his cufflinks and tailored suits, and I fell in love with the idea of our perfect image together. He loved the idea of me being a news reporter and I loved him loving it. I stopped trying to decide if the major was right for me and dove in headfirst.

Toward the end of our junior and the beginning of our senior year, we began making our Idaho exit strategy. We would get married and jet off to the coast to begin our careers. I had wanted change and when I found it, I molded myself to it. Parker saw me only from when I had already begun changing. Other than a few bits and pieces about my past life, he only knew the Kelsey at college. Could four years of college erase a lifetime of memories? Erase a lifetime of a person's core identity? Did I really want it to?

I kept telling myself that I didn't care about Cade. This wasn't about him. It *couldn't* be about him. I had no idea where we stood. While a big part of that had to be true, deep down, I *did* care about him. That was the problem. A big problem. It turns out when someone goes Crocodile Dundee and shoots a mountain lion that's about to rip the size six meat off your bones, it's rather difficult to push that person out of your mind. I even looked it up... it's perfectly reasonable that a person forms emotional attachments to someone who has helped them. Saved them. Perfectly normal. I wanted to believe that it wasn't *him* I was attached to; it was just what he did. That was all. Nothing else. He had always been, and always would be, a jerk.

But that was a lie.

Against my better judgment, my heart seemed very interested in reliving the way his arms felt, the heat in his body when he pulled me in for a hug, or the softness in his voice when he told me he liked having me around. Then I would see Parker's face in my mind and feel ashamed. While no physical lines were crossed, something had shifted, bringing with it a new awareness of Cade, one like never before. Or quite possibly, it had always been there. Even at our worst, I could begrudgingly admit a certain pull... a lure toward him. It wasn't just physical, but some sort of emotional fascination.

Our pranks and bickering had created a dance, with rhythm and steps for us to follow, keeping us together but separate. Heat and Ice. But now... I had played with fire. Not enough to get burned, but the snaps and sparks toyed with me—mocking me. Cade Williams had never been the plan. I didn't know if he would ever *be* the plan.

No. This decision was *not* about Cade.

This was about me.

I don't quit things. I was raised to be a finisher. To see it to the end. 'Can't do things halfway on a farm,' my dad would always say. Cows can't get half-fed or half-milked. The fields can't be half-harvested. Once semester in high school, I mistakenly got put into a welding class. That's right, welding. The fusing together of metals with heat. I had signed up for a movie class (the type where I would have to watch a movie and write a paper on it), but somehow welding had been put on my schedule. So, I stayed in welding. I had attended the first class and knew the teacher was now counting on me. Not really. In my heart, I knew he couldn't have cared less whether I stayed or transferred out, but in my mind, transferring meant I was a quitter. Heck, I was involved in a prank war for twelve years (and counting) that caused me repeated personal humiliation because I couldn't make myself stop.

I had said yes to Parker. Pledged to give him my life. Spent three years with him, dating, studying, and planning a life together. I had molded and adapted myself into what I imagined would be the perfect companion to him. The problem was, he knew nothing about what I'd done, how much I had changed, or who I was before. *That* was entirely on me. The qualms I had about my welding class were nothing in comparison. Guilt wracked my body. I didn't want to hurt him. The idea that someone could be hurt or even devastated by a choice I made very nearly made me reconsider. Could I spend a life-time with someone not meant for me, to avoid hurting them?

And then the dress. It was so stupid to be worrying about the dress at a time like this, but I had pledged to wear it. I promised I would do whatever it would take to fit into the dress. Even with my dislike of Parker's mother, I still couldn't bear the thought of her angry or worse, disappointed in me. Why was it that the people you walk the most on egg-shells with are the ones you are the most nervous to disappoint? She deserved none of my anxiety, but still, the thought was distressing to me.

The next morning, after a long, tear-filled discussion with my mom, and a relieved squeeze on my shoulder from my dad (the best he could do at awkward girl affection), I called Parker. He had been packing to go overseas. His dad's company was paying for him to go to China for a three-week conference and work trip.

"Hey, babe," Parker's term of endearment pricked at my ears through the phone. "The company car will be here to pick me up in just a few minutes. Did you need something before I go? Do you mind if I just call you when I get there?"

There was my out. It would be so easy to wait. To tell him later. He was busy packing to leave the country. It wasn't fair for me to drop something like this on him before a big work trip, but the need to alleviate the pressure building in my chest was much greater than my usual cowardice.

So, like a band-aid, I ripped it off without giving Parker any warning.

"Parker, this isn't right."

A slight pause. "What's not right?" he asked, his tone guarded.

My thumping pulse was ricocheting in my ears. Last chance to turn back.

"Us."

I heard a decisive suitcase zipper in the background before he said, "Last I checked, we were pretty right for each other."

My eyes closed as I leaned my head onto the headrest on my bed, taking a deep breath. This was the moment that would change both of our lives forever, and saying it out loud sucked. "I wish I could be there to say this to you in person, but... I think I made a mistake. I can't... I'm so sorry, but I can't marry you."

There was torturous silence on the other end of the line. I imagined him sinking stunned onto his bed, next to his suitcase packed for three weeks in China. Finally, he spoke.

"What do you mean? Why?"

I sighed. Why, indeed. Where do I even begin? "I thought it was what I wanted but being home has made me realize our plans are wrong for me. I'm different from what you know." I fumbled through my words, unable to properly explain myself, and making more of a mess.

A snort of derision came through the phone. "What are you talking about? We made those plans *together*. We fell in love *together*. I was just there a week ago. I know we were fighting a little, but that can't be a deal-breaker. What made you *all of a sudden* think this?"

"It's been building for a while inside, but I didn't realize how much until I came home."

"Is this about *him*?"

I closed my eyes, my heart ripping in two. "No."

"Is this about the *freaking* dress again? You said you wanted to wear it."

"No." I sank further back onto my bed, burying my face with a pillow. "It's not. It's about me and coming home to realize, I was wrong. I don't think I'm the right fit for the life we wanted."

He scoffed into the phone. "I guess, I'm just not sure how you've changed *so* much in a month and a half since going home."

"I changed completely in the four years I was at school. You only know that person, not the person I was for eighteen years before that."

Silence fell between us. I imagined him weighing the pros and cons of this revelation, measuring and analyzing the data, and finding it inconclusive. I object, your honor.

"I can't... I guess I'm just a little pissed off. So, you were *lying* to me our whole relationship?"

"No. At least, I don't think I was. I was that person too, I thought." I threw my hand over my face. This was such a mess. I had no idea how to explain myself. Turns out, I didn't get a chance to.

"Great. Three years of our life wasted on each other. Thanks for that. I've gotta go."

"Parker, I'm so sorry, I..."

He hung up.

After laying in my room in contemplative silence, I told my dad I was taking a day off. He seemed relieved, since he had no idea what to do with me in this disheartened state and told me to take what time I needed. Thankfully, my mom got the hint I didn't want to talk, so other than bringing me a sandwich at noon, she left me alone. I stayed in my room, flopped on my bed, and ignored the world.

I wished Parker hadn't hung up so fast. I wish I could have more adequately explained my feelings, but maybe it was better this way. He would be in China for three weeks. *If* we spoke again, and the image of a very expensive dress poking out of my closet needing a new home, made me think we probably would. Hopefully, time would heal the anger. I hated being the bad guy. I wish I could have told him it wasn't me; it was my stupid heart that was the problem. If only I had gone to California, it would have been *years* before I realized what a mistake I had made.

The next day, I went to grab an apple out of habit. I held it in my hand for a long moment, staring at the healthy ball of vitamins. I grabbed my keys, stepped out onto the porch, and pitched the apple against the maple tree in our front yard. Watching it explode and fall to the ground filled me with zero satisfaction (it was kind of disappointing actually), but it added a nice symbolic touch to my life. Then I got into my car and drove to The Ranch House Diner and proceeded to scarf down a double bacon cheeseburger, a large fry, and a Pepsi. It felt amazing until about a half-hour after eating it. Apparently, it would take some time before my stomach could handle that much grease.

Emotions all over the board jabbed at me over the next few days, but the feeling that stood out the most was... liberation.

20

New Summer Checklist (circa - current)

1. Figure out what to do next
2.
3.

A person couldn't avoid work for too long on a farm, at least if they had a dad like mine. Thankfully, it was tractor work to be done and I was more than happy to make money sitting alone in a piece of farm equipment, not speaking with anyone. By the last week of July, the grain had been harvested, leaving rows of straw to bale. Which would have been fine, but the only tractor available had no cab attached, which meant sitting in an open tractor in the hot air, pulling the baler behind me, compressing the dry straw into bale cubes. It was a miserable job for several reasons, but mostly because, on a day like today with not a stitch of breeze flowing, the straw pieces took to the air and stayed there. With a bandana strapped around my face and my hair a sweaty, tangled disaster, I was a hot mess. A hot, sweaty, and extremely itchy mess.

So very itchy.

My dad had sent Cade and the boys out to turn on the sprinklers in a field a few miles away. So, the boys got to play in the cool sprinkler water while I sat in the sweltering heat in a mental battle of wills, trying to fight the urge to scratch off my entire body.

It had been one week since I broke up with Parker. Once the word of our demise spread around the farm, it felt as though I had been diagnosed with leprosy. The boys gave me a wide berth (probably terrified that I might cry or talk about my feelings) which I had been grateful for. Even though I had been the one to call it off, there was still a lot I was processing through. I had an angry ex-fiancé in China for two more weeks. I didn't feel like the engagement had the proper closure our relationship needed. I had a degree in a field I no longer wanted, and where my life once had direction at the end of the summer, now I had none. I was confused about my purpose in life, and a bit apprehensive, but I refused to let the nerves about my new situation get me down. If all else failed, I would implement the cat lady plan a bit earlier and move in with Tessa in Boise.

Cade had made himself scarce. Anytime work on the ranch happened to throw us together, I got polite nods and a few smiles, but nothing like the heat from the cattle drive. Which was fine. Honestly, I expected it. Cade and I together... was a joke.

My dad zoomed around behind me in the hay stacker, picking up the straw bales. He sent me a sympathetic wave as he passed me, heading back toward the house with his full load. If he trusted anyone else to drive his stacker, he would have traded places with me in a heartbeat. Finishing my last row of the miserable straw, I turned my sights and tractor toward the house. The sweat *clung* to my body, attracting every straw particle from the air and making me itch in places a lady didn't scratch. My mouth felt as if a piece of cotton had been stuffed inside of it all day.

I may as well have been in the Sahara Desert without water for how enticing the sprinklers in the neighboring field looked to me as I drew closer. Unable to help myself any longer, I threw the tractor into park and jumped down to the ground. Seeing no one around, I yanked my bandana out from around my neck and peeled off my shirt, watching the straw bits fly into the air. Tugging the ponytail out of my snarly hair, I grabbed one of the sprinkler heads and pelted my whole body, starting with my face. Just me and my bright pink sports bra in the middle of the open field. Finally clean, I backed a few feet away from the nozzle and stood with my arms raised and my head tilted back as the water from three sprayers hit me slowly from different angles. The *cha-cha-cha* sound of the sprinklers relaxed me into a semi-induced coma.

From a distance, the rumble of the stacker made its way closer to me. My dad had seen me do this plenty of times, and I was too relaxed to care. He would probably be here to join me after he gathered the last of the straw. It felt so amazing; I would probably wait for him. The stacker grew louder as it neared. I opened my eyes and smiled, waving as he drew closer.

Wait.

Shading my forehead from the sun, I squinted my eyes to clear my view. My dad hadn't been wearing a blue shirt. And he wasn't wearing a baseball hat.

I locked eyes with Cade as the stacker closed in on me. My body burned with humiliation, but for all my pride I stood tall, keeping my eyes on his face, which wasn't wearing his usual cocky grin. I felt his eyes rake quickly down my body and back up again. Tingles erupted down my spine as his eyes left trails of heat in their wake. A smile tugged at his lips before he turned his head and pulled his hat down over his eyes as the stacker passed. Grabbing my wet shirt laying over the wheel line, I quickly yanked it back on over my head and stumbled to the tractor.

Since when did my dad teach Cade the fine art of driving his *precious* stacker?

Later that evening, I was in the barn, grabbing some tools for my dad, when I glanced at the chalkboard on my way out. Stopping short, I did a double-take. A slow, burning ran from the tip of my head, stopping for a moment in my belly, before moving down to my toes. Though, neither Cade nor I played any pranks that day, there was a notch scrawled below *my* name with today's date and Cade's initials.

T wo days later, after feeding cows, my dad pulled Cade and me aside. "Alright you two, I need you both to take the loader out to Willow Creek to finish fixing the fences. I've got the bucket loader loaded with new posts, and the holes are already dug, you four just need to drop them in, pound them in the dirt, and re-tie the wire to the posts. Jake and Dusty are already up there with the tractor and a four-wheeler, in case you need it."

My mouth dropped. "Willow Creek? That's five miles away."

Dad looked at me with his eyebrows raised. "Yup."

Cade snickered, but I would not let my dad off that easily. "There's only one seat in the loader. I'll take a four-wheeler."

"Dusty took one, and I need the other one here."

My stomach clenched in... apprehension. Yes. Apprehension. Not excitement. Not even a little bit. I tried another angle. "How about I take the truck?"

Dad shot me what could be interpreted as a sympathetic smile, but I wasn't quite convinced. "Sorry Kels, I need that."

"My car, then."

"With all the rain we've been getting lately, it's too muddy out there, the only thing getting through is the loader." He turned to

Cade. "Son, go start the loader and get it warming up. Kels will meet you there in a minute."

Son? He was calling him son now?

"Yes, sir." I could feel Cade's laughing eyes on me, but I kept my gaze firmly locked on my dad. He turned and strode toward the loader.

Once he was out of earshot, I made my case, glaring at my dad and folding my arms. "Dad. I just broke off an engagement. I'm not sitting on Cade's lap to drive *five miles* up a bumpy road. You have to think of something else for me to do."

"Kels, I rode in the loader to the north corral with Dusty yesterday. There was plenty of room to sit on the armrest."

"Then why don't you ride with Cade?"

His lips twitched the slightest bit before reminding me gently just who was boss. "I've got to be here. I've got a guy coming to deliver some grain in a few minutes. You'll be fine. Go."

I had to hand it to him, his look remained stoic, firm even, as he motioned me toward the loader—toward Cade—but his eyes had a hint of a twinkle.

"Kels, hold up."

I paused, turning around to look at him again. He scratched his head and put his hands in his pockets before taking them back out again. "Listen, I just wanted to say that I'm sorry about what happened with that kid."

"Parker." I folded my arms, scoffing a bit even, as I had to laugh.

"Sure. I just want you to know, I'm real proud of you. Your mom and I had been worried about this ever since you started dating that boy. He was a nice enough kid. He might make somebody else a good husband, but he wasn't for you, was he?"

I swallowed, not sure why I had tears welling up in my eyes. "No, he wasn't."

"I'm glad you were finally honest with yourself, kiddo."

He started to turn away before I stopped him with my words. "Dad, why were you and mom so worried? What did you see about me and Parker that made you feel that way?"

His eyes pierced into mine as he rubbed his chin thoughtfully. "You were always so fun and full of life growing up. You just had this brightness about you—this fun, loving light. Then you went to college and when you came home, you were so different, so serious all the time. Then, all of a sudden, you were marrying a kid who took himself just as seriously. What I'm trying to say is, that's not a bad thing, it can be good, but... you lost your spark, Kels." He motioned toward Cade sitting inside the loader. "And I noticed every time I threw you and Williams together, you got it back. It was so fun to see, I couldn't help myself."

My mouth dropped open. I moved to swat his arm. "You dirty dog. I wondered why you kept putting us together."

He grinned, sidestepping my advances. "My conscience is now clear. All right, enough of this mushy stuff. Go fix my fence."

As I approached the lumbering machine, Cade was already sitting in the cab. I could feel his eyes on me as I grew closer, so I made sure to hide any trace of my residual smile from my talk with my dad. I put my foot in the first rung of the ladder and hoisted myself up.

My dad was a use-it-until-it's-broken kind of guy. Even if it gets broken, he's the type of guy to fix it again and again until it's *really* broken. Even at that point, the brokenness is negotiable. He's had this front loader on the farm since before I was born. The dang thing had been tweaked and fixed and put back together so much, it was a real shocker it still worked. Technically. If you consider driving some-where in the seven to eight mile per hour range, working. Which meant that this 'innocent' ride my dad was forcing me to go on, would take us close to forty-five minutes.

Cade was sitting with his arms resting casually on the top of the wheel. He wore a short sleeved, button-down plaid shirt with a base-ball hat slung low over his forehead. He did not look sexy with his hat on. Not even a little bit. I was not at all worried about myself being locked in a tractor for almost an hour with Cade. He leaned forward and held the door open for me when I reached the top rung of the ladder.

"Hey, Red."

"Cade."

He scooted over in his seat and motioned for me to sit on the three inches left of his chair, which left me to wonder where the rest of my hips were supposed to go. The invitation in Cade's amused eyes answered my question, scaring the crap out of me, so I sat on the armrest.

"Chicken," Cade said as I closed the door tight. He revved up the engine and began inching us forward. Inching, because that is literally how fast six miles an hour feels in a loud, noisy piece of machinery.

I shifted in my seat. The cab inside the loader narrowed up the sides, which meant I couldn't sit up straight. My head and neck were bent at a weird angle, and the armrest jabbed indecently up one side of my rear end.

I turned behind me to check our progress the same time Cade hit a huge bump in the road. The movement jolted me off my seat (although the word *seat* is quite a generous term) and right onto Cade's legs.

"Red, why are you playing hard to get? I offered you this seat when you got here."

I scrambled off of him and back to my bike seat, looking behind us to see the crater we must have fallen into. Instead, I discovered that the bump in the road was just a small hole, which had been on the *opposite* side of the road. He would have had to aim for it to...

"Are you *trying* to hit all the potholes?"

"Who? Me?"

I grabbed an armful of his shirt. "No pranks in the loader or I swear, I'll make your life miserable."

"My mind's still blank from the last prank you played on me."

His teasing eyes fell on mine and my stomach flipped sideways, remembering the fervor in his gaze as I rinsed off in the field.

"That wasn't a prank. I thought you were my dad."

"Ew. This isn't Kentucky."

I pushed at his shoulder while he laughed. "Until you've bailed straw in an open cab tractor on a hot day, you don't understand the torture. The clothes come off at the end."

"So, this happens every year then? When's the next showing? Is there another matinee I can catch?"

"Shut up," I said, my smile breaking free.

I adjusted so I sat only on my right bum cheek, the left having gone officially numb.

"Do you want me to trade you seats for a bit?"

I turned to look at him. "Did you just volunteer to do something nice for me?"

"Don't let it go to your head."

My eyes narrowed, studying him closely. "I don't buy it."

He held up his hands in protest. "I swear. It's just a gentlemanly offer."

"Well I don't see one of those around here, so I think I'm okay for right now."

Another lurch in the road had me falling, once again, stomach first onto Cade's lap. His quick reflexes stopped my face from smashing into the right side of the tractor. He helped me to sit up, his sudden warmth and nearness kicking my nerves into overdrive. I tried to rise, to go back to my numbing corner of the cab, when his arm snaked around me, pulling me back onto his lap.

Instantly, I tried to resist his warmth, his sweetness, but he held tight.

"Settle down, hotshot. Just try this for a bit. It's got to be better than the armrest."

"You're thinking way too highly of yourself."

"Believe me, I am hating this as much as you are."

His low drawl in my ear raised the hairs on my neck. I looked at him then, his arm clamped around my waist, my back and side pressed up against his stomach, and my heart gave the tiniest thrill. The tiniest *hint* of a thrill really. Practically nothing. It definitely didn't have anything to do with the sudden smile he flashed me as he pulled me closer. Nope. Not at all. My heart had just finished stomping on another and was closed for business for the next fore-seeable future.

We rode in silence for a stretch, neither of us speaking. Our only conversation sounded through darting glances and self-conscious smiles. It turned into a game of sorts, each of us sneaking glances at the other, only to flit our eyes out the window before being caught. I couldn't keep my eyes off of him. Not just his face, but his strong hands at the wheel and the tight muscles and veins peeking out of his forearm. It turns out, I didn't need words with Cade to make my heart pound and my temperature rise.

"If you relax a bit, you might feel more comfortable."

I glanced down at my body. My arms were folded, and I was facing forward, trying to keep us a respectable, working distance apart, even though I was literally sitting on his lap. It was ridiculous that my dad had me ride in the loader such a long way with Cade and he *knew* it. I would not let him have any satisfaction (or me, apparently).

"I'm fine."

"Liar."

Looking over at him, I asked, "What do you mean?"

He let out an impatient scoff. "You look like you're on your way to church."

I smirked. "Some of us are more comfortable at church than others."

He rolled his eyes. "You have some serious trust issues."

My mouth gaped open. "What? What trust issues?"

"Are you serious?" He shook his head. "Look at you. Arms folded, sitting straight as a board… everything closed off." He glanced down at my feet. "Even your ankles are crossed."

"So. What does that matter?"

"You keep the world out. Open up and let the sunshine in, Red. I'll only bite a little bit."

I glanced at his posture, even with me on his lap, his legs were sprawled out in front of him, his left arm draped across my waist, while his right arm rested casually on the steering wheel. He had the look of a man ready to take on the world, assured and confident. I found myself a bit jealous.

"So, what do you suggest I do?"

Cade shifted me again. He grabbed my right hand and swung it around over his head, dropping it onto his shoulders. He leaned down and uncrossed my ankles and pulled my feet and legs over his lap. So now, the old armrest was my backrest, my butt sat low in the three inches of space on the chair beside Cade, and my arm draped across his shoulders with my legs dangling from his lap. This sudden, but smoking hot maneuver, had not been anticipated by myself, so in a matter of seconds, I went from being a choir girl on her way to Sunday service to draped across his lap like somebody 'in da club.' With my arm now around his shoulders, if I wanted to, I could very nearly lay my head across his chest and smell his cologne under his neck. If I wanted to. Which I didn't. Obviously. Closed for business.

He gave me a lazy grin, shifting me closer, his arm resting comfortably on my knee, his hand at the wheel. "Red, sometimes we have to do things for work we just don't want to do."

I smiled, blushed a fiery red, and fought off the butterflies chasing around in my stomach for the rest of the drive. Trying to resist Cade Williams when he got his flirt on was like eating pancakes without slathering it first in maple syrup. It could be done, but then all you had to eat was dry, bland tasteless pancakes. And I hated dry pancakes. I could almost hear my dad laughing from here.

21

Reasons Cade Williams is the worst
(junior high - current)

81.

82.

83.

A t least once a summer growing up, Tessa and I had a long-standing tradition of spending the night on the trampoline at my parents' house. It had been three years since we'd had our last outdoor sleepover, and we were determined to hold on to one more

childhood ritual before being swept away by the conventions of
adulthood.

While my plans for marriage had fallen through, there was a
good chance I would be getting a real job sometime this year, or
possibly going back to school, and I may never have summers off
again. I wasn't sure I was ready to let all of this go just yet. I had just
reacquainted myself with the farm, and soon I'd be leaving again,
coming back only for a long holiday or weekend. The future made
me both anxious and excited, and a little sad. It was the end of a
wonderful phase of life, with a childhood so many could only wish
for, and I couldn't help feeling a bit melancholy as Tessa and I
climbed onto the trampoline and snuggled down into our sleeping
bags under a bed of shimmering stars.

"It is so hot," Tessa said. She flopped her legs out of her sleeping
bag. "Nobody knows we're out here, right?"

"I didn't tell anybody."

We had agreed to keep our sleeping arrangement quiet from the
men on the ranch to hopefully avoid any mayhem, so we snuck out to
the trampoline long after Jake and Dusty had left for the night. I
could only imagine the fun the boys would have if they knew we were
out here. Logan, who was home for the weekend to go to some family
event with Courtney, was the one I was worried about in particular,
but he went to bed thirty minutes before we snuck outside.

"You were smart to wear a tank top." Tessa eyed my shirt
longingly.

"I'll probably regret it in the middle of the night, but I couldn't
stand the thought of putting anything with sleeves on my body."

"So, how are you doing? With the Parker thing?"

I tucked a piece of hair behind my ear. "I'm good. I've felt the
rainbow of emotions, but mostly, I'm good. It feels right. I just need to
figure out what to do now.

There was a moment of silence before, she asked, "Can I tell you
something? I didn't know how to tell you before, but now seems like a
good time."

My body clenched. "Yeah."

"I'm glad you broke up with Parker."

I sucked in a breath. I sat for a moment, not knowing what to say, but Tessa wasn't finished.

"You were different around him."

"At the time, I thought that was a good thing."

"I loved the old Kelsey before Parker, so I saw no need for changes, but I've just noticed how much more fun you've had this summer, being away from him. You never used to laugh much around him. You were always so serious and worried about what your hair looked like, or whether Parker would like your outfit. You'd spend all day in the library. Not that those things were bad, but it's just nice to see you acting more like yourself again. Although, I think we have somebody else to thank for that."

I smiled and shook my head slightly. The sound of the sprinklers and crickets settled over us then as I thought on her words for a moment.

"How are things with you and Cade lately? I haven't heard you complain about him in a while."

After the mountain lion ordeal on the cattle drive, I hadn't told Tessa anything else. I couldn't tell her about the chat around the campfire and my body still burned up thinking about his hug. I mean, it was just a hug. But... that hug. Even if I *could* find the words to explain what happened that night, the words would only cheapen it somehow. I couldn't even begin to describe the loader ride to Willow Creek.

"We haven't talked much. So, nothing to complain about there." Ugh. I should have gone with something else; Tessa would see right through that.

She laughed softly. "Did you know that I was always jealous of you and Cade back in high school?"

I rolled over to gape at her. "Of me and Cade? Why? We fought all the time."

"I wouldn't call it fighting. A fun, hot guy in our class was constantly seeking you out, even if it was to tease you. I never had anything like that."

"He sought me out to make my life miserable. And yes, you did. You guys were friends. Behind my back, I might add."

She held up her hands in protest. "We sat by each other for *one* class and you never let me hear the end of it! Do you want to know what we talked about most of the time?"

No. Yes. Maybe. "I mean... if you want to tell me..."

"I'll give you one wild guess. He didn't come up with *all* his own pranks."

My mouth dropped open. "Are you serious?!"

Tessa laughed, blocking my kick to her leg. "I just helped with a couple of them. But what I'm trying to say is that even in high school, it was so obvious that he liked you. If you guys could have just stopped with all the pranks, there would have been a lot more fireworks. Do you realize how much of *our* relationship was spent talking about Cade?"

My hands crept upward and cupped my burning cheeks. As much as I tried to stamp down my feelings, my heart betrayed me with shameful delight at her words. "I'm guessing it was much more than I ever realized." How many nights had we spent plotting and scheming... all for Cade. I hadn't ever thought about Tessa's feelings. I had just figured she was right there with me.

I shook my head slowly, thinking back on our childhood. "Tess, I'm so sorry. I was always so wrapped up in revenge that I never thought about how it affected you. How much I let him get between us. I promise, I never meant to hurt you."

"I know. Don't feel bad, he..."

We both gasped as two buckets worth of water fell from the sky above us in slow motion, drenching us and our sleeping bags within seconds. Coughing and sputtering, we rolled over onto our stomachs to see Cade and Logan standing there, with satisfied grins filling their faces. Mortified, I recalled the last few minutes of our conversation and hoped they hadn't heard much. As Cade's amused gaze found mine, I slowly shook my head, a dangerous smile on my lips, and revenge clouding my vision. I would worry about that later. This was a time for war.

"Ready?" I whispered to Tessa, wiping the water out of my eyes.

"They are so dead," was her reply.

We both reached under our saturated sleeping bags and found our own super-size soakers, filled to the brim with freezing water we had prepared for such an occasion. Jumping off the trampoline, we chased the boys around the yard like children, shooting them with our weapons, all the while squealing and laughing and soaking up those last days of summer.

I could have pretended not to feel a thrill of delight when Cade caught me in his arms, pulling me back against him to steal my gun. I could have pretended not to feel the heated graze from his fingers on my bare stomach in the struggle. I could have pretended not to feel the warmth in his gaze when he turned me around to face him.

But I didn't.

I felt everything: the look in his eyes as he leaned closer, chaos and laughter and water flying everywhere around us. My eyes closed, my lips parted, waiting... until suddenly... I felt myself blasted with the soaker all down the front of my body. I could have pretended not to see the wink he threw me, or feel the smack on my butt he gave me as he moved around me.

But I didn't.

I felt everything.

The dirty cheat.

"What's the bet tonight, boys?" I asked as I joined Cade, Jake, and Dusty on the basketball court after chores a few nights later.

Cade looked up as I approached, and did a casual perusal of me with his eyes, lingering a bit longer on my legs before he said, "What's with the knee highs, Red? Bringing the nineties back?"

I made a face at him as Jake and Dusty each chuckled. I glanced down to tonight's basketball outfit. Since we played nearly every night and my laundry could not keep up, the shorts were an old pair my sister Amanda had left behind. They were a bit shorter than my usual basketball shorts—hitting me about mid-thigh. I had felt a bit self-conscious, so when I found some old knee-high soccer socks in my drawer, I couldn't resist.

"Actually, old man," Dusty said over his shoulder to Cade, while shooting a three-pointer, "knee-highs are coming back. All the girls in Eugene wear them now." Which, to be fair to Cade, Eugene was typically about five to seven years behind the times. If this was just now hitting Eugene, who knows what the real fashion was everywhere else.

Cade made a face. "Why?"

"Maybe they don't want guys ogling their legs all the time," I interjected, sitting on the concrete to stretch.

Cade jerked his eyes off my legs and mumbled as he turned away, "Then maybe they should wear pants." He joined the boys under the basket, while I pretended I didn't hear him, and that I wasn't blushing.

"So, here's the bet," Jake began after we had each taken a few warm-up shots.

"Oh, here we go," I said, rolling my eyes good-naturedly.

Jake laughed. "Don't worry, Kels, I think you'll like it."

"Well, maybe not at first," Dusty interjected, jabbing Jake in the ribs, snorting with laughter.

Cade walked over to us. "So, what's the plan? Somebody gonna have to run through Tom Bingham's pasture, buck naked?"

"I'd hate for you to put ol' Tom's cows through that again," Jake said.

Cade puffed up his chest and flexed his muscles. "It's true. They'll never be the same after seeing all this."

"Alright, what's the bet, ladies? We're burning daylight here," I taunted as I peeled my gaze away from Cade's physique. I stole the ball out of Jake's hands and took a shot, trying to look cool. Airball.

"The teams are me and Kelsey versus Dusty and Cade." Jake grabbed the ball from my hands before I could embarrass myself again. "Now, this is important. I'm only going to tell you what happens when a team loses. To find out what the winners get, you have to wait until after the game."

"I don't want to play if I don't know what I'm playing for," I said.

"It's all good, I promise." Jake smiled at me. An all-knowing, mischievous, gleam, with an edge sort of smile. The kind of smile that makes a person feel... unsettled.

"I'm not eating anything gross."

Technically, I have never had to eat anything gross, but last week I had to watch Jake grind up an earthworm into a smoothie. I still dry heave a bit in my mouth whenever I think about it.

"You'll be safe then."

Jake looked over at Cade. "You in?"

Cade nodded. "Let's hear your terms, man."

"Alright, drumroll please... If Kelsey and I lose, she has to go on a date with Cade, while I do her chores."

———

The game was intense. Crazy intense.

For me.

Because it was rigged.

Watching Jake lob a backward granny shot through the air was my first clue. Jake 'forgetting' Dusty wasn't on his team was my second. But it was about the time Jake faked a sprained ankle while handing the ball to Dusty to 'steal' that I decided to kick it in gear. Yelling at Jake did nothing. All I got in return was a cocky, knowing grin thrown in my direction.

I had been set up.

So, I determined I'd win without him. But, I was only 5'6 and every one of those boys (except Dusty) was well over six feet tall.

Rebounding and shooting became a problem. Once Cade got over the initial shock of the bet, he seemed to settle into the idea of me losing quite quickly. No doubt planning all sorts of torturous things for me on our date. Thanks to Jake's cryptic rules, I wasn't sure it would be any better for me if I actually won the game, but I had to try, my pride demanded it, and there was no way I would ever let them know that the thought of going out with Cade secretly thrilled me.

Another breakaway three-point swished by Cade. The game ended when the first team scored twenty points. The score was nineteen to seven. It was over for me, but I kept my head high while my insides quivered with nervous anticipation. It was our ball and Butterfingers Jake was bringing it down the court. Hopping up and down as he dribbled like a five-year-old, he pretended to wait for me to be open. Which I was. Very open. Too open.

Suspiciously open.

Just as Jake lobbed the ball in my direction, my feet left the ground as Dusty swooped in from behind, locking me in a giant hug and pinning my arms down. Cade "stole" the ball, ran to the basket, and dunked it for the win.

Dusty set me down and ran over to the boys to join them in their celebration. Dropping to my knees, I threw myself down on the concrete, sulking dramatically.

Cade squatted down beside me.

"What's the matter, Red? You just won yourself the best date of your life."

I groaned.

Jake smirked at me. "I've never been so excited to lose before."

"You guys are the worst."

"I'm sorry we lost it, Kels. I don't know what happened back there."

I stood up, brushing off the dirt with trembling hands. Excited hands. But now was not the time to give that away. "You're such a punk," I told Jake. "You better get comfortable doing my chores. I'm going to tell my dad I feel like cleaning all the barn stalls tomorrow."

He laughed. "Worth it. The look on your face when we started playing was priceless!"

Cade stood, staring at me with a knowing grin on his face.

I glared at him too, holding back the smile threatening to escape. "Were you in on this too?"

"Nope. I was just as surprised as you were." Turning, he spoke to Jake, "But you did say she has to do anything I say, right?"

"Yup. And she has to be happy and nice the whole time." Jake grinned, slapping Cade on the shoulder. Then, shooting Cade a warning look, he added, "Anything within reason, man."

"Happy *and* nice? This really will be a date to remember."

I made a face at Cade while he laughed. "Well, Red, I'd better take off so I can plan the perfect night. You like mushrooms, right? And extreme sports... skydiving, bungee jumping, cliff diving...?"

I gave him my best withering glare. "I'm not scared of you."

He raised his eyebrows. "Challenge accepted. I'll pick you up at 6 tomorrow. Bring a change of clothes... I have a feeling we're going to pack a lot of... activities into this date."

When he sauntered toward the bunkhouse, I turned to Dusty and Jake, giving them both a friendly shove. "A date with Cade? What were you thinking?"

Jake shot me a smug grin. "This has been a *long* time coming."

"What?"

"You heard me. You guys are so pathetic and disgustingly into each other. You're driving us crazy, so we thought we'd nudge you along."

I let out a huff in response, but couldn't think of anything to retort.

"And now that you've finally broken up with what's his name, we wanted to get you back on the market."

"What was the prize for the winner?"

Jake smirked. "It didn't matter cause you were going to lose either way, but Cade's prize was that he gets to take you out, while Dusty does his chores."

"You're pretty proud of yourselves, aren't you?"

"Just remember who you have to thank at the wedding," Dusty said as he threw his arm around me while they walked me to the house.

"Maybe I'll just marry one of you."

"Hmm... " Dusty stroked his chin in contemplation for a moment. "Naw, you're too mean. I like my women to adore me and bake cookies all day long."

"I'll make you cookies."

Dusty shuddered. "Please don't."

"If no other guy will take you, I'll keep you in mind," Jake said as I walked up the front steps.

"You guys are so sweet."

"Remember," Jake called out as I stepped inside. "You have to be nice and do whatever Cade says."

"Within reason," I shot back, just as the door closed.

22

Qualities I want in a ~~Husband~~ Man
(circa junior high - revisited)

~ Handsome
~ Dark hair preferable, ~~but will settle for blonde if there are~~
  ~~dimples~~
~ Makes me laugh
~ ~~Rich~~
~ Be a good dad (play with kids) - Inconclusive - but, if he's
  anything like his dad...
~ will help me wash dishes
~ Loves to cook (Inconclusive data)
~ Treats me nice
~ Feeds me when hungry
~ Knows how to ride bareback (definitely need to investigate)
~ ~~Does not like to prank~~

W hat exactly was one supposed to wear on a surprise date
with a guy I secretly liked but openly despised? When I had
asked Cade that morning what I should wear, he just smirked and
told me to bring a jacket and a swimsuit. I had half a mind to scrap

that last part. What woman on earth likes to prance around in a bathing suit on a date? But at the last minute, I stuffed my gray and teal one piece in my backpack. As for my outfit, I decided on a pair of skinny jeans, brown ankle boots, and a loose-fitting, rose-colored top. Hopefully, it gave the impression of dressy, but without caring too much. I curled my hair into loose beach waves and added a touch of mascara and lip-gloss because apparently, I did care a little.

I gave myself one last look in the mirror before turning to leave my room when I heard tapping at my window. Figuring it was Dusty or Jake coming to give me last-minute instructions, I pulled back my curtains.

A handsome Cade, wearing jeans and a fitted, dark blue t-shirt, and his ever-present baseball hat, stood outside my window. With an over-the-top, alluring grin, he held out a handful of dandelions still covered with dirt.

I shook my head slowly, biting my lip as I opened the window. My heart picked up speed while anticipation blasted through my body.

"Hey, Red." Giving me a quick once over, he gave a low whistle. "You clean up pretty good."

"Thanks. You're not so bad yourself. Ever heard of a door?"

"Dusty told me every girl dreams of guys throwing rocks at their windows." He handed me the dirt-crusted bouquet.

"Thanks. Dandelions are my very favorite weeds." I smiled and placed the weeds on my desk.

Cade was grinning as I awkwardly attempted to crawl out my window without looking like an idiot. Somewhere between getting my legs out, with my upper body still stuck in my room, I felt his hands at my waist, holding me steady as I dismounted with all the grace and finesse of an elephant. He released me as I hit the ground.

"Did you pack extra clothes?" he asked.

Groaning, I looked behind me at the backpack sitting on my bed, just out of reach from the window. Although my room was on the ground floor, the windows were up just high enough to be awkward.

Rolling his eyes, he put both of his hands on the windowsill and, like a cat, lifted himself into my room.

"You're either surprisingly agile, or that's not the first time you've done that," I said, drily.

He smirked. "Let's assume it's the first one."

He grabbed my bag and began walking back toward the window when he stopped. Looking around my bedroom slowly, a wicked smile growing on his face.

"Cade... let's go." I gave him my best warning voice, but he acted like he didn't hear me. Prowling around my room, he took his time looking at old high school photographs I had taped to my walls.

He raised his eyebrows suggestively as his hand rested on the top drawer of my dresser. "Underwear drawer?"

"Don't you dare."

"Let me just see if I need to change your name."

"Cade!" My body heat skyrocketed as every inch of me blushed a fiery red. I could very well run into the house and pull him out of my room, but I had too much good bait in that bedroom to take my eyes off him, even for a second.

Laughing, he started toward the window again, but as he rounded past my bed, he did a double-take at my journal sitting on my nightstand.

"Is that a diary?"

With my level of hysterics rising rapidly on the inside, I forced myself to remain outwardly calm.

"No."

"Oh good, then you won't mind if I take a quick peek then," he said as he walked toward the incriminating book.

"Cade Williams, don't you dare!"

He paused in his pursuit. "If I leave now, you're going to have to owe me one." He raised his eyebrows and stared at me before speaking slow and dangerous, "Do you want to owe me one?" Meandering closer to the window, he stayed within easy reach of the keeper of all my deepest, darkest, secrets.

My eyes drifted to my book. Though it mostly held recorded scuttles throughout our childhood, he was featured throughout that book a disconcerting amount. Too risky.

"Fine. I owe you one. Get out of my room."

"I guess there's always tomorrow, right?" he said as he crawled through the window.

"Nope, there isn't. That book definitely won't be there tomorrow."

He chuckled, leading me to his truck.

"Where are we going?"

"To get ice cream."

"Ice cream? Should I have eaten dinner before you picked me up?"

He opened the passenger door for me and scoffed as if I had offended his manhood. "I'll feed you dinner, Red. We'll just be too far out of town to get ice cream afterward, so we're getting dessert first."

I smiled to myself as I climbed inside his truck. The smell of fresh-cut hay mixed with a warm summer breeze filled the cab, along with a faint hint of his delicious cologne. Bits of hay and grain littered the floor, probably from his boots. A pair of ear pods were strewn on his dashboard next to his phone, and a pack of mint gum. I couldn't help but compare the truck to Parker's immaculate sports car he ran through the car wash at least once a week. When Cade's body settled into the driver's seat, and the rumble of the engine filled the evening, I knew without a doubt which vehicle was the clear winner.

The ride to town was uneventful but full of banter. We exited his pickup and were heading toward Daisy's ice cream shop when Cade stopped suddenly and pulled me to the side of the big store window.

"Woah, change your mind about the ice cream?"

He darted a quick glance through the window. "Does Robin Miller work here all the time?"

I peeked around his shoulder through the window, spying the woman in question looking bored at the counter. "I think she fills in sometimes. Her cousin owns Daisy's."

He leaned with his back against the brick building, looking very unsure of himself, which wasn't normal.

"What's going on?"

He stuck his hands in his pockets before taking them out to adjust his hat. "I went on a couple of dates with her earlier this summer and now she won't quit calling me. She's a nice girl and everything, but I don't know what to do. I've told her a few times now that I'm not interested. She showed up at the bunkhouse the other night. She left me another voicemail yesterday. She won't stop. It's like three or four times a week."

Jealousy... and... relief flooded my body. So *she* was Cade's mystery date. It wasn't nice, but Tessa and I have occasionally called her the town boa constrictor with how she attaches herself to guys and never lets them go. Many of our guy friends in high school had been caught in her coils.

He turned to me with his eyebrows raised. "How set are you on eating ice cream?"

I smirked. "Afraid of your girlfriend seeing us together?"

"She's not my girlfriend. She's more in the realm of a stalker."

I didn't have any real reason to be jealous. They went on a couple casual dates. He was not interested. He kindly told her that, but the thought of her not leaving him alone made my blood boil. Not a rolling boil like a crazy person, but a light simmer. Small bubbles. Either way, I was going to help. I folded my arms and looked at him.

"I'm willing to cash in on my 'debt'."

"Huh?"

"What I *owe* you for not snooping around my room."

He smiled. "Oh that. What's your plan?"

"We walk in there like we're on a date."

"Which we are," he interjected.

"And that's it. She'll see us together and maybe she'll finally get the hint."

He nodded slowly, his hand stroking his chin. "Not bad, Red, but I think for a target like Robin, we're gonna have to really sell it."

The look in his eyes turned gleaming with a side of mischievous, which made my heart race. "What do you mean?"

"I think we need to be more than just a date. We need to pretend we're together."

"Together, like *together* together?"

"Like hand-holding, butt grabbing, making out..."

The look I shot him didn't deter him one bit.

"You owe me, remember," Cade said, a smile playing on his lips. "I didn't want to cash that in this early, but..."

I regarded him for a long moment, keeping my elation carefully in check. "Fine. Hand holding only. The other options wouldn't be convincing."

He leaned in close to my ear as he opened the door for me and whispered, "I bet I'd convince you pretty quick." A blush rose to my cheeks as I felt the light smack on my butt as I passed him. I jabbed him in the ribs, but he only snickered and grabbed my hand as he walked me to the counter.

Trouble. That's what this was. Trouble. The chills and tingles erupted fiercely up and down my entire body when his hand closed over mine. If I didn't keep my guard up, I could wind up getting my heart stomped on, without him even aware of my misery.

Robin greeted us behind the counter. And by greeting, I meant a smile for Cade and a stare that could skin a cat tossed in my direction. There was almost enough tension in the air to make me want to release my hand from Cade's.

Almost.

"Hi, Cade," Robin said, a little too brightly. She glanced at me. "Hey, Kelsey."

We both said hi in unison. There was a long, awkward pause until Cade pulled me to the side in front of the freezer cases. I'm not sure how it happened, but somehow, my back ended up pressed against Cade's stomach as he hugged me from behind. He casually leaned over my left shoulder to browse the ice cream flavors.

"Laying it on a little thick, aren't you?" I whispered in his ear.

"I don't hear any complaints."

Before I could answer, Robin demanded behind the counter, "Are you guys dating or something?"

We both looked in her direction, but Cade spoke first. "Yeah. It's still new, but it seems to be going well."

I started pulling away, but my sorry attempt to escape flew out the window when he leaned over and kissed me quickly on the cheek before releasing me. "What flavor do you want, Red?"

It was all too familiar. Too right. Too natural. Too wrong. SO wrong. Wasn't it? I concentrated all my efforts on keeping my erratic elation in check. This was Cade Williams, for heaven's sake! Was I really on a date with my lifelong enemy? The destroyer of childhood happiness?

"Rocky Road," I said.

He smiled approvingly. "Robin, we need two cones with two scoops each of Rocky Road." Turning back toward me, he said, "I'm sure glad you didn't say bubblegum, or this would have been the world's quickest date."

"Hey, Robin, I'd like to change my order," I started to say, laughing as Cade pulled me into him and covered my mouth with his hand.

My stupid, flighty heart soared. This was going to be a very interesting night.

"Did you bring a sweatshirt?" Cade asked as we walked across my dad's farm after our ice cream run.

"A jacket, why?"

"You're going to want to put it on for this next part."

"What are we doing?" I asked, pulling my jacket out from my backpack.

He just smiled as he opened up the garage door to the shop. Walking inside, he sat on the blue ATV. The roar of the engine quickly filled the room.

A squeal of delight escaped my lips as I ran to the red four-wheeler. It felt like ages since I had gone on a four-wheeler ride. Growing up we mostly used them for work-related purposes, but I had always loved to ride all over the farm when the workday was over.

"Nope. This is my date. We take one four-wheeler." Cade motioned me to come toward him. I smiled slightly to myself as I made my way over to him.

"Well, you can't blame a girl for trying."

"To do what?"

Cade's eyes met mine as I reached him. My mouth dropped open to say something—not sure what.

"I thought so," he mumbled as his eyes darted down to my lips for the briefest of seconds. "Front or back?"

My eyes narrowed. "Back."

Taking my backpack from me, he stuffed it and his bag into the large toolbox sitting on the front grill of the ATV. Scooting forward, he held my arm steady as I climbed on behind him. Once I was settled, he backed out of the shop. Turning the machine, he revved the engine and pealed out, my legs flying upward as the momentum pushed me backward. My arms shot out, wrapping a death grip around Cade's waist.

"You did that on purpose."

"Did what?" Cade feigned innocence, but his left hand took hold of my right, as it laid across his stomach. I tucked my other hand inside his jacket pocket. My heart warmed and with no resistance left in me, I nuzzled my head closer until it rested lightly on the back of his shoulder.

Confusion and a strange calm came over me as we started climbing the trail up the mountain. I didn't know what it all meant, but at that moment, I was so messed up in my head that I was toying with the idea that this could make an excellent new normal. If Cade was playing some elaborate prank to win the war at the end of the summer, he would get the ultimate prize to finish me off.

My heart on a chopping block.

We ran out of trail when we reached the top of the hill. Dense pine trees surrounded a large patch of open meadow. A deep breath of mountain air filled my lungs as my soul was nearly bursting at the seams with memories from my happy childhood. I was happy to note that being here with Cade felt... normal. Or at least not as strange as I had anticipated. Cade climbed off the ATV and began rustling around in the toolbox in front of the four-wheeler seats. Grabbing a grocery sack full of something, he started toward the trees.

"Let's go, Red," he called over his shoulder. "I'm not done with you yet."

Smiling, I hopped off and ambled toward him, no longer caring that I had no idea what was in store for me. At this point, I was pretty sure I would follow him anywhere.

"Is this the part where you kill me?" I asked as we reached the trees. A gasp left my lips as I discovered a homemade fire pit, filled with firewood, kindling, and two camping chairs surrounding it.

"This is the part where I feed you," he said as he flung his sack on a camp chair, knelt by the woodpile, and began working on building a fire.

I could only stare at him. Not moving. It wasn't the fact that he was starting a fire, although watching a man build a fire was one of the most attractive things in the world. It wasn't the fact that he had brought a sack full of hot dogs and chips, even though roasting hot dogs over a fire was one of my favorite things to do. It wasn't even the fact that this guy, who had been tricked into this date yesterday evening, had still found the time—in between chores—to not only ride all the way here to set up the fire pit and chairs but to actually plan a date. A date that by all definition should have been dedicated to making these few hours in my life dreadful and humiliating, not wonderful.

It was the fact that he had done all of those things for me.

Me.

His lifelong antagonist. The thorn in his side. The anchovies to his pizza. The girl who lived for revenge and to make his life miserable. Until recently, I had kind of figured the feeling was mutual. Oh, he started a lot of the pranks, to be sure, but I had never hesitated to give it right back. Sometimes I would be laughing, sometimes I'd be furious, sometimes indifferent, but always... always, I'd be thinking about *him*. I hadn't even begun to realize how much a part of me he had become until suddenly, it was hard to imagine a life without Cade Williams.

He glanced up and caught me staring. Even then, I couldn't look away. He raised his eyebrows in question. I forced myself to swallow any of my usual sarcastic remarks that would kill the sweetness of the moment.

Clearing my throat, I asked, "What can I do to help?"

"So, what other form of torture do you have in store for me on this date?" I gave him a teasing smile to soften my question.

We were leaning back in our camp chairs, situated next to each other, having just finished eating. He had even remembered to bring mustard so the dinner was a win in my book. Roasting hot dogs together actually yielded a surprising amount of pleasant conversation, with Cade asking me questions about growing up on the ranch and my life in Moscow.

"Swimming. Or skinny-dipping depending on whether or not you brought your swimsuit."

"Oh, I definitely brought something to swim in."

He raised his eyebrows appreciatively. "Bikini?"

"Parka."

He rolled his eyes but smiled. "Eh, I don't care about swimming anymore."

My face burned with delight. My toes tingled. I hadn't noticed how close we were sitting until now. It felt a natural distance while we were eating, but now... I felt and observed every move he made. He shifted his arm. He leaned forward. He adjusted his baseball hat. All of these things I might not have noticed had our chairs been further apart, but that close, I felt, saw, and obsessed.

"See something you like, Red?"

He grinned at me with interest, as I startled.

"You wish," I said, shifting in my seat.

"We can go swimming if you want. That pond is just down the trail."

"I don't care."

Neither of us moved. We sat quietly, enjoying the beautiful sky streaked with orange and pink. The roaring fire had calmed and was giving way to the softly glowing embers below. The evening had grown chilly so we moved our chairs closer to the fire. Crickets were chirping. The crackling sounds of a campfire filled the air. Our legs had brushed on contact, stretched out near the fire, but neither of us drew away. The night was—in a word—cozy.

"Truth or Dare, Red?"

He looked over at me with a gleam in his eye. An unspoken challenge singed the air between us.

I groaned.

He smiled.

23

Journal Entry (circa - high school)

I had a ~~dream~~ nightmare that I kissed Cade Williams. All I will write for posterity's sake is that it was, surprisingly, a very nice kiss. Kind of hot, actually. Went on for about three minutes. Okay, it was closer to five.

"Doesn't matter what you choose," Cade said. "Either way I win."

"Truth." I grimaced, covering my eyes with my hands.

"Ahhh... let me think." Cade leaned back in his chair, sighing dramatically. "So many things I'd like to know."

"Do we get a pass?"

"We each get one pass."

"Get on with it then." I couldn't decide what would be worse, truth or dare. At least truth would involve me staying seated, not eating anything gross, and keeping all of my clothes on.

"I've got it. Have you been completely honest in this little prank war we've got going on?"

The dirt at my feet became fascinating.

"You didn't forget to add on a point for me, maybe?" Cade goaded, leaning closer.

At this point, I had all but turned the other direction in my chair.

"Did you have any incidents in the tractor a while back?"

"That's two questions!" I flung around to his laughing face.

"I think they're both the same." He grabbed my arms to keep me facing him. "Answer up or pass."

"Oh fine. I owe you one stupid point."

"What happened?"

"Your dumb mouse ran up my leg and I had to strip down to my underwear while *freaking out* and driving the tractor to get it out."

Cade burst out laughing so hard he fell out of his chair. Watching his shaking shoulders on the ground, I was tempted to kick him, but ended up giggling behind my hand instead.

Finally, he sat back down, wiping his eyes.

"Are you finished?"

"Not quite. Just so I can picture the whole thing accurately, were you wearing the reds or a different color this time?"

"Shut up," I said, my face in my hands, hiding my grin. "Your turn. Truth or Dare?"

"Dare."

Crap. I was the worst at picking out things like a dare on the spot. "Um... stand up and sing 'I'm a Little Teapot' with the hand motions."

He rolled his eyes. "Pass."

"Really? You're wasting your pass on that? It's an easy one."

"That's all you got for me? Sing a song?" He shook his head. "You'd better be careful picking a dare from me. Your turn."

"Well, on that note, most definitely, truth."

He studied me for a moment, his mind calculating. "Does your diary have my name in it anywhere?"

Swallowing my sudden nervousness at the question, I slipped a smirk on my face and answered. "Yes. I made sure to document it all, just in case anything ever goes to trial."

He snorted. "Anything recent?"

Curse my skin and its ability to create a blush quick as a wink. "That's two questions. I don't have to answer that one."

A slow grin crossed his face. "I think you already did, Red. I pick truth."

"Fine. How did you get a hold of my black bra?" When Cade started to laugh, I grabbed his shirt and threatened, "And if I find out you went into my room and went through my drawers, I will kill you. Or I'll tell my dad and *he'll* kill you."

He held up his hands like a white flag. "I promise, it wasn't anything like that. I found it lying out on the grass by your car. You must have dropped it when you moved home from school."

My mouth fell open. Tessa had told me to put all my underthings in a sack so nothing would fall out, but I insisted they would be fine sitting loose in my laundry basket.

I poked his arm. "You kept it that long!"

"I didn't even know if it was yours for sure, but it gave me such a great idea for your laundry, I couldn't resist holding onto it for a while." His eyebrows rose slightly as he added, "So... B cup, huh?"

"Next question!"

His deep laughter rumbled and for a moment. I forgot my embarrassment and let the sound cover me like a warm blanket.

The game continued onward, each of us trading truths at request. It turned out to be the perfect game for a potentially awkward first date.

"Alright. Why did you decide not to try out for the minors?" I asked him. "I already know you didn't want to play, but I want to know why. I thought all guys dream of fame and riches."

"Every guy does. Heck, I still do." He flashed me a smile. "But you can play for the minors for years with crappy pay, always hoping to get drafted into the majors, but the chances are pretty slim."

"Doesn't your brother still play?"

"Yeah. He plays with the Sea Dogs in Portland."

I waited for more but none came. "But didn't you want to try it? Just to see? You were good enough."

He nudged my shoulder with his. "Thanks."

I nudged him back. "Why?"

"The game was a dead-end for me. I knew I needed to make a change." He looked at me like his pathetically short and cryptic answer might pass my examination. I gave him a look to continue.

He sighed. "I played for four years at Colorado, and the first couple years were fun. Busy, but we had a good group of guys. But this last year, I realized that my whole life was baseball, and the closer I got to graduation it stopped being a game and started being a business." He rubbed the back of his neck with his hand. "Anyway, even with all that, I was still set to try out. Just to see what happened, but when it got closer, I kept thinking about my dad."

"Your dad?"

"Yeah. If I did get drafted for the minors, I'd be on the road all the time. It would be hard to help raise a family if I'm not there. My brother lives for baseball and just got his second divorce. He has two kids with two different moms. His life's a mess. It's hard on his kids. I'm not interested in that kind of life. So, I got thinking of other... ideas and career options, which brought me here."

My chest warmed at his admission. "Your dad was a great guy."

He nodded, staring into the fire.

"So, you want a family then?"

He looked at me like I had grown two heads. "Yeah. Don't you?"

"Yes. It's just hard to imagine the guy who once taped a paper onto my back that said 'For an average time call...' as a dad."

Chuckling, he said, "I forgot about that. You're not so innocent yourself, you know. Somewhere, poor Jenny Miller has a fake diamond ring she got on a date with me." He tapped my foot. "But I can still imagine you as a mom. A good one, too."

My heart both burned and hammered as our conversation took a steep turn. I sat very still, somehow afraid that any movement would release all of the butterflies swirling around in my belly. I tried to steer us back to safety. To normalcy.

"Have you liked working with Stitch?"

"Yeah. I like being around cows and ranches. I've never wanted to be stuck working in a stuffy office anywhere." He smiled at me then, no doubt thinking about our argument from earlier in the summer.

"Would you ever want to coach?"

"Oh yeah. One day, me and my wife will have enough kids to fill a baseball team. That's the dream."

I laughed. "What is that, ten kids?"

"Just nine, but I could play catcher, so we could squeak by with eight."

Goosebumps traveled up and down my arms and legs when he glanced at me saying the word "we." He couldn't have meant it how my body seemed to take it, but for some reason, I had to remind myself quite often that night that this was *Cade Williams*. I tried to think of all the dirty, rotten things this handsome, funny scoundrel had ever pulled on me, but then he smiled and I forgot everything all over again.

He nudged my arm. "Your turn."

"Truth."

"Chicken."

I bumped his leg—his warm, solid, muscular leg, which happened to be leaning into mine. Which caused my heart to beat faster. Which caused my breathing to be more shallow and a bit more erratic, but I chalked it all up to being nervous for my next question.

"Where do you see yourself in ten years? What's your dream life?"

Of all the questions in the world, I was least expecting this. The very question I had been asking myself the past few weeks. I stared quietly into the fire for a few moments. Never in a million years had I anticipated a date with Cade to end up here, around a campfire, on the verge of spilling all my secrets. But the heat from our bodies kept me warm, his eyes were curious, and heaven help me, I wasn't moving.

I drew a breath. "This."

"What? A campfire?"

I laughed softly. "Sure, that too." Feeling unsure of myself more than ever and with a shaky voice, I bared the most secret part of my soul to Cade Williams. "I would love a ranch, some animals, a few kids, and a husband, all tucked away on a piece of property outside of town. Maybe a few willow trees and a creek, and a white house with a big porch." I gave him a small smile. "But that's not asking for much, is it?"

He shrugged as he looked back toward the fire. "Depends on who you're asking. Did your fiancé know about this?"

The smile left my face. "Ex-fiancé. No. He couldn't have. I didn't even know it until I came back home. I acted differently at school. I *was* different at school. I wanted so badly to be... different at college than what I was in high school, that I changed. I spent so much time chasing an idea in my head, that I forgot to see if it actually fit. I let myself forget about what *this* life meant to me. Until I came here and got reminded of how much I do love it." I shot Cade a wry smile. "This life seems possible here, but at school... I don't know, it just seemed more old-fashioned, I guess."

"It seems that way, but somebody has to do the ranching in this country, it might as well be you. But I thought you were all set to be a news anchor?"

Cade threw another log on the fire and the newfound flames drew me into a trance. It already seemed like a lifetime ago when I was planning to move to Santa Cruz with Parker. I used to imagine myself living the big city life. My high heels clicking on the pavement. Dress suits and important meetings in tall buildings. Lunch dates. Co-workers. Astonishing the world one news report at a time. But here, now, wearing an old jacket with dirt in my hair, sitting in front of a campfire in the mountains... it seemed like someone else's dream because I couldn't imagine anywhere else on earth I'd rather be.

"I've been thinking more about *teaching* communications. I'd have to go back to school and get a teaching certificate, but I'm afraid the big city news anchor idea died with Parker."

He leaned forward, popping his knuckles. "And how are you feeling about your breakup?"

"I should be more broken-hearted. I feel bad that I blindsided him but looking back, there were so many warning signs. I wanted to come home instead of being with him, I didn't want to make any wedding decisions, he never fit in with my family, the whole dress thing..." I trailed off before adding, "I should have been heartbroken, and while I was sad about how it all played out, the biggest emotion I have felt so far has been relief."

Cade watched me for a few moments before he said, "Good."

We sat in the quiet for a moment, breathing in this newly charged air between us.

"Are we still playing?" I asked. "Because it's your turn. Truth or Dare?"

"Truth. Because you're a pansy when it comes to dares."

Two could play this game. I took a deep breath. "Alright. What happened on Prom night?"

"Pass."

"You already wasted your pass. I told you to sing."

Cade's head fell into his hands. "You really want to do this now?"

I held my arms out. "What time would be convenient for you?"

Cade sat up in rigid, uncomfortable silence. "What do you know about that night?" he asked.

"All I know is that as I stepped out into the hallway from the school gym trying to find Mike, I saw you take his shirt in your hands and punch him hard in the face. Then Mike punched you back and it went on for a few more minutes, even when I was yelling at you to stop. Then we all got kicked out and prom night was ruined." My words spat out more bitterly than I had anticipated. It had been four years, time had lessened the wound, but reliving the night again with the culprit right in front of me brought the heat, once again, bubbling up inside of me. "When I confronted you at your house, you still wouldn't give me any reason. So I had to think it was personal against me, like everything else you'd done to me our entire lives."

Cade shook his head. "You were so mad that night, you wouldn't have believed me if I did try to explain."

"Try me."

"What?"

"I'm listening now."

He put his head down a bit lower as he adjusted his baseball hat. For a moment, both of us were lost in our memories of that day. I had driven to Tessa's house that afternoon so we could get ready together. The room had quickly exploded with clothes all over the floor, makeup, and the two of us singing and dancing to the latest country song on Tessa's playlist. We had both been shocked at our dates. Mike Ramsey from the baseball team had asked me out. While he certainly had a reputation among our school (and community) as a hothead, he had been nothing but nice to me. He had light brown hair, a medium build, and a nice smile. I said yes.

Tessa was going with Tom Jones, and there was a big group date of friends going with us. I had been surprised to discover that our group also included Cade. He was going with Marissa Hill, a very peppy cheerleader. Knowing Cade would be in our group had made me nervous, but Tessa assured me that she would keep an eye on him. It would be a low blow to play pranks on a girl on her prom night, even for Cade.

There was just something so magical about Prom. The last dance as seniors. We were weeks away from graduating. We got to dress up in beautiful dresses and look fancy for our dates. I had been deter-mined to put aside my feelings for Cade and just enjoy the evening.

We had arrived at the prom only ten minutes earlier when the fight broke out. We were all kicked out, both boys were bleeding heavily, so Tessa and I caught a ride home with another couple from our group. Everybody was annoyed, and nobody had answers. After being dropped off at my house, I changed my clothes quickly and jumped in my car to drive to Tessa's house to commiserate over our lost night.

I had told myself to drive straight to Tessa's house. Begged, even, but with shaking hands and a stomach clenched in tight knots, I found myself taking a left when I should have turned right. No good would come from this. But I was hurt and angry and it just so happened that Cade's house was only a little bit out of my way.

His house was dark when I parked my parents' Buick next to Cade's truck in the driveway. The porch lights were off and, because he lived on a lone country road with no close neighbors, the darkness felt eerie. I leaned forward onto the steering wheel as I made out at least one light on in the house. I just couldn't understand why? They were teammates. Why would they be fighting? The only thing that made sense was my anger. I eased myself out of the car and slammed the door behind me.

I used the glow from my cell phone to guide me up the front steps and onto the porch. I balked at the thought of knocking. Knocking seemed too polite, too mild. Cade didn't deserve politeness. Before I could determine the type of sound that would alert Cade of my presence, light flooded the porch before me. My eyes squinted shut at the sudden blinding intrusion but flicked open once again when I heard the door unlatch.

Cade stepped out, meeting my eyes, forcing me to take a step back. If he was surprised to see me there, I would never know. All I could think about as I stared at his face, his eye blackened and his cheek red with scratches was that this boy was here on earth only to torment me. Prom night. A night that should have been fun and full of memories had now been blackened forever. Years later, when friends would reminisce about prom, it wouldn't be dresses and dates and dances that would fill my memories, it would be turning the corner to see Cade attacking my date in the hallway. It was always him. Every bad memory of my childhood had Cade Williams in it. And I was so tired of it all.

He brushed past me and turned to face me as he leaned against the porch railing. His arms were folded. He wore a pair of jeans with a metal band t-shirt. If it wasn't for the gel still in his hair, all the clues that he had been at Prom would have vanished. Except for the shiner on his face.

"Why?" I asked, my bravado quickly fading as I studied the beginning of a black eye on his face and the red scratches across his cheeks.

"Why what?"

"Why? Why do you... do this? Prom night? I can't go anywhere without you pulling some sort of crap on me. I just want to know why. What did I ever do to you?" I folded my arms and waited for his answer.

"Ramsey's a tool."

"So, he must have said something stupid to you and so you punch him? Get us all thrown out of the dance before we even start? Or did you say something to him? Making fun of me? Is that it? Was that your plan?"

His jaw clenched, but he remained silent. Stoically so. Even when I pressed up closer to him in my anger. Trying to intimidate him, I guess, but his heat emanated between us and caused me to catch my breath, not at all helping in my attempt of a scare tactic.

I pushed at his arms, but still, he didn't move. "Say something."

"There's a lot you don't know about Ramsey."

"Well, I guess I won't be finding out anytime soon, will I? Thanks to you."

"Yep."

We stared at each other then. My chest heaved in frustration with his cryptic answers. My entire life had been his playground.

"Why do you hate me so much?" It was a pathetic question, and I felt dumb asking it because it sounded like I cared what he thought of me and I didn't. Not really. I just wanted all of this to stop.

At that, his eyes softened as he looked at me. The back of my eyes burned with unshed emotion, so I pinched my arm hard to take the focus off of the tears that I was *not* going to allow to fall at that moment.

"You think I hate you?"

A harsh laugh barked out of my throat as I threw my hands in the air. "What am I supposed to think?"

He was quiet as he studied me. So I stared right back. What had happened to him? To us? The pranks were mean in grade school, such as the nature of kids and a boy convinced I had started a war against him. In junior high, I started giving it right back, but it was after his father passed away in high school that the teasing went full force. The pranks became grander and I had to work harder to keep up. I wasn't innocent, not by a long shot, but I had boundaries. Prom night was one of them.

"You've made school bearable for me."

I grunted in exasperation. "Oh, that's nice. I'm glad I could be your punching bag." I moved to leave when he pulled my arm back and maneuvered my body to be in front of him again. The smell of his cologne met my nostrils and out of nowhere, I wished I could be pressed even closer to him if just to smell it again.

"You made school fun. You took my mind off of..." He broke off. Was he about to say his dad? "I know I probably pushed it too far, but I only ever meant it in fun. I always thought you liked getting me back." His words were choppy as he spoke, as if he wasn't used to having to explain himself or apologize. If this happened to be an apology. I couldn't tell for sure, but his next words gave me pause.

"I don't hate you. Far from it."

I shook my head as I looked up at him. "Then why...?"

His breath caught as he stared at me, now standing closer than ever. My heart stammered danger, danger, danger to my head, but even as he took one step closer, my feet refused to retreat. His eyes touched my lips. My chest felt like it would explode and my beating heart took flight.

Headlights flashed onto us as a car pulled into his driveway. We both turned toward the light. He sighed and ran his hand through his hair as his mom climbed out of her car and slammed the door. She was dressed in her waitressing clothes and looked as though the night at the diner had been long. "Cade, are you alright, honey? What's this I hear about you getting kicked out of the dance?"

Cade looked at me. "You'd better go. I'm sorry your night was ruined."

Numbly, I walked past him and toward my car. I said hello to Mrs. Williams as I passed her and then drove away, leaving Cade to answer for his own choices.

Cade cleared his throat, bringing me back to the present. That night on his porch was the last time I had spoken to him until this summer, and I couldn't help but wonder what else he had wanted to tell me.

"Sooo," I prodded.

He leaned forward in his chair, adjusting his hat. "Ramsey and I had played baseball together all our lives, and our senior year, we were fighting for the same position."

"Catcher?"

He nodded. "He's an idiot, a hot head, always trying to start something with somebody. I usually stayed out of his way, but off the field, he started noticing..." Cade trailed off for a moment, glancing at me before clearing his throat and starting again. "Noticing who I spent my time with. And then he asked you out to prom."

My breath caught as I sat in anticipated silence, staring at him, waiting for more. "Yes. I know that." He struggled to find the words he was looking for. Finally, he just quit and looked at me helplessly. I almost wanted to laugh; I had never seen him so out of sorts.

"What? Just say it."

He sighed and adjusted his hat. "Now, hear this the right way. You were hot and fun, and any guy would have wanted to take you, but Ramsey taking you was more personal."

"Why?" I was honestly confused, as much by the drive-by compliment as the reason for Ramsey taking me out.

"I know he wanted to take you to prom for a lot of reasons, but I know at least one was to get back at me for taking the catcher position."

"Why would he be getting *you* back if he took me? We never dated. Far from it."

"I know, but we had something... the guys noticed too." Cade took his hat off his head, ran his fingers through his hair, and put it back on his head again. "You were always... mine... to tease... you had always been mine and... I don't know, Red. I think they knew I was a bit... possessive of you. Well, at least Ramsey figured that out."

I swallowed, my heart pounding at his broken statements. Had he liked me? In high school? There had been a moment standing in front of him at his house the night of prom where the thought had entered my mind. Emotions were charged that night, the details were easily fuzzy, but after that, he had kept his distance. The last few weeks of school held no more pranks between us.

"Then why did you fight?"

"He started saying stuff about you. Things he wanted to do to you." He breathed out a laugh, rubbing his hands over his face. "It feels so stupid to say it like that. I don't think he would have...he was probably just baiting me, but... I was already on edge that night, so when he started talking..."

Those simple statements hovered in the air between us as he waited for me to grasp his meaning. And then he continued, rocking my world completely.

"What you saw that night was the tail end of a warning I gave to him."

The fire snapped. I jumped. Cade, probably grateful for something else to focus on besides this conversation he never wanted to have, added another log to the fire while I grappled with understanding. I had been so stupid.

"Why? Why would you do that for me?"

He looked at me like I was crazy. "I'm glad you think I'm the type of guy who can stand back and watch some jackass molest an innocent girl."

Reaching out, I grabbed his arm. "No, I didn't mean that, it's just... why didn't you tell me after it happened?"

He shrugged. "We didn't have the type of relationship where I could tell you something and you'd believe me. That was probably my fault."

"Why did you let me think such horrible things about you? I said the most terrible things to you that night."

"It didn't matter."

"Yes, it did."

"I just figured I owed you one, for all the crap I did to you growing up."

"Why were you already on edge that night, Cade?" I pressed, needing him to tell me what he wasn't.

Cade looked at me for a long moment, his eyes taking their time trailing up and down my face, settling on my lips, before he said, "Because... Ramsey ended up being right about me. I didn't like watching you with another guy. With him. With anyone else."

My breath drew up short and all the questions and words jumbling around in my head vanished. I opened my mouth to say something and closed it again. Words seemed... insignificant to the warm rumblings in my chest and belly.

"Your turn. Truth or dare, Red."

Something shifted between us. My eyes were locked on his gaze and unwilling to break the trance. We had spent the entire date climbing a hill. Now that we were at the top, we could either fly down in exhilaration or fall down in heartache. Or my specialty, which would be to not go down the hill at all. The old me would stay at the top, where things were safe, and mouth off some wisecrack to ruin the moment. A place where I didn't have to choose and nobody got hurt. I shivered a bit as Cade's gaze turned warm. My heartbeat sounded like a herd of horses to my ears. I hoped Cade couldn't hear it. There was something in his eyes, calling to me, goading me, *begging* me to fly down the hill with him—to choose something instead of nothing. Something I found I couldn't resist when I whispered, "Dare."

A smile touched his lips briefly. "That night with the mountain lion—before your dad got there. We started something. I dare you to finish it."

I sucked in my breath. Holding my body perfectly still, I studied his face and found no trace of teasing or mocking. His eyes simmered with something else. Something...vulnerable and hungry. I wanted to shake myself awake. This was Cade Williams. And I was falling for his bait. Hook, line, and a stupid, sinking heart.

"I could pass you know," I said, softly.

"You could."

Turning his body toward mine, he reached for me, trying to pull me closer, the awkward arms of our chairs blocking his advance. He stood up and reached for my hand, pulling me up and into him, both my hands landing on his chest. I watched them move up and down with his breathing for a moment before my gaze moved to his face.

"You want it exactly how it would have played out in the woods, then?" I asked.

"If you have the guts." His taunting voice was ragged as he leaned his face closer, nudging me along.

I moved slowly toward him, my heart beating out of my chest and just when I was about to press my lips to his, I darted to the side of his face and kissed his cheek.

Growling lowly and catching my laughing face with both of his hands, he shook his head. "Not this time, Red."

His hands fell to my neck and drew me slowly closer as if I were a skittish squirrel who might dash away at any second. My laughter faded as his hand feathered across my cheek in a soft caress. Feeling shy, my gaze dropped down to my feet. What were we doing? What was he doing? Without all the teasing, I was just a big pile of confusing emotions.

"Kelsey."

His low voice brought my face back up to his. The instant my name fell from his lips, he became the potter and I the clay—putty in his hands. His eyes explored my face—taking in each unruly freckle scattered about my cheeks and nose, and settling on my lips. Ever so gently, his fingers followed suit. He took his time with me—soothing my doubts with the softest of brushstrokes. His thumb caressed my bottom lip, teasing and fondling it until I drew in a ragged breath, my racing, impatient heart not able to bear much more of such delicious agony.

Then he kissed me.

Kissed me quite well, actually.

Cade's hands left my face and wrapped around my back. Soft lips touched mine, tender and sweet, testing the waters, as we both surrendered to a taste so long denied. I melted into him—warmed by his heat and ignited by his touch. My hands traveled up his chest, past his shoulders, and clung to his neck, my fingers toying with the hair peeking out from his baseball hat. Frustrated at such limited access, I pulled the hat off his head and dropped it unceremoniously on the ground while his arms wound even tighter around my body, pulling me closer, and kissing me senseless.

Our passion turned fiery as the kiss intensified, while years of pent-up desire and frustration exploded between us. We were flying down my imaginary hill at an exhilarating speed. I had no flashbacks of our rocky history. No memories of our past. Cade Williams, the boy, didn't enter my thoughts. It was Cade Williams, the man, kissing me now.

It was a few long moments into the kiss before I realized I hadn't tried to resist. There was no game between us here. No pranks. The instant his lips touched mine, I softened, kissing him back with a ferocity that didn't even startle me. It came so natural and smooth and easy that all my questions and worries regarding Cade were silenced by the sweetness.

There were so many things I wanted to say with this kiss. So many things that were difficult for me to say any other way. I kissed him for saving my life. I kissed him for making me laugh, for putting me in my place, and for teasing me. I kissed him for making me feel special. And for this date. This glorious and magical and most confusing date that I wished could go on forever. But mostly, I kissed him for me, because I was starting to wonder if Stitch really was right about that fine line between love and hate.

24

Journal Entry (circa - University of Idaho)

I put my feet on the dashboard in Parker's car today, and he asked me to take them off. He's really worried about scratching it, even though I just had my socks on. He really loves that car. Good thing he's cute.

The next morning started like any other. After milking the cows, the boys and I were gathered at the north corral, feeding hay and grain to the cows. The only difference was the fact that Cade and

I had gone out on a date the night before, which led to barrels of fun for the two *other* pesky cowboys in my life.

"Hmmm... your lips are looking a bit puffy this morning." Jake looked at me innocently as we kicked hay into the manger. Glancing over at Cade, he asked, "That's not your doing, is it?"

"Oh yeah, how was the hot date last night?" Dusty smacked his lips together in the air. "You two love birds finally resolve your issues of the past, I don't know, fifteen years?"

"Ha. Ha." I tried to keep it cool while I stole a glance at Cade.

A smile was playing on Cade's lips as he carried another hay bale to the manger. "I don't know about that, but I do know she had a hard time keeping her hands off me all night."

Jake smiled delightedly at me. "Really?"

"No, I didn't," I exclaimed, kicking at the seat of Jake's pants.

"We didn't even get to the skinny dipping I had planned, because she just wanted to cuddle up by the fire." Cade was laughing as I tried my very hardest to glare at him.

"I guess you'll have to go out again then," Dusty added, giving Jake a high five.

The two cowboys all but disappeared, however, when Cade caught my eye and slowly nodded at me.

Um... yeah.

All was forgiven.

In truth, I had wondered if the four-wheeler ride home would be awkward after we had kissed. As we finished feeding the last of the cows, I smiled as I remembered a moment the previous night, asking Cade that very same thing.

"Is it going to be awkward the rest of the date now?"

"What?"

"You just kissed me and we still have a long drive home."

"I don't know. How about you don't be awkward and then I won't be awkward."

"Oh great. You should have just kissed me at the doorstep. Then we go our separate ways with no awkwardness."

"We could try the doorstep thing too."

After a cozy ride back down the mountain, snuggled in front of Cade with his arm wrapped around me, we did try the doorstep thing too. I can firmly report that I have no objections to either method.

We spent the rest of the day split up, with odd jobs around the farm. Later that afternoon, the four of us met back at my dad's truck to have a shooting competition. Kissing or no kissing, it was high time I showed these boys what shooting guns really looked like.

We were talking smack and scrounging up the last of the shells and clay pigeons and throwing them into the bed of the truck when a cloud of dust flying down the lane caught our attention. The four of us turned to watch.

I peered closer while warning bells in my head began to ring. The first clue that something was wrong was that instead of the usual pickup most locals drove, it was a car. Not just any car, but a sleek, sports car. Definitely not from around here.

The second clue was the speed at which the car was flying up the lane. Unless there were cows out or someone was running late to the high school football game, most of the people in Eugene weren't in a big hurry.

The main clue, however, the one that had my stomach clenched and the feeling of dread in my stomach, was the color. A lime green sports car. The car I was never allowed to drive. The car that took me on dates to fancy restaurants and expensive theaters. The flashy, pompous car that could never compare to a certain beat-up, old pickup. The car that, as hard as I tried, never really felt like me.

It was also the car that was very nearly here, rounding the bend in the lane. I watched it slow as it passed the house, then tensed visibly as it kept moving toward the barn. We had been spotted.

I swore.

The boys looked at me. I avoided all of their gazes while I mentally calculated the distance to the stables and how long it would take me to hop on Ace and fly out of there. I needed time to gather my thoughts. What was he doing just showing up unannounced like this? I guiltily remembered the handful of voicemails and texts I hadn't opened from him in the past couple of days. I had been so blissfully consumed with Cade and our date that I hadn't wanted to deal with Parker yet. It looked like, ready or not, I would have to deal with him today.

"Is that...?" Dusty started to ask but fell silent as the ostentatious car pulled in to park beside my dad's pickup.

"Yeah," I breathed.

A hush came over us as we waited for the driver of the car to emerge.

Jake held up the shotgun. "Want us to rough him up for ya?"

Dusty snickered while I snuck a glance at Cade. He was staring at the car with no expression on his face. He looked at me, raised his eyebrows, folded his arms, and leaned back against the pickup. By the looks of it, he wasn't going anywhere.

The green door opened and out stepped Parker Gillette.

The scent of expensive cologne and mint gum drifted out from his car. His blonde hair had been freshly cut and his smile, though cocky, seemed a bit shaken. From his Rolex watch, designer jeans, and two-hundred-dollar sunglasses, it was clear he didn't belong here. He must have felt that too. I tried not to flinch as he took off his sunglasses and turned his sharp eyes on me—slowly taking in my boots, baggy size six jeans, muddy T-shirt, and messy hair in a bun. A far cry from my polished school persona.

And then he spoke. "Hey, babe."

I swallowed. "What are you doing here?"

"Well, I wondered if you were dead since I left a thousand messages and never heard back from you." He crossed his arms over his chest as he took in the rest of his audience. Dusty sat in the passenger's seat of my dad's truck with the door flung open, inserting bullets into his pistol. Jake stood on the bed of the truck with a shotgun in his hands. His final gaze settled on Cade.

For all the tension in the air, Cade looked remarkably calm, sticking out his hand toward Parker. "Hey, man. What brings you here?"

Parker ignored his hand and looked at Cade as though he were the mud on his Italian leather boots. "That's not really any of your business, is it?"

Cade snorted. "Looking for a job?" He made a show of looking Parker up and down. "Not the clothes I would have chosen to feed cows in, but hey, it's your money, right?"

I didn't miss the money jab pointed my way and resisted the urge to roll my eyes. Parker smiled patiently, as though he were explaining something to a toddler. "Yeah, see, that's the thing about getting a real job, you can make the big bucks to afford a new shirt, buddy."

"You? Or your daddy?" Cade grinned, but there was a definite hardness in his eyes.

The two men faced off for a moment before Parker looked over at me. "Babe, can we talk?" He looked around at the gun-toting cowboys and added, "Alone."

Why was he still calling me babe? I don't think the notion was lost on any of the boys either.

The sound of Jake's shotgun being cocked made all of us jump. At my frigid stare pointed his way, Jake just grinned.

Oh heavens. Showdown at the Lost River Corral.

Parker cleared his throat and looked back at me, asking a little more urgently, "Can we talk somewhere?"

In the back of Parker's cocky facade, I could see how unsettled he was. The past few weeks of hurt and heartache were hidden in the shadows of his face. I felt sorry for him. I had done that. Me. I had broken his heart and he deserved an explanation. He didn't deserve to be intimidated by my overprotective, redneck bodyguards just for showing up.

"Yeah, let's talk." I led him toward the barn, refusing to acknowledge the annoyed glares thrown my way.

"Why didn't you call me back?"

Why? Because my traitorous heart had already moved on and was busy being enamored by somebody else.

"I'm sorry. I've been busy here." Not a lie. Cade and I had been very busy.

"I know I was mad when I hung up on you, but I just needed time to think. I was hoping you'd at least give me a chance to win you back." He sent a pointed glance back toward my posse at the truck, who made no pretense of minding their own business. "Or maybe you already found your replacement for me right here?"

Though my cheeks reddened slightly, I owed him no explanation. "They work for my dad."

Parker scoffed, his eyes still lingering on them. "If we were in the old west, I'd have three bullets in my back right now."

"Nobody would shoot you in the back, Gillette. Real cowboys aim for the chest," Cade drawled behind us. Dusty and Jake snickered.

Glaring at Cade over Parker's shoulder, I yelled, "I got this."

My ex's face seemed a few degrees whiter than a minute earlier. I drug him farther away from the firing squad. "What do you want, Parker?"

"Can I take you to dinner tonight? I want to talk to you about some things."

"No. I'm sorry. You can say what you need to right here."

He gave a sidelong glance at the boys, who were now talking amongst themselves, sending occasional glances our way.

"Okay. Can we at least go somewhere a gun isn't aimed at me?"

"Sure, let's talk on the porch."

We walked toward the house, an awkward distance between us, until I remembered my manners. "How was your trip?"

"It was okay, considering I had my heart ripped out of my chest ten minutes before leaving."

I shut my eyes. "I'm so sorry, Parker." We had reached the porch by this point and I motioned him to sit in one of the rocking chairs, while I took the swing.

"Was it the dress? Babe, I'm sorry about my part in all that. If I could go back, I would have just told my mom we weren't interested. I feel horrible thinking about how much extra pressure that put on you. My mom feels bad too."

His phone rang. He glanced at the caller ID and then looked up at me with an apology written on his face.

"Babe, I'm so sorry but I have to take this call. My work needs some information I researched. It will just take a minute." I nodded at him, motioning for him to take his call.

Parker stood and moved to the other side of the porch while I rocked in the swing, staring out toward the orchard. Parker's words floated over to where I sat and a vision of life with him unfolded before my very active imagination. There were suits and ties and business meetings, date nights interrupted by cell phones and bosses, two token children, nannies, and expensive vacations to fancy desti-nations. A mirage in the distance but up close, a life with very little substance. At least for me. A place of hustle and bustle. Where work time, parent time, and playtime existed separately.

I thought of my own upbringing. Where the days were filled working alongside my family. Where work and play blended together as one. Certainly, happiness could be found in both versions of life. My sister Amanda was proof of that. She had eloped with her own Parker. Currently, they lived in a high-rise apartment in Seattle with my four-year-old niece, Hannah. They had a nanny and both worked in corporate downtown, and she loved it. They got along happily. It was her dream. It had just taken me a while to realize that it wasn't mine. I had been so close to throwing it all away. Cade was right, I hadn't been asking the right questions to the right person.

Parker ended his call and sat next to me on the swing. I made a little room for him. He took my hand in his. I made it feel like a limp noodle.

"Kels, I want you to know, I think we can work this out. If it was the dress or my mom, we can fix all of it. Heck, we can even do your courthouse wedding and barbecue picnic thing if you really wanted."

He fidgeted in his seat, looking at me with a hopeful expression. It looked out of place on a face that usually exuded confidence. His eyes were pleading with me to say the words to get us back on track, to get past the uncomfortable few weeks.

But I couldn't say the words. My heart was no longer in it. It was no longer his. I wondered if it ever really was.

"Parker, I came home to Eugene this summer because something was missing and I didn't know what it was. We had both talked and dreamed of a big life in California and of me being a news anchor, and for so long, I had convinced myself I could be happy in that life. A part of me loves the idea of it all, but being home this summer helped me realize that a much bigger part of me wants something simpler. *This* felt like home to me. When I left home to go to college, I wanted to be different. I had an idea of who I wanted to be. So I changed. I dressed, looked, and acted differently. That's when you met me, when I was trying to mold myself into something that, deep down, wasn't really me."

He rubbed his hand through his hair. "Okay, but you're still you. Even here. You can be who you are in California too, you know. If you don't want to work in the city, then don't. Whatever it is, we can work it out, I want *you*. Not a fake you."

I closed my eyes as a sense of peace filled my heart at my next words. "I don't want that anymore, Parker. I'm so sorry. I promise you, when we were making plans, I was completely invested. It was only when it came time to make the jump, I realized I couldn't do it. I shouldn't do it when I want something else."

He was silent for a moment before blowing out a shaky, disbelieving breath. "Are you serious?"

"Yes." I had never been so certain. And even though Cade played a part in helping me discover what I had really wanted, I could say with certainty that, with or without Cade, this choice was right for me. I knew it deep down in my soul. I had come home.

Parker's face was etched with confusion and disgust. "What do you want then? Was your degree all a waste?"

I smiled gently. "Nothing will be wasted. I want this." I motioned around toward the farm. "I want to live in a small town where everybody knows my business. Where everybody waves when you pass by, and where a traffic jam involves a tractor. I want my children to grow up in the country surrounded by animals. I want them to have chores where they feed and care for something other than themselves. I want to go camping in the summer and sledding in the winter. I want family and grandparents nearby. I want this life."

A sad smile filled his face as he shook his head slowly. "I can't give you that. But I could get you a horse, would that help anything? Or we can bring your horse to Santa Cruz. There's a horse stable not too far from the house."

I wanted to laugh, but he was looking at me so earnestly, I couldn't. "No. I'm sorry."

He nodded, slowly. "Okay but hear me out. What if I told you I got you a job in Santa Cruz? At the top news agency in the city?"

I looked at him, slightly bemused. "And did you?"

"Yeah. I pulled a few strings."

I laughed. It was all so cringe-worthy. Was he like this before? Was he serious? Had he heard a word of anything I had just said?

Just then, the redneck posse of Cade, Jake, and Dusty walked by the porch on their way into the house. Jake and Dusty's loud voices broke into our conversation.

"Hey babe, let's go get some grub," Jake said as he walked the steps up to the front door.

"Yeah, babe, that sounds great." Dusty followed Jake as they opened the door and walked into the house.

Despite myself, I bit back a smile while I shook my head slightly. Cade followed a second behind, his hat on low and his hands in his pockets. He glanced over at us and I saw in his eyes what we must have looked like. Smiling, holding hands, and swinging on the porch together. He glowered at me as he moved toward the front door. My mom must have invited them all in for lunch. I met his annoyed stare with one of my own, holding his eyes until the front door closed. A girl could only deal with one childish male at a time.

Parker cleared his throat.

"What if I told you that if we did marry, I don't want to wear Jennifer Harris's dress?" I asked.

He grinned, almost as if he were anticipating that question. "I'd say that's good cause her wedding is back on and she wants the dress back."

"Are you serious? Can she do that? What if I was already set to wear it?"

"My mom didn't want to ruffle feathers, and since we weren't sure if the dress would work for you or not, we figured you would probably be relieved. So, I've come on an errand from my mom to get the dress back and convince you to buy something you'd love just as much, on us."

"On us?"

"Since you weren't planning on the unexpected cost of the dress anymore, we want to buy it. Whatever dress you want, babe." He smiled at me, satisfaction clenched in his eyes.

I sat there, amazed at the nerve of him. The nerve of his family. The nerve of this rich, above-all-reproach family, who could make deals and demands on a whim, as long as it served them. I had given Parker exactly zero ideas that I would be taking him back, but in his delusional thought process, there couldn't be any possible way I would turn him down. If it didn't make me so angry, the cluelessness would be almost endearing.

"Thank you for the offer, but I'm going to pass." I stood up from the chair, releasing his hand from mine, and moved toward the door.

"You don't want us to buy you a dress?" His voice was casual, but underneath, I detected a hint of panic.

I turned and met his eyes. "I'm not going to marry you, Parker. It's over."

"Babe." He stood up.

"Please don't call me that. We were wrong for each other from the start, and that was my fault. I am truly sorry for hurting you."

"We had good times too, Kels. We were good together. Or have you forgotten?"

"We did. And thank you for those times. But I'm still saying no." I put my hand on the doorknob before turning back to him. "I'm going to grab your dress and the ring. If I were you, I'd just wait out here. I think you'll be safer."

25

~~What I Should be when I Grow Up~~
Career Options (circa - current)

~ ~~Personal Trainer (ha)~~
~ Veterinary Assistant
~ ~~Writer~~
~ Teacher
~ ~~Lifeguard~~
~ ~~Dairy Farm Manager~~
~ Professional cowgirl
~ Assistant to a Veterinarian

Later that evening, I went for a drive. It took a bit more convincing for Parker to take back the ring. In the back of his mind, he kept thinking I was only playing hard to get. He couldn't understand why I was giving everything up, for nothing. I thought I might have to threaten to go and grab my shotgun before he finally left in a frustrated huff. In the end, it seemed our relationship was more of a matter of pride to him than any strong feelings we had toward each other.

While meandering through Eugene, I tried calling Tessa. I could have used some girl talk. So much had happened in the past twenty-four hours, there were so many emotions I needed to sort out and I didn't know where to start. Just my luck, she didn't answer. I didn't want to go home yet, but I was out of places in Eugene to drive, so I took the cutoff road just before the turnoff to our lane. The old, dirt road would lead me directly to the pond where the boys threw me in a few weeks earlier.

As I drove closer, I discovered a familiar truck already parked there. I hadn't spoken to Cade since he spotted Parker holding my hand on the porch swing. Tingles erupted all over my body as I noticed Cade sitting on the hood, leaning back against the wind-shield watching the sunset. The stars would be filling the sky soon and I suddenly had a strong desire to go stargazing.

I pulled my car up and parked it next to his truck. When he still didn't move to acknowledge me, I summoned all the courage of my heart and stepped outside.

Though he didn't look at me, I detected the slightest smile brush across his lips as he moved his arms back behind his head, staring at the sky.

I slammed my door shut.

My eyes raked over his body stretched out on the truck; from his jeans to his fitted gray t-shirt and dirty baseball hat with his shaggy brown hair poking out of the sides. He looked perfect. Taking a deep breath, I moved closer.

"You're in my spot."

Still not looking at me, he said, "You're welcome to try to get it back." The challenge in his voice tinged the air, but I was all smiles by this point.

I walked over to the side of his truck where he finally met my gaze. "Did you get back together with Casanova tonight?"

"Nope. But I'm officially broken up with him. Again."

At my words, Cade slowly leaned over, held out a hand, and pulled me up onto the truck beside him. He may have pulled me up too fast, or maybe I didn't make the effort to stop, but somehow, I landed almost fully on top of him, stopped only by my hands at his chest. But his eyes were shining as he maneuvered me next to him, leaning back onto the windshield, his arm tucked snug around my shoulders.

I didn't resist one bit as I curled into him, my hand settling easily onto his chest. His heartbeat pulsed steadily in my ear—both of us soaking up this newfound closeness for the second night in a row. The summer sun had mostly set, with only a few streaks of pink left in the sky. The north star twinkled in front of us. Soon our view would be filled with stars.

"So, will our big date get me another mention in your journal?"

I rolled my eyes while playfully tapping his chest. "I told you, I document everything for evidence."

"What were you and the city boy talking about on the porch?"

"How wrong we were for each other."

"Really?"

"At least, that's what my side of the conversation was."

"You looked pretty cozy when I walked by."

"Just telling an old friend goodbye."

Cade shifted, snorting in mild derision. "He was so wrong for you. I can't believe you were going to marry him."

"How did you know that? You'd only met Parker twice in your life."

"Yeah, and I figured it out in two seconds. What took you so long?"

"I don't know," I mumbled, snuggling closer.

"Did you think about getting back together with him?"

"I knew the second he stepped out of his car that it was still very over."

Cade groaned. "And you decided to keep that knowledge all to yourself?"

I gave him a delighted smile. "Well, I think my amazing performance earned me at least a couple of points on the board."

I laughed as he growled and pulled me in even closer, my head tucked just below his chin. The crickets chirped in the distance and the sound of the sprinklers filled the air. The evening had turned a bit chilly so I nestled into his chest. I felt a light kiss on my forehead and everything in my world fell into place. Because against all odds, and in the most unbelievable way, I had fallen in love with Cade Williams.

Those next few weeks with Cade were wonderful. Amazing even. We dated, laughed, played pranks, played basketball with the boys, and cuddled on the porch swing most nights after chores. I was already mourning the loss of summer. Not just summer. I was lamenting the loss of a certain cowboy who confused me, made me mad, made me laugh, and delighted every part of my soul all at the same time.

The problem was that Cade would be going to Vet school. He had been accepted back into Colorado State University and his semester started in a few weeks. Every time I brought up school, he changed the subject. None of that mattered when his arms were wrapped around me and we always had more time. But as I now had only a couple of weeks left, I needed to know where we stood, what his plans were, and whether or not they involved me.

Having a summer love always seemed so fun and romantic in the movies. I had only bad things to say about it now. Especially since we had wasted most of the summer fighting and pranking. Or as Cade liked to call it—working his magic.

"Hey Red, why'd you run off? We were about to start a basketball game. You in?"

He found me in the orchard. I'd taken a walk by myself, hoping to be missed. Looks like it worked.

"Not right now."

"What's wrong?"

I wasn't sure how to word all the thoughts and feelings ready to explode out of me, so I remained silent.

He moved closer. The smell of his cologne reached my nose.

I took a few steps backward before he could touch me. "No, stay over there."

"Why?"

"Because we need to talk, and I can't do that with your cologne messing with my head."

"You think I smell good?" Cade was all smiles as he took another step toward me.

"Go take a shower and wash it off, and then maybe we'll talk."

"Now you're thinking of me with my clothes off? That's inappropriate."

I tried pushing him away, but he was stronger and pulled me in closer. His breath tickled my ear when he said, "You know, I've been meaning to talk with you about something."

Hope bloomed in my chest. "What?"

He pressed his body close to mine as he backed me into a tree, his face centimeters away. His eyes danced around my lips as his mouth pressed a gentle kiss on mine in between each word. "One. Final. Prank."

My brain barely registered his last statement before Cade bent down, threw me over his shoulder, and broke into a run. I squealed as my head dangled upside down facing into his back with my legs flapping in the wind. I knew beyond a shadow of a doubt where we were headed.

"Any last words, Red?" he asked as we arrived at the pond, a sense of deja vu enveloping me.

"You know, you're really doing me a favor. I was just headed this way."

He laughed. "Nope. Not buying that." Shaking me gently, he

asked, "Nothing you want to say? The water's freezing. You're gonna hate it."

I tried to kick myself free. "You've already gotten a point for throwing me into the pond. This just makes you look lazy."

"Nice try." Cade squeezed me tighter. "You know... if you're interested, maybe we could make a deal. I'll trade you this prank for something real."

"Why would you make a deal?"

At that point, I was *still* hanging upside down behind his shoulder. My rear pressed right next to his face. I just wanted this over. The closeness, the teasing, the knowledge he was moving away... it was all too much.

"If I put you down, will you promise not to run away?"

"Sure."

I think Cade knew that if given the chance to bolt, I would, but he set me down anyway, grabbing my face with his hands, stepping in close for a smooth, hot and delicious kiss. Well played, Williams. I had lost all desire to run now.

"So... what's the deal?" I mumbled against his mouth when I pulled away to take a breath.

"I've been thinking."

"Oh heaven help us all."

He moved to pick me up again when I laughed and ducked away. His arms reached out and pulled me back into him.

"As I said, I've been doing some thinking."

I smirked at him, and he rolled his eyes.

"I'm moving back to Colorado. And it gets pretty cold there."

I froze. My body tensed. My heart pounded. He glanced over at me, clearing his throat nervously as he continued. "And I've gotten pretty used to you being wrapped around me on the porch swing every night."

"Oh really?" I failed miserably to keep the hope out of my voice.

"Yeah."

Taking a deep breath he said, "I was wondering how you'd feel about coming to Colorado. It wouldn't be hard to find you a job, or you could go back to school and get your teaching certificate if you wanted. And you could keep me warm when it gets cold."

My heart wanted to leap outside of my chest, but I played it safe. It was best to know his true intentions before my heart got crushed both inside and on the surface. "I could just buy you a blanket. That would take care of you just fine without me"

"Dang, woman," he growled, tucking my hair behind my ear. "You don't make things easy on a guy."

"Well maybe if I knew exactly what you were trying to say, I could help you," I told him sweetly.

"Fine. I want you to come with me as my girlfriend."

"Why? You think I'm going to do all your homework?"

He raised his eyebrows. "Well, I didn't think about that, but it's not your worst idea."

I shook my head as I smiled softly at him. "We fight too much."

Cade grinned. "It's not fighting if we're having fun."

"That can't be good for a relationship," I said, testing the waters as I pulled away from him. I needed to make him play his cards.

"That's what makes all this work, Red." He grabbed my waist and pulled me right back into his arms. My hands betrayed all previous resistance efforts and went straight to his chest. Though my insides were alive with excitement, my face was a mask. Silent and rigid. His eyes narrowed and briefly touched on my lips before he dragged them upward.

"You and me. We both like a challenge. We can both be a pain in the butt. Some of us more than others." He gave me a look and squeezed me tighter. Balking, I tried to move away, but he held me fast. "But at the end of the day, no matter who wins, I can't wait to do it all over again the next day. You're the first person I want to talk to when I wake up. I lose way too much sleep at night trying to think of ways to get a rile out of you, make you laugh, torture you, kiss you..."

Can a chest explode from happiness? My body, once tense and stiff, now felt light as air, floating away on some cloud overhead. I was looking everywhere but at him, but I held on tight and drank in his words.

"Kels... I'm in love with you."

Startled, my eyes flew to his.

"When I first saw you this summer, I began to wonder if I always had been...if it always was you." His forehead wrinkled and his mind seemed far away. He ran a hand through his hair. "I came here with a pretty good idea of what I wanted. I just wasn't sure how to get it. Even back in high school, whether we were fighting or pranking... you were the one I wanted to be around. And that terrified me. I didn't know how to handle my feelings, so naturally, I made everything worse."

"Naturally."

He snorted, shaking his head at me. "But I found that I like getting a rile out of you. Spitfire Red's my favorite color." He grinned at me as he placed his hands on my cheeks and leaned his forehead against mine. "Did you hear me? You drive me crazy in all the best ways. One day I want to give you that white house on a ranch. I love you, Red."

Those were all the right words. Not only the right words, but they were also from the *right* man and that made all the difference. The grin I'd been holding back burst onto my face as I threw my arms around his shoulders, ducking my head into his chest, too timid for words. His arms came around my waist as I reveled in the feel of his tender confession.

We stayed that way for some time before I grew the courage to speak, pulling myself out of his embrace. "I came home this summer thinking I knew exactly what I wanted too, but the longer I was here, the more confused I became. I thought that having you here was only going to make it worse, but, then, the more I was around you, the more clear everything became. When I was with you, I knew exactly what I wanted." I smiled sheepishly. "Even when I couldn't admit it. And even when you were filling my room with fish and my tractors with mice."

He chuckled but his attention once again was focused on my mouth. "If I kiss you, will that make it all better?"

I pretended to think. "If you make it good."

"Oh, it'll be good," he mumbled as he brought his lips to mine. Gentle at first. Warm and wanting, but also savoring. My hands left his forearms and made their way over his shoulders. He pulled me in even closer, trapping me against him, deepening the kiss. One of his hands moved to caress my cheek. I pulled back for a moment to whisper shyly, "I love you too."

He smiled for a moment against my mouth before we lost ourselves once more.

It was a few long moments before we came up for air.

"Hmmm... maybe... seven out of ten?"

"What?"

I wrinkled my nose. "That kiss. Seven out of ten?"

Grinning, he pulled me close again. "Well shoot, we can't have that."

This time, when Cade released me, after several long, ten-out-of-ten moments, he seemed uncharacteristically fidgety and nervous. He glanced at me briefly before I pulled his face down to meet mine once more.

He broke away. "Alright, that's it. I don't know if I'm going to make an idiot out of myself, but I gotta do this." His confidence had lifted once more as his arms snaked around my waist. "Kels, I know we haven't technically been dating for a long time, but..." he shook his head, "Ah hell, I've been dating you my whole life. I just didn't know it. Will you just marry me? And then you can come to Colorado as my wife."

My breath caught, disbelieving. He stared at me expectantly, waiting for my reply. I thought I knew... but I had to be sure. "Is this a prank? Your proposal?"

He deflated a bit and shook his head, biting back a smile. "Given our history, I probably deserve that question." His arms circled once more around my waist, tugging me closer to him, whispering these next words in my ear. "But I am *all in*. Completely serious and one hundred percent in love with you." He pulled back and looked in my eyes. "I didn't know it then, but all my misguided pranks toward you throughout our entire lives were just to get me to this moment. It's always been you." He pressed his forehead against mine, and just when I thought my heart couldn't explode anymore, he said softly once more, "Marry me, Red?"

A smile stole across my face. Confetti and fireworks seemed to burst down from the clouds at just that moment. "Yes! Yes! Oh my gosh, yes!" I threw my arms around his shoulders and kissed him deeply, with a fire and intensity that frightened me.

I pulled away abruptly. "Wait, did you mean get married before you go to school? Or after? When?"

Cade chuckled as he tucked another piece of hair behind my ears. "Is yesterday too soon?"

"My mom is going to kill me."

"Kels, we can get married whenever you want. If you want a big wedding and we need to wait until winter break that's fine. But if you don't, I'd be fine with that too. More than fine." He grinned wickedly as he gathered me in his arms. "Just think about how much warmer I'd be with you in my bed."

My cheeks flamed with delight at his words. I thought of the beautiful pasture with the large willow tree and the creek. Cade's eyes were gentle as I looked up at him. He would look perfect wearing his cowboy boots in the grassy field. Visions of Tessa and Amanda standing next to me, in long bridesmaid dresses the color of a dusty, pink rose. Me, standing in a white, flowing, off-the-shoulder gown of satin and lace, holding a simple bouquet of soft pink and cream peonies. It was all so simple. Perfect.

"That gives us two weeks to plan a wedding, right? If we want a honeymoon before school."

He raised his eyebrows, "Oh we most definitely want a honeymoon."

"Then I'll go to Colorado as your wife."

It's amazing how in the space of a conversation and a few delicious kisses, your whole world can change. It's also amazing how in the space of one summer you can have two fiancés, but that's the thing about love stories—sometimes it takes a wrong turn to go in the right direction. Sometimes *home* is exactly where you left it.

All my worries, doubts, fears, and insecurities vanished while he wrapped me up in his arms. With the right man, my worries turned to calmness, my doubts to faith, my fears to bravery, and my insecurities to confidence.

My competitive and impish nature, however... remained pretty much the same. We were standing near the four-foot drop into the water's edge when I broke from his lips. "Cade?"

Suddenly missing my mouth, he squeezed me tighter, nuzzling his face down into my neck. "Mmm?"

I kissed his cheek, leaned in close to his ear, and whispered, "Is the prank score still tied up?"

His body stiffened as he started to pull away from me, but not before I gave him a big smile... and a hard push over the edge.

I stood on the side, laughing, my hands covering my mouth, as chaos in the water ensued. He sputtered and laughed and shouted mild obscenities in my name as he tried to pull me in. Squealing, I swatted his hands away from my legs and gave myself a moment of triumph before I jumped in after him.

I had some very passionate apologizing to do.

EPILOGUE

THE ONE WHERE CADE FINDS MY JOURNAL

Reasons Cade is the Best
(written by Cade)

2,345. Super SEXY

2,346. Rock hard, smoking hot bod

2,347. Full of charm and charisma

2,348. Takes his shirt off while he's working outside in the heat (See line 2,346)

2,349. ~~Forgave Red for puking her guts out all over him in second grade~~

2,350. He's the best kisser

2,351. Married Red in her dad's field underneath the willow in front of the whole town ~~(to everyone's surprise)~~

2,352. ~~Agreed to the 'no pranks' rule on the wedding day~~

2,353. Gave Red her white house (still working on the ranch part)

NOTES FROM THE AUTHOR

Me and my dad milking cows (circa — 2006)

I was raised on a small dairy farm in Idaho. While growing up, the love of the farm life seeped into my soul in the best way possible—though I didn't fully grasp just how much until I had left home. Some days were dirty and gross and covered in manure. Some were long and hot and left you wanting to strip down and rinse off in the field. Eventually, I realize how lucky I was to be able to move wheel lines, milk cows, drive tractors, spray weeds, and fix fences in the fresh, country air. Milking cows was not a glamorous job, but it was a sacred one. It was where I would have the best conversations with my dad and he would offer advice and tell stories and we'd have discussions about everything going on in my life. It was a place where I fought, laughed, and got into water fights with my siblings. It was a place with amazing acoustics where I'd sing my little heart out to every country song on the radio.

I've heard it said that if you want to be a writer, begin by writing what you know. So I wrote bits of my family life into this story. My dad and Kelsey's dad are two peas in a pod. My mom is sweet and wise like Kelsey's mom. I had a big teasing relationship with every-one, though I never had a good enough poker face to play pranks. A mouse once crawled up my leg while in the tractor. We had an irriga-tion ditch we would swim in when we were kids. We used to sleep out on the trampoline under the stars. And like Kelsey, there was a time in my life I was dating somebody (casually) that wasn't right for me. He was nice and I had no real reason not to date him, but when I brought him home, he just didn't fit.

Sometimes it takes coming home to find yourself.

Just to be clear, I have never preg-tested a cow before. Never used the long plastic glove, so to speak. I have never wanted to, but I have seen it done a thousand times. But I really think that we as a romance community are not doing enough to talk about it, so I'm glad I could do my part and paint you all a visual.

Thank you so much for reading this fun little piece of my heart. I hope it brightened your day and left you with a smile.

ALSO BY CINDY STEEL

ACKNOWLEDGMENTS

So many people have been instrumental in bringing this book out into the world. Here are just a few of them...

My husband and boys... who give me the time and space I need to write each day and then fill up every other second with hugs, adventures, kisses, and laughter—and let's be honest—some crying, fighting, bugs, fake snakes, and lots of dirt. SO much dirt.

My sister, Lisa. Thank you for holding my hand the whole way through this novel, starting at its initial concept to the million edits, changes, and re-writes. Thank you for all your amazing advice, input, and your shared love for Cade and Kelsey. You are simply the best.

My mom. Thank you for reading this book and loving it. Thanks for your edits and ideas to get this thing polished and shined. I love you so much.

Karen. My writing bestie. When I got serious about getting this book out into the world, you were the first person I wanted input from. Thank you for reading it and giving me the best feedback that made all the difference.

My critique group. Karen, Whitney, and Hollijo. It's been the

BEST year getting to know you all. Thanks for all the help, critiques, edits, and encouragement.

My beta readers...Rachelle, Karen, Julie, Christy, Micah, Morgan, Lisa, Joy, Whitney, and Jenn Lockwood. Thank you for your time, edits, and excitement for this book!

My ARC readers and Bookstagram friends. This community on the social media web has been so kind and accepting and all-around lovely. Thank you for believing in me and taking the time to read my books and share them with others. You guys have changed my world for the better. Thank you.

My cousin Shelby for saying yes when I asked if I could photograph her and her husband for promotional pictures. You guys are the cutest.

Spencer, Jenelle, Annie, Leah, and Kate. There was a time a while back where you guys offered to take my kiddos for a whole day. I had been so stressed with finalizing all the details of this book and you guys were lifesavers. You couldn't have known how much I needed you that day, but I thank you a million times over. Thanks so much for all you do for us and for loving my kiddos.

Hayleigh at Editing Fox. You are such a kind editor with great feedback. I appreciated all of your ideas.

Amy Romney. Thank you for being willing to proofread for me and your great feedback. I would thank you for making me do scary things on vacation but I wouldn't mean it.

Melody at Whim and Joy. Thank you for your time in making the covers for this series shine.

And finally...thank YOU for reading, sharing, posting, loving, and reviewing. It means the world.

ABOUT CINDY

Cindy Steel was raised on a dairy farm in Idaho. She grew up singing Garth Brooks and Reba McEntire songs at the top of her lungs and learning to solve all of life's problems while milking cows and driving tractors —re-writing happy endings every time.

She married an Idaho boy and is the proud mother of two wild and sweet twin boys and a sweet baby girl, which means she is now a collector of bugs, sticks, rocks, and slobbery kisses. She loves making breakfast, baking, photography, reading, and staying up way past her bedtime to craft stories that will hopefully make you smile.

She loves to connect and get to know her readers! She is the most active on Instagram at @authorcindysteel, and her newsletter, but occasionally makes her way to Facebook at Author Cindy Steel, and her website at www.cindysteel.com.

Made in United States
Troutdale, OR
05/24/2025

31625972R00159